EDWARD EVERETT HALE

His Level Best
and
Other Stories

The American Short Story Series

VOLUME 18

GARRETT PRESS

936 02

Library of Congress Catalog Card No. 68-55677

*This volume was reprinted from the 1872 edition
published by James R. Osgood & Co.*

First Garrett Press Edition published 1969

The American Short Story Series
Volume 18
© 1968

Manufactured in the United States of America

GARRETT PRESS, INC.
Publishers
250 West 54th Street, New York, N.Y. 10019

PREFACE.

THE first of these stories has never before been published. The others have had a circulation more or less limited in different journals.

"The Queen of California," as will be seen, is my translation, from the "Sergas of Esplandian," of every passage relating to the imagined island of "California." Since the first publication of that translation the principal public libraries of this country have obtained copies of that romance.

E. E. H.

November 30, 1872.

CONTENTS.

——◆——

HIS LEVEL BEST.

[STRICTLY speaking these notes are only part of a story. They are fragments, taken not quite at hazard, from the diary of an unfortunate gentleman, now resident in the poor-house, a cultivated man of amiable disposition, and formerly of comfortable or sufficient property. How he lost that property his own memoranda will show us.

If any one should ask me what this memoir teaches, I should have to say, as I should say of most life, that it teaches a great many things. I suppose it teaches the folly of a constant remark, that if people mean well all will go well ; but I should not print it here to teach that simple lesson. If it teaches, also, the absurdity of the pressure which some of the organizations of society make upon the best of its individual members, I shall be glad of that. Most of all, I hope that it may teach some young man or some young woman that it is better to do the whole of one duty than a part of many ; that it is better to compel society and to make circumstance obey you, than it is to yield to fashion or to dictation the use of your talent, of your money, or of your time.]

MY story begins where most stories end, — with a wedding.

It begins with my wedding. My wife was married at the same time.

Our friends all said that the circumstances were most auspicious. Certainly I thought so. I loved her. She loved me. Better than either, we had not been attached in youth, and so were not beginning to get tired of each other. We were not like each other. That, as my Aunt Joanna said, was so much the better. She said that, when she bought a box of hooks and eyes, she was always disappointed if they proved to be all eyes or all hooks. She said that a hook and an eye held together much more firmly than two hooks did, or two eyes.

I had a little property, perhaps sixty-two thousand dollars, and a trifle of three hundred and ninety-seven or thereabout more. My wife had an independent property in her own right of sixty-one thousand nine hundred and one dollars. It seemed as if I were a little the superior in this, but on her wedding-night one of her uncles gave her a five-hundred-dollar bill, which made her rather the richer of the two.

No one gave me anything on our wedding-night, with a single exception which I shall mention. She had a great many presents. Her father gave her to me, and she was not a thing. I counted that much the best present of the occasion.

My wife and I had no causes for dissent, and we have never quarrelled from that hour to this. We have faithfully followed each other's fortunes. True, we have been parted, but not by ourselves. I am now in the Male Department of the poor-house, Dormitory

B, native whites. She is in the Female Department, also Dormitory B, native whites also. The children are in what is known as the Nursery Department, also Dormitory B, native whites also.

We have been married seven years, and have known no material difference of opinions. Tiffs we have had, but not quarrels. I own to tiffs, but I do not own to quarrels. There was no reason why we should quarrel. We both had good appetites and good health. We were both fond of books, and yet we did not always want to read the same book at a time. We had the same views on papal infallibility, on the doctrine of election, on regeneration, on the fall of man, on the vicarious atonement, on baptism, and on the future life.

In a paper to be read before a mixed audience, I do not think it proper or desirable to state what those views were ; but mine were hers and hers were mine.

We went to the same church, we taught in the same Sunday school, and believed in the same — minister.

Under these circumstances we were married. There was a large attendance, and the minister married us first-rate. I have no fault to find with the minister. Then they all congratulated us. I sometimes wonder if they would congratulate us now, if they came down to see the poor-house some day with the Board of Overseers of the Poor, and I should be detailed to see to their horses, and my wife to wait at table when they had the collation. But they congratulated us then.

Then her uncle gave her the five-hundred-dollar bill,

in a little aside, and he told her that she had everything heart could wish, — a pretty home and a good
husband. He meant me. Then he said she must not
be unmindful of others, but must be willing to do whatever other people wanted her to do for the good of
those around her, indeed, for the good of the world.
And she cried a little, and she said she would.

Then, in a little joking, her father came to me and
said he thought I ought to be sufficiently obliged to
him for giving Gertrude to me. But he was going to
add to the obligation. Then he took out a little bit
of paper. I thought it was a check. He made a little
speech, in which he said that he had got much comfort,
and I think an occasional nap, from reading regularly
the " Evening Post," which was the leading evening
paper of our town. He had been to the office that day
and subscribed for it for five years in my name. And
this bit of paper was the receipted bill of the publisher
for five years.

It was not a check.

I observed, while he was doing this, that my father
was handing Gertrude a little bit of paper. All the
people thought that was a check. But it was not. It
was not the same as mine, however. My father always
read in the morning the " Daily Times," which was the
leading morning paper of our town. He had subscribed
for that for six years in her name, and he was giving
the publisher's receipt to her.

By and by the wedding was done. The minister

kissed her and he bade me good by. "Boothby," he
said to me, "I don't know when I have seen such a
lucky fellow. The best of it is, I know you won't be
selfish. You will not hide your talent in a napkin.
You are not one of the kind to say *no — no — no*, because you have a pretty house and a pretty wife. Now
you have a position in society, you must assist in all
good objects."

"In all good objects!" At the moment it did not
occur to me how many *all* meant, and I said, "I'll
do my Level Best, Doctor." So he went away, and I
have done that very thing ever since, as I said I would.

By and by they were all gone, and we took a carriage and drove to our new home.

———————

LIFE began on us very gently. We were not to
receive our friends for a fortnight. Those of them
who remembered our existence thought we had gone
on a journey. Really we were journeying round the
town in each other's company. We had an excellent
breakfast the first day, which did honor to my wife's
housekeeping. Then I read aloud the new daily to
her, while she washed her new cups and saucers. I
never read the paper so conscientiously before, and so
I was surprised to find how many duties I owed to
society, which I had never before performed, indeed
had never thought of. You see that is what the newspaper is for. It is the keeper of the people's conscience,

and it tells them all what in the aggregate everybody
thinks they ought to do. So as I read on Gertrude
and I found that there was no danger but even the
day of the honeymoon would be eventful enough, if
we only did what all people of conscience and intelligence were expected to do, and if we kept up to the
demand which an enlightened public opinion made
on the people of our town.

Thus the " Daily Times " said that morning : " All of
our readers who are interested in fine art should go
to-day to witness the ' Court of Death,' which is on
exhibition for the last time at Watkins's Hall. This
noble painting will be rolled up at nine this evening,
previous to its transfer to the private gallery of the
Emperor of Russia."

So Gertrude and I agreed that, as we were really
interested in fine art, we would go at noon. The
newspaper said we must go, and we had rather go at
that time.

Then, in another column, I read that " every intelligent person knew that it was quite time that something was done to prevent cruelty to animals in the
city ; that all such persons were invited to meet at
the Coliseum Hall at one." The editor expressed his
conviction that they would all go.

I told Gertrude it would be a nice opportunity to
meet all the intelligent people in the town, whom I
had never met together, and we agreed to go there at
one.

Then it said, under the "musical" head, that it was
sure the readers had not forgotten that the fourth Symphony Concert was to take place that afternoon. It
was quite right about me; for, as I never knew it before, I could not have forgotten it. It said that all
persons who had any love of music ought to go, if
only to encourage the deserving conductor; and that
they would be more than rewarded by the performance
of the Eleventh Symphony in D-Flat; and that all the
rest of the music would be thrown in for nothing. So
Gertrude ordered her dinner earlier than we had intended, for the "Times" said that if we did not go early
we could not get seats. This proved to be a mistake;
but we acted on the editor's misapprehension.

These three engagements made, I went about my
affairs and Gertrude about hers. We did not mean
to torment each other, as Maria Theresa and her husband did, because he had nothing to do.

But I had not been at my new desk in my new study
five minutes, wondering what I should do with my new
ink and my new papers, when there was a tap at the
door and my new wife came in. She was very pretty,
— did I say so before? She had on a lovely pink morn-
ing-dress, and a trig little collar round her neck, and I
thought the best thing I could do was to kiss her. But
she said no, I must not do that; that she was sorry to
interrupt me, but this was business. A poor girl had
come begging. She was the oldest of seven sisters,
and her father had been killed on the railroad, and her

mother was in the insane asylum. Her rent was be-
hindhand; she needed seven dollars, and a gentleman
whose name she had forgotten had given her six, and
had recommended her to come to us for the seventh.

Neither of us could think who this gentleman was.
But we were not going to be stingy the day after our
wedding. So we had the girl in, and I made notes of
her story. I was sorry to find that her breath smelt
a little of gin, which showed a defect in her education.
I told her we would come and see her, that we never
gave any money at the door, and I took down her address. She had forgotten the name of the street she
lived in, and the house had no number, but it was
convenient to the Catholic church and was across the
way from the grocer's. Her landlord was named James
Flaherty, and I could not miss the house, she said. So
I agreed to call before night, and I felt pleased that I
could do something so soon to carry out my promise
to the parson.

So that day was quite fully occupied in advance,
even before we started on it. We had not much correspondence yet, only a few letters to write in answer
to presents. I wrote some for Gertrude while people
did not know her handwriting. We found that, by a
misunderstanding, two letters, signed Gertrude Boothby, went to Mrs. Senator Foster, and two to Horace
James. But this was better than if it had been the
other way.

I went to the post-office before going to the " Court

of Death." I found there a notice that our class would meet to pass resolutions of sympathy with Green's widow that evening; also that the graduates of the Dummer Academy would meet to organize on Friday evening; the trustees of the Humane Society had elected me a member, and would meet Saturday evening; that I was chosen into the Historical Society, which would meet Monday evening; and that all the citizens of the town would meet to take measures to prevent the drainage job on Tuesday evening. There was another notice that they would all meet at another place, to concert measures for carrying forward the great sewerage improvement, the same evening. It was rather difficult going to both, but the halls were not far distant from each other, so I put down both on my memorandum-book.

[Mr. Boothby's notes go on from day to day of the honeymoon, showing that he and his Gertrude did not in the least lack the joy of eventful living. He describes at some length his difficulty in finding Mary Williams, convanient the Catholic church, opposite the grocery. Indeed, in that effort he failed entirely, though he invested an hour in it. Before many days he and his wife established a system of memoranda, and of division of labor. She read aloud the " Evening Post " to him while they were so fortunate as to have any time together, and he, who had a knack at whittling, carved his cigar-boxes into parlor ornaments. Then he made little notes of what was expected of every good citizen, of every lover of his race, of all ladies of fashion, of any man who had a heart bigger than a sixpence, of all the descendants of John Cotton, of whom he

was one ; of all the family of Elder Brewster, of whom his wife
was one ; of all members of the *human* family, to which they
both belonged ; of the residents in Ward XVI. ; of the people
who were affected by the bone-burning nuisance, of the loyal
members of the Church of Christ, of the active members of the
Republican party, of persons interested in the temperance reform, of gentlemen who did not mean to have politics made a
trade of, and of such lesser calls as the evening paper made on
him and on her. They then sorted these out, and arrayed them
as best they could. When they could go together, they did.
If no gentlemen were admitted to these meetings, she went
alone. When no ladies were admitted, he went alone. Eventually, lack of time compelled them to discharge all such duties
separately, from the mere impossibility of being in more than
four places at the same time. But they did their level best, and
attended as many as was possible.

Mr. Boothby soon saw that if he had committed himself to
any profession, he would have had no time for these public cares
and pleasures ; but, on the other hand, he had not been married
six months before he found the unexpected necessity of the most
careful bookkeeping and economy, that he might meet the pecu-
niary calls with honor, which his gallant determination to do his
level best made upon him. His diary of a few hours will best
illustrate these calls.]

March 11, 1863.

Professor Tournefort is just entering on his grand
enterprise for publishing colored pictures of all the
humming-birds in the southern tropics. The paper
says it will be of immense credit to the United States
that this book shall be published here. Even the Emperor of Russia refused to undertake it, the expense
was so large. But now the Academy of Naturals has

taken it up, and it is hoped that every man of public spirit will order a copy. It is only twenty-five dollars a year, and may last thirty-four years. Sent my check to honorary treasurer.

Paid assessment to the Natural History Society. Wish I could ever get to their meetings. Asked the collector what advantages members had above non-members, when I found I had to buy the Transactions as other people do. He told me members only were admitted to the library on Tuesday afternoons, all other days being the public's days. *Mem.* To go next Tuesday afternoon.

Paid assessment to Technological Society, to Genealogical Society, to Philological Society, to Anthropological Society, to Theological Library, to Physiological Institute, and to the Logical Necessity. They have taken a suggestion of mine, and all now employ the same collector, which is a convenience, one check and visit answering for all.

Interesting call from the agent for the College for educating Mammals. The State will give them a hundred thousand dollars, if they can raise another hundred by subscription. I am afraid they have to pay a pretty large commission to their agents. Subscribed twenty-five dollars, which seemed to be what they expected. The man said he should like cash, because he " wanted to buy a new vest and pair of pants." So I gave him the money, though I don't see what that has to do with it.

Rev. Mr. Izaaks came in. He is secretary for the
Society for teaching Children not to eat with their
Knives. He brought a line from our good Dr. South,
saying that he hoped that all the members of his
parish whom God had blessed with abundance would
do something for this estimable man. I did not quite
see why subscribing to the society should help the
secretary. But Dr. South probably knows. Gave five
dollars as an annual subscriber.

Paid annual subscriptions to Humane Society, Hospital for Children, People's Reading-Room, Hospital
for Infants, Scandinavian Emigrant Society, Hospital
for Girls, Old Women's Home, Hospital for Boys, Old
Men's Home, Hospital for Young Persons between Ages
of Fourteen and Twenty, Old Colored Women's Home,
Hospital for Adults, Old Colored Men's Home, Hospital for Aged Men, Home for Indians and Turanian
Races, Hospital for Aged Women, Home for Discharged
and Disconnected Aryans, and the newly-founded Home
for Kanakas. This last is a very interesting charity.
The whalers bring home these from the Sandwich Islands, and they cannot bear the climate here. As none
of them are rich, they have, of course, never paid taxes
for ten years, so they cannot go into the poor-house.
How singular it is that the poor-house should be an
institution mainly for the support and relief of prop-
erty-holders ! This makes it necessary to have a separate asylum for the Kanakas.

And so on.

[After a year's experience at this very unsatisfactory averaging of one's duties to the world, Mr. Boothby seems to have thought of another course for a moment, to see if there were not a best better than a level best. He seems to have thought for a moment that a man's own judgment of his duty was better than any public's judgment ; that a man had better right to divide his own time than any newspaper had ; and that it was better to do one thing throughly or thoroughly, than to help a hundred men to do a thousand things languidly. But I am sorry to say that he tested this about a certain great concert, to which neither he nor his wife wanted to go. She said it was the fashion, and they must go. So they went. But she said she thought he might give up looking in at club every afternoon. But when he said, " Everybody did," *she* gave way. He bid in tickets for the first performance at the opera of " Debt and the Devil," because Gertrude said, " They say that everybody is going." Boothby asked who *they* were, and Gertrude could not tell ; but he found out afterwards that it was Mr. and Mrs. Grundy, whom he did not know, and indeed never saw. She said there was a man named Jawkins, who said so too.

There are some curious memoranda of Mr. Boothby's on what he calls the tides. He means the general laws which bring in on one day all the assessment people, on one day all the Western College people, on one day all the foreign professors, on one day all the bores, and on one day all the butterflies.

It will never answer to read his speculations in full, but I will select a few illustrations from a letter of Introduction Day.]

" VERY odd ; I had just got to my desk when a gentleman came in, — a Swede, with a letter to me from Fergus, our Vice-Consul at Nord-Koping. I have not seen Fergus since we graduated. This gentleman speaks no English, but we got on quite well in German. A very interesting man. Asked him to dinner.

Very odd; I had just got back to my writing when an interesting man came in, — a Bohemian, late professor at Buda, turned out on account of his views regarding the Sacrament. Brings me a letter from Acs, Kossuth's chaplain. He spoke no German, but we talked in Latin. *Mem.* He will dine with us to-morrow.

Very odd; I had just resumed my letter to Fisk and Hatch, when a gentleman brought me a letter from Rev. Mr. Cozzens, the missionary. This is a Dutch planter from Table Bay. Very interesting man. Does not understand English nor French, but we made out by signs very well. Says he will dine here to-morrow.

After he left I began my letter again about selling out my 10-40s, when a dark-colored gentleman came in, who proved to be a Japanese prince, with a friendly note from an old friend, Matateeset. Spoke no English, but knew a little French, and we got on quite well. Says he will take tea with us or dine in a friendly way some day this week.

After he was gone I went back to my letter; but it was too late for the midday mail, and so I went to the monthly meeting of the Soldiers' Home, where I am vice-president. Sat there an hour, but we did no business for want of a quorum.

[I asked Mrs. Boothby about this dinner-party on the last visit I made to Dormitory B, Female Department (white females), and she gave me a very interesting account of it. In his eagerness to do his very best by these gentlemen intrusted to him from different parts of the world, Mr. Boothby had forgotten that the plumber was to be in the house the next day, to take down the range and the water back, and that they were to have a cold dinner. Or, more accurately, Mrs. Boothby, in *her* determination to do the right thing at the right time, had ordered the plumber to come, and had not mentioned it to her husband. As they were to have a cold dinner and no company, Mrs. Boothby had thought it a good day to have two dress-makers, who would dine with them. Fortunately these young women were both deaf and dumb. Mrs. Boothby arranged as well as she could. She sent to a restaurant for her dinner, which *was* a little cold, and they got through very well. Just as they were sitting down, her aunt and her aunt's sister and the sister's two children happened in, on their way home from Rye. So they had to put another board into the table.

Just as they got through the oysters, Dr. South, the minister, dropped in, with a Brahmin gentleman, one of the first-fruits of the Serampore mission. He never expected an invitation, they were always so glad to see him. " I was a little afraid the dinner would not hold out," said poor Mrs. Boothby to me, as she told me the story, " but my husband did not care. He said we were doing our best, and we could do no more."

I asked Mrs. Boothby how the gentlemen talked with each other, — if there was no difficulty about language. She said there was a little trouble when the Bohemian professor addressed the deaf-and-dumb dress-maker in Latin, but that in general they did very well. Mrs. Boothby herself said nothing. The Dutch planter talked Dutch across the table to the Japanese prince ; the Japanese prince spoke French to Mr. Boothby ; Mr. Boothby spoke German to the Swede ; the Swede spoke Danish to Dr. South ; and Dr. South spoke Latin to the Bohemian. He said nothing after his failure with the dress-maker. None of

them talked in their own languages, but all did their best, —
their level best. The only misfortune was that they had been
seated as it happened, and the conversation had to be across
the table.

But Mr. Boothby said it was impossible, in our modern civilization, to choose on what day letters of introduction should
come. You must do the best you could with them, and that
was all.]

GOOD-HEARTED though he was, poor Mr. Boothby sometimes
got a sad repulse. He had written to Asaph Ferguson to ask
him to subscribe to the Kanakas' Hospital, and he got this rebuff, which I find preserved among his papers.

DEAR JOHN : — I will see you hanged first. If you
go on as you do, befriending every cause only because
it is a good cause, I am likely to see you hanged. You
say you do your level best, and I believe you. Now
level best is a sort of best I despise as much as I do
level country. I had rather have a sort of best which
knows what ups and downs are.

Boothby, which do you like best, a horizon where
there are four or five mountain-peaks and as many
valleys between, or one which is a dead level ? You
like the mountains best. So do I. I hate your Indiana prairies.

Boothby, your practice reminds me of poor Stickinthemud's preaching. It is all too good. He begins
on a high plane, — too high, as I think, — and then
he goes on and on and on and on, like a canal-boat

on one long level, and we all go to sleep and we all wake up, and we wonder why he has not done. But Robert Collyer begins where we are, and goes up and up and up, and we try to follow him, even to the gate of heaven. The first thing we know, we are almost there. But in a minute he is down again, just on our own level, and he has got some little baby in his arms who stumbled before, and but for him would have been lost; and then it is up again, up again, up again, till those who are pure in heart enough see God. But he will not stay even there. He is down again, seeking the lost and looking after them. So next thing you know he is at your workshop door in his talk again, and has you in his hand, and coaxes you and leads you, and leads you and lifts you, till you are in the clear air once more, and see as you are seen and know as you are known. Up and down, up and down, up and down; that is better than Stickinthemud's high level.

I wish to heaven, Boothby, you would give up your level best; and even if you had some days of mere getting ready, why there would be some things which you would do terribly well.

[BUT I cannot see in his notes that poor Mr. Boothby ever acted on this lesson. It came too late. Indeed, if he had acted on it, I should not be telling you the story now. His wife's health broke down, before many years, under her exertions. It was not the charities, she said to me, once when I was in Department B (W. F.), so much as it was the lessons.

Great numbers of people came who wanted to open classes. There was a new method of learning German, and no one who had any interest in modern literature was excusable, the " Post " said, if he did not join the class.   Then there was a man who had invented a new short-hand, which was " the reform of modern times," and he explained to Mr. Boothby and his wife that if they did not take lessons, it was because they were selfish cumberers of the ground, who did not believe in the Golden Rule.   There was a French gentleman, a professor in the University of Paris, who was starving.   Mrs. Boothby offered his child a frock, but she would not take it because it was alpaca, and her father would not allow her to wear any but silk. So Mrs. Boothby asked what she *could* do, and she found that their susceptibilities would be least injured if she went to the class in French conversation, and so on.   She went to so many classes for the benefit of the teachers that she got, poor woman, very little benefit herself, unless dreadful headaches, earned in the cause, did her some good morally.   Mr. Boothby took no lessons, except in boxing, fencing, and the use of the broadsword ; but he subscribed annually to the Lyceum, the Parker Fraternity, the Bay State Course, the Citizens' Course, the Mercantile Course, the Tremont Temple Course, the Berkeley Course, the North End Course, and the South End Course, and so, as you see, his education was not wholly neglected.   He did not go to the Lowell Lectures, unless they had them in the afternoon.]

HERE is one terrible story, — almost too cruel to print here, — which will show how impossible even a man as generous as he finds it to hold to his best determination.   It will show how there are cases in which " the man is greater than humanity," when the duty next your hand appears to you greater, and therefore is greater, than duty to all the world beside. There was one of Boothby's many societies, to which he gave not only his purse but his heart. It was the old Washingtonian Society. Boothby was not President or Treasurer, nor Past Grand nor Most Worthy there. He was only a High Private,— the best thing, I think, that a man can be, — nothing less and nothing more. He liked to go in and see the new recruits, and hear them tell their stories. One night a man named Breck came in,— handsome dog, taller than Carter, and weighing a hundred more than he does, — hair black, lip well cut, and really loving eyes, — and *he* made a little speech. He said liquor had damned him, but, so help him God, he would never touch anything but water again. Boothby sat near him, shook hands with him when he had done, said something kind; but he saw the poor wretch was only a bundle of bare nerves, that he was speaking on nerve, living on nerve, and was no more able to stand to his oath than is a fly to take the load of Atlas. Boothby asked where he was going. " Going," said the poor creature, " where should I go ? Home ? I have lost my home forever."

" Then," said Boothby, " come to mine." And he hurried him out of the hall. He found a cab a square away, and they rode home, none too soon. He got poor Breck a cup of tea and another, but it was hard work to get him to bed.

Not twenty minutes, before Boothby heard a crash

there ; rushed up, and all his fears were true. The
poor fellow was wild with horror. He was crouching
in the corner ; he was chattering, he was hissing, like
a beast or a bird ; he was shivering, and tearing his
shirt to pieces. When he saw his friend with a lamp
he cried out with joy, " You have saved me, you have
saved me." The good man soothed him, calmed him,
humored him, put him to bed again, and promised not
to desert him, not to take the light away again ; sat
chafing his hands and crooning to him. If he might
only go to sleep. Sleep ! No ! No sleep for him.
The horrid phantoms of the pit — snakes and scorpions, flies and hornets, dragons and griffins — seemed
all around him again, and it was almost by force that
his friend held him down, by every change of de-
vice that even for an instant he dispelled the visions.
He rung for a servant. Before an hour was over he
had Morton, the doctor, there. For an hour or two
more they two worked together on the poor wretch,
and when Morton left at midnight, it was to say, " It
is life or death with him. If you see him asleep for an
hour or two before morning, you save him ; but if not,
no." And so poor Boothby girt himself for a night of
horrors. He told poor Breck I know not how many
stories of adventure. He pretended to read to him
novels, by Scott, and Dumas, and Dickens, making up
the tale as he went on. He repeated " Marmion," and
" The Corsair," and the " Lord of the Isles." He sang
to him old hymns. And yet, with every ten minutes,

poor Breck would start in agony, and cover his head with his blankets, and beg his friend not to desert him now the devils had come again. Then that friend prayed with him. And the poor shattered brain and nerves, that would still themselves to nothing else, would be hushed for prayer; and lips that knew more of oaths than of devotion could calmly say, as when he prayed by his mother's knee, " Lead us not into temptation, but deliver us from evil," and " Now I lay me down to sleep." And there was a Spirit with those two that heard and answered. As the clock struck half past five, the watcher turned to give to the patient the stated sedative, and was sure then, thank God, that he was sleeping! Sleeping! And for five minutes he slept, ten, half an hour, an hour. Surely that *is* daylight. Yes, it is daylight, and he sleeps on. Seven o'clock, eight o'clock, and he sleeps on.

My friend had given orders that no foot should mount that stairway till Morton, the doctor, came. It is his wife's story which I am to follow now. At half past seven a common councilman rang at the door. " Husband down, Mrs. Boothby ? " " He has a sick friend." " Call him just one minute; my horse won't stand." " Indeed, Mr. Williams, I cannot call him." " Not for a minute ? " " Not for a minute." And the councilman went away in a rage. " Boothby was always a selfish dog." The builder next door came. " Please, ma'am, ask the old man to step out a minute about our fence." " Indeed, Mr. Cade, he is with a sick friend." "O, only a minute, you know!" "I *cannot* call him at all, Mr. Cade." "Then he may go to hell, for a purse-proud aristocrat as he is." Ring the third. "Would Mr. Boothby be so kind as to head the call for the Woman's Suffrage Convention?" Indeed, Mrs. Wolstoncroft, he is with a sick friend." "Then if you would just take the pen up to him." "I do not dare disturb him, madam." And Mrs. Wolstoncroft goes away, raging at an excuse so shabby for a dereliction of duty so cowardly and so mean.

"I lost my election to the Senate," said Boothby; "I had a nuisance built next my garden; I was abused like a pickpocket in two or three conventions. But somehow I did not care. Poor Breck pulled through. We got him on quassia and iron. And, what was more, we got him to believe in men and women. That was best of all."

"You saved him, if you lost yourself," said I.

"Very much so," said he, pluckily; "but that is what comes to a man when he fails to do his level best."

And I thought worse things might happen to him.

———

[IN that adventure poor Boothby made one friend. I think he never made another. A great many people used him, but nobody but Breck loved him. Now I certainly do not say that making friends is the business of life, but I have learned that the depth and sincerity of a man's friendships are the best test of his success in life. Now friendships come only where you have given your whole self to your friend in the occasion which has

called you together. If you only give a part and retain something, you make an acquaintance, but you make no friend. Mr.
Boothby, in his level life, made a great many acquaintances, but
only one friend, as it proved, alas, when the crisis came, and
he made him by violating his rule of life.

The result, in this regard, is a little like that of a missionary-
meeting, where nobody pledges his whole life to the cause, but
where a hundred people pledge each the ten-thousandth part of
a life. The result of such a meeting, if you will multiply the
fraction by the number of the assembly, is a strenuous effort to
save the hundredth part of a soul. But, alas, souls are indi-
visible !]

I HAVE intimated already that Mr. Boothby's readiness to do his level best for each and every scheme, —
or, in the phrase of his beloved pastor, "to help all good
objects," — made serious inroads in his finances at an
early date. His diaries are full of allusions to these
difficulties, now difficult to comprehend. He soon found
his outgoes larger than his income. He had, however,
plenty of acquaintances who were bank directors, and,
for a man of assured position like him, it was not difficult to borrow money, — only temporarily, you know,
— while he always had some scheme of economy which
was going to set all right and square in another year.
Or, on the other hand, when he relucted from asking
such accommodation, it was always easy again to sell a
few 5-20s or 10-40s, to take up any note which fell due
or to make his bank account look respectable. Only
this relief, unfortunately, reduced the permanent in-

come. He had always — and knew he had — his wife's
property to fall back upon, although he was ashamed
to think of that. Yet it was a comfort, of course, to
know that if anything did happen to him, and to what
he was pleased to call his investments, she and the
children would be all safe, indeed well off, with her
sixty-two thousand dollars.

In this calculation there was but one mistake, which
was this, that it was all wrong from the beginning to
the end. Mr. and Mrs. Boothby had started on the
theory that they were to be wholly independent of
each other in matters of money. He did nothing
about her property, and she nothing about his. True,
they disliked to trade with each other at breakfast.
He did not like to say, "My dear, if you will give
me a cup of your coffee, I can pay you for it with a
nice cut of my beef," as is the way with those who
logically carry out the modern theories. So they arranged that he should pay the bills one month and she
another; and, until the last, they tried to surprise each
other with new and dainty devices for the table. But,
for the rest, they lived up to the lofty idea of individ-
uality. He would not tyrannize over her, nor would
she grape-vine around him.

It is to be hoped that great good may come to society from this mutual understanding of theirs. But
unfortunately great misery came to them. For Boothby's dividends grew less and less, his notes payable
became larger and larger, the annual expense of house-

keeping grew with the number of his children, and
the demands of the various societies, the Ontological
and Frontological, and the rest, knew no end. Then,
in the midst of his perplexities for money, certain
thunderbolts would fall unexpectedly. Thus, he was
never ready for taxes ; and all of a sudden, because our
Southern friends wanted to be let alone, there came
two tax-bills in a year instead of one. Then he had a
great many memorial statues to subscribe to. He could
never remember the days when the mortgage payments
on his house were due. And as for his life insurance,
as long as he paid it at all, it seemed to him as if
he paid it every Monday. Still his wife and children
were not beggars, he said. There was Gertrude's property to fall back upon.

But at last the last bolt fell. Some of his notes had
been protested. The money for his mortgage was long
overdue. He brought himself to sell off his last ewe
lamb, — some 5-20s which he had nursed as his heart's
blood. As he returned from down State Street, where
he had been for this purpose, to his amazement he saw
Gertrude getting into a cab. Her veil was down ; but
it was surely she. He knew that blue bow and that
sea-green merino. He stopped the driver, threw the
door open, and sprang in to find her sobbing.

"My own heart," said he, "what is the matter ?"

"O my dear, dear John," said she, with her head on
his shoulder, "your poor Gertrude is a beggar !" And
then she told him all.

What with subscriptions, and stockings for Alfred, and testimonials, and shoes for John, and regular contributions, and petticoats for Fanny, and benefit concerts, and bonnets for Jane, what with this that was necessary, and that that was not necessary, poor Gertrude had worked through her little competency side by side with John, and she had just now met her last rebuff, a little before he met his. She had been down to Baring and Rothschild's to order the sale of her last 7-30s, only to be told that they were all sold on her order three months before. Poor Gertrude, she kept all her accounts in her head, and so she was ten thousand dollars poorer than she thought she was. That is, she possessed nothing but a loving heart, a loving husband, and four loving children.

"Dear Gertrude," said John, after she had had her fit of crying out, "you have spent all your money. I have spent all mine. You have sold all your stocks. I have sold mine. You have not a penny. Neither have I. But you have done your level best. And so have I."

"Have we nothing, then, dear John?"

"Dearest, when the house is sold, when our debts are all paid, we shall still have

"A SETTLEMENT."

"Pray, what is a settlement?" said Gertrude.

"Dearest, because we have been rich, because for five years we have paid taxes, because we have lived ten years without removing our home, the town will care for us now in the poor-house.

" Had we been poor, dearest, had we had to move for work from place to place, the town would now have turned us out of its borders."

" And we have each other," said Gertrude. " We have not meant to do wrong. We meant to do right."

And so was it that they found themselves with their children in the poor-house.

Yet I, as I have looked over these papers, have thought that if Mr. Boothby had learned or tried to do one thing well, instead of doing all things poorly, it would have been better for him. Had he forged bolts well, or painted carriages well, or set types well, or had he well tied up bleeding arteries, or set broken arms, or had he well painted pictures or preached the Gospel, and then to one and another Peter, asking him to try politics, or social science, or general philanthropy, if he had said, " Get thee behind me, Satan," I think he would have done better. Of my own daily duties, I find I look back every night with most satisfaction to those rebuffs I give every day to men who want to hang back themselves while other men are working. I say to them, " Put your own shoulder to the wheel. There is no Jupiter and no Juno to help you, no God of whom I know, unless you give your own life to the cause in which you would enlist me." They say to me,

"It is only your name we want," as they said to poor
Boothby. And I say to them, "You will never have
my name, you will never have any honest man's name,
unless you have him and the whole of him." And I
have written out these notes in the faint hope that
I might persuade some young woman or some young
man that it is better to do one thing well than two
things by halves ; better to learn one thing thoroughly
than to get a smattering of two ; better to stick to one
duty till it is finished, than to make two beginnings ;
better to stand loyally to the post God has pointed out,
than to try to serve here and there and everywhere.
There are no secrets which yield to commonplace or
superficial inquiry. But there are none which do not
answer the resolute student, who pledges his life to
his investigation. There are no evils healed by the
commonplace resolutions of commonplace conventions,
where a hundred people offer each the thousandth part
of a life for the endeavor. But no one evil stands
against the resolute purpose of one loyal man. Let
society tell you, in its namby-pamby editorials, what
is everybody's business, and you will find laid down
for you in its neutral colors a picture of very level
backgrounds, of very vague middle distances, whose
foregrounds are crowded with undecided groups of
dreamers, who are all preparing to begin to try. But
do *you* tell society how *you* mean to serve mankind,
find your own place and strike your own blow, and
society will meekly obey each true word you speak,
and will fall into order at your requisition.

Hold to the level best which the commonplace of society demands of you, and you come out on the quagmire flat of the dismal swamp of worthless indecision.

Ask God to show your duty, and do that duty well; and from that point you mount to the very peak of vision. It may be that you plant there another beacon-light for the world !

THE BRICK MOON.

FROM THE PAPERS OF CAPTAIN FREDERIC INGHAM.

I. — PREPARATION.

I HAVE no sort of objection now to telling the whole story. The subscribers, of course, have a right to know what became of their money. The astronomers may as well know all about it, before they announce any more asteroids with an enormous movement in declination. And experimenters on the longitude may as well know, so that they may act advisedly in attempting another brick moon or in refusing to do so.

It all began more than thirty years ago, when we were in college ; as most good things begin. We were studying in the book which has gray sides and a green back, and is called " Cambridge Astronomy " because it is translated from the French. We came across this business of the longitude, and, as we talked, in the gloom and glamour of the old South Middle dining-hall, we had going the usual number of students' stories about rewards offered by the Board of Longitude for discoveries in that matter, — stories, all of which, so far as I know, are lies. Like all boys, we had tried our hands at perpetual motion. For me, I was sure I

could square the circle, if they would give me chalk
enough. But as to this business of the longitude, it
was reserved for Q. to make the happy hit and to explain it to the rest of us. .

I wonder if I can explain it to an unlearned world,
which has not studied the book with gray sides and a
green cambric back. Let us try.

You know then, dear world, that when you look at
the North Star, it always appears to you at just the
same height above the horizon or what is between you
and the horizon : say the Dwight School-house, or the
houses in Concord Street ; or to me, just now, North
College. You know also that, if you were to travel
to the North Pole, the North Star would be just over
your head. And, if you were to travel to the equator,
it would be just on your horizon, if you could see it at
all through the red, dusty, hazy mist in the north, —
as you could not. If you were just half-way between
pole and equator, on the line between us and Canada,
the North Star would be half-way up, or 45° from the
horizon. So you would know there that you were 45°
from the equator. There in Boston, you would find it
was 42° 20′ from the horizon. So you know there that
you are 42° 20′ from the equator. At Seattle again you
would find it was 47° 40′ high, so our friends at Seattle
know that they are at 47° 40′ from the equator. The
latitude of a place, in other words, is found very easily
by any observation which shows how high the North
Star is ; if you do not want to measure the North Star,

you may take any star when it is just to north of you,
and measure its height ; wait twelve hours, and if you
can find it, measure its height again.   Split the difference, and that is the altitude of the pole, or the latitude
of you, the observer.

"Of course we know this," says the graduating world.
"Do you suppose that is what we borrow your book
for, to have you spell out your miserable elementary
astronomy ?"   At which rebuff I should shrink distressed, but that a chorus of voices an octave higher
comes up with, "Dear Mr. Ingham, we are ever so
much obliged to you ; we did not know it at all before,
and you make it perfectly clear."

Thank you, my dear, and you, and you.   We will
not care what the others say.   If you do understand
it, or do know it, it is more than Mr. Charles Reade
knew, or he would not have made his two lovers on the
island guess at their latitude, as they did.   If they had
either of them been educated at a respectable academy
for the Middle Classes, they would have fared better.

Now about the longitude.

The latitude, which you have found, measures your
distance north or south from the equator or the pole.
To find your longitude, you want to find your distance
east or west from the meridian of Greenwich.   Now if
any one would build a good tall tower at Greenwich,
straight into the sky, — say a hundred miles into the
sky, — of course if you and I were east or west of it,
and could see it, we could tell how far east or west we

were by measuring the apparent height of the tower above our horizon. If we could see so far, when the lantern with a Drummond's light, " ever so bright," on the very top of the tower, appeared to be on our horizon, we should know we were eight hundred and seventy-three miles away from it. The top of the tower would answer for us as the North Star does when we are measuring the latitude. If we were nearer, our horizon would make a longer angle with the line from the top to our place of vision. If we were farther away, we should need a higher tower.

But nobody will build any such tower at Greenwich, or elsewhere on that meridian, or on any meridian. You see that to be of use to the half the world nearest to it, it would have to be so high that the diameter of the world would seem nothing in proportion. And then, for the other half of the world you would have to erect another tower as high on the other side. It was this difficulty that made Q. suggest the expedient of the Brick Moon.

For you see that if, by good luck, there were a ring like Saturn's which stretched round the world, above Greenwich and the meridian of Greenwich, and if it would stay above Greenwich, turning with the world, any one who wanted to measure his longitude or distance from Greenwich would look out of window and see how high this ring was above his horizon. At Greenwich it would be over his head exactly. At New Orleans, which is quarter round the world from Green-

wich, it would be just in his horizon. A little west
of New Orleans you would begin to look for the other
half of the ring on the west instead of the east; and
if you went a little west of the Feejee Islands the ring
would be over your head again. So if we only had a
ring like that, not round the equator. of the world, —
as Saturn's ring is around Saturn, — but vertical to the
plane of the equator, as the brass ring of an artificial
globe goes, only far higher in proportion, — " from that
ring," said Q., pensively, " we could calculate the longitude."

Failing that, after various propositions, he suggested
the Brick Moon. The plan was this: If from the surface of the earth, by a gigantic pea-shooter, you could
shoot a pea upward from Greenwich, aimed northward
as well as upward; if you drove it so fast and far that
when its power of ascent was exhausted, and it began
to fall, it should clear the earth, and pass outside the
North Pole; if you had given it sufficient power to
get it half round the earth without touching, that pea
would clear the earth forever. It would continue to
rotate above the North Pole, above the Feejee Island
place, above the South Pole and Greenwich, forever,
with the impulse with which it had first cleared our
atmosphere and attraction. If only we could see that
pea as it revolved in that convenient orbit, then we
could measure the longitude from that, as soon as we
knew how high the orbit was, as well as if it were the
ring of Saturn.

" But a pea is so small ! "

" Yes," said Q., " but we must make a large pea."
Then we fell to work on plans for making the pea very
large and very light. Large, — that it might be seen
far away by storm-tossed navigators : light, — that it
might be the easier blown four thousand and odd miles
into the air ; lest it should fall on the heads of the
Greenlanders or the Patagonians ; lest they should be
injured and the world lose its new moon. But, of
course, all this lath-and-plaster had to be given up.
For the motion through the air would set fire to this
moon just as it does to other aerolites, and all your
lath-and-plaster would gather into a few white drops,
which no Rosse telescope even could discern. " No,"
said Q. bravely, " at the least it must be very substan-
tial. It must stand fire well, very well. Iron will not
answer. It must be brick ; we must have a Brick
Moon.

Then we had to calculate its size. You can see, on
the old moon, an edifice two hundred feet long with any
of the fine refractors of our day. But no such refractors as those can be carried by the poor little fishermen
whom we wanted to befriend, the bones of whose ships
lie white on so many cliffs, their names unreported at
any Lloyd's or by any Ross, — themselves the owners
and their sons the crew. On the other hand, we did
not want our moon two hundred and fifty thousand
miles away, as the old moon is, which I will call the
Thornbush moon, for distinction. We did not care

how near it was, indeed, if it were only far enough away to be seen, in practice, from almost the whole world. There must be a little strip where they could not see it from the surface, unless we threw it infinitely high. "But they need not look from the surface," said Q. ; "they might climb to the mast-head. And if they did not see it at all, they would know that they were ninety degrees from the meridian."

This difficulty about what we call "the strip," however, led to an improvement in the plan, which made it better in every way. It was clear that even if "the strip" were quite wide, the moon would have to be a good way off, and, in proportion, hard to see. If, however, we would satisfy ourselves with a moon four thousand miles away, *that* could be seen on the earth's surface for three or four thousand miles on each side ; and twice three thousand, or six thousand, is one fourth of the largest circumference of the earth. We did not dare have it nearer than four thousand miles, since even at that distance, it would be eclipsed three hours out of every night ; and we wanted it bright and distinct, and not of that lurid, copper, eclipse color. But at four thousand miles' distance the moon could be seen by a belt of observers six or eight thousand miles in diameter. "Start, then, two moons," — this was my contribution to the plan. "Suppose one over the meridian of Greenwich, and the other over that of New Orleans. Take care that there is a little difference in the radii of their orbits, lest they 'collide' some foul day. Then, in most places, one or other, perhaps two will come in sight. So much the less risk of clouds : and everywhere there may be one, except when it is cloudy. Neither need be more than four thousand miles off; so much the larger and more beautiful will they be. If on the old Thornbush moon old Herschel with his reflector could see a town-house two hundred feet long, on the Brick Moon young Herschel will be able to see a dab of mortar a foot and a half long, if he wants to. And people without the reflector, with their opera-glasses, will be able to see sufficiently well." And to this they agreed : that eventually there must be two Brick Moons. Indeed, it were better that there should be four, as each must be below the horizon half the time. That is only as many as Jupiter has. But it was also agreed that we might begin with one.

Why we settled on two hundred feet of diameter I hardly know. I think it was from the statement of dear John Farrar's about the impossibility of there being a state house two hundred feet long not yet discovered, on the sunny side of old Thornbush. That, somehow, made two hundred our fixed point. Besides, a moon of two hundred feet diameter did not seem quite unmanageable. Yet it was evident that a smaller moon would be of no use, unless we meant to have them near the world, when there would be so many that they would be confusing, and eclipsed most of the time. And four thousand miles is a good way off to see a moon even two hundred feet in diameter.

Small though we made them on paper, these two-hundred-foot moons were still too much for us. Of course we meant to build them hollow. But even if hollow there must be some thickness, and the quantity of brick would at best be enormous. Then, to get them up! The pea-shooter, of course, was only an illustration. It was long after that time that Rodman and other guns sent iron balls five or six miles in distance, — say two miles, more or less, in height.

Iron is much heavier than hollow brick, but you can build no gun with a bore of two hundred feet now, — far less could you then. No. Q. again suggested the method of shooting off the moon. It was not to be by any of your sudden explosions. It was to be done as all great things are done, — by the gradual and silent accumulation of power. You all know that a fly-wheel — heavy, very heavy on the circumference, light, very light within it — was made to save up power, from the time when it was produced to the time when it was wanted. Yes? Then, before we began even to build the moon, before we even began to make the brick, we would build two gigantic fly-wheels, the diameter of each should be " ever so great," the circumference heavy beyond all precedent, and thundering strong, so that no temptation might burst it. They should revolve, their edges nearly touching, in opposite directions, for years, if it were necessary, to accumulate power, driven by some waterfall now wasted to the world. One should be a little heavier than the other. When the Brick Moon was finished, and all was ready, IT should be gently rolled down a gigantic groove provided for it, till it lighted on the edge of both wheels at the same instant. Of course it would not rest there, not the ten-thousandth part of a second. It would be snapped upward, as a drop of water from a grindstone. Upward and upward; but the heavier wheel would have deflected it a little from the vertical. Upward and northward it would rise, therefore, till it had passed the axis of the world. It would, of course, feel the world's attraction all the time, which would bend its flight gently, but still it would leave the world more and more behind. Upward still, but now southward, till it had traversed more than one hundred and eighty degrees of a circle. Little resistance, indeed, after it had cleared the forty or fifty miles of visible atmosphere. "Now let it fall," said Q., inspired with the vision. "Let it fall, and the sooner the better! The curve it is now on will forever clear the world; and over the meridian of that lonely waterfall, — if only we have rightly adjusted the gigantic flies, — will forever revolve, in its obedient orbit, the Brick Moon, the blessing of all seamen, — as constant in all change as its older sister has been fickle, and the second cynosure of all lovers upon the waves, and of all girls left behind them." "Amen," we cried, and then we sat in silence till the clock struck ten; then shook each other gravely by the hand, and left the South Middle dining-hall.

Of waterfalls there were plenty that we knew.

Fly-wheels could be built of oak and pine, and hooped with iron.   Fly-wheels did not discourage us.

But brick ?   One brick is, say, sixty-four cubic inches only.   This moon, — though we made it hollow, — see, — it must take twelve million brick.

The brick alone will cost sixty thousand dollars !

The brick alone would cost sixty thousand dollars. There the scheme of the Brick Moon hung, an airy vision, for seventeen years, — the years that changed us from young men into men.   The brick alone, sixty thousand dollars !   For, to boys who have still left a few of their college bills unpaid, who cannot think of buying that lovely little Elzevir which Smith has for sale at auction, of which Smith does not dream of the value, sixty thousand dollars seems as intangible as sixty million sestertia.   Clarke, second, how much are sixty million sestertia stated in cowries ?   How much in currency, gold being at $1.37\frac{1}{4}$?   Right ; go up. Stop, I forget myself !

So, to resume, the project of the Brick Moon hung in the ideal, an airy vision, a vision as lovely and as distant as the Brick Moon itself, at this calm moment of midnight when I write, as it poises itself over the shoulder of Orion, in my southern horizon.   Stop ! I anticipate. Let me keep — as we say in Beadle's Dime Series — to the even current of my story.

Seventeen years passed by, we were no longer boys, though we felt so. For myself, to this hour, I never enter board meeting, committee meeting, or synod, without the queer question, what would happen should any one discover that this bearded man was only a big boy disguised ? that the frock-coat and the round hat are none of mine, and that, if I should be spurned from the assembly as an interloper, a judicious public, learning all the facts, would give a verdict, " Served him right." This consideration helps me through many bored meetings which would be else so dismal. What did my old copy say ? " Boards are made of wood, they are long and narrow." But we do not get on !

Seventeen years after, I say, or should have said, dear Orcutt entered my room at Naguadavick again. I had not seen him since the Commencement day when we parted at Cambridge. He looked the same, and yet not the same. His smile was the same, his voice, his tender look of sympathy when I spoke to him of a great sorrow, his childlike love of fun. His waistband was different, his pantaloons were different, his smooth chin was buried in a full beard, and he weighed two hundred pounds if he weighed a gramme. O, the good time we had, so like the times of old ! Those were happy days for me in Naguadavick. At that moment my double was at work for me at a meeting of the publishing committee of the Sandemanian Review, so I called Orcutt up to my own snuggery, and we talked over old times; talked till tea was ready. Polly came up through the orchard and made tea for us herself there. We talked on and on, till nine, ten at night, and then it was that dear Orcutt asked me if I remembered the Brick Moon. Remember it? of course I did. And without leaving my chair I opened the drawer of my writing-desk, and handed him a portfolio full of working-drawings on which I had engaged myself for my "third"* all that winter. Orcutt was delighted. He turned them over hastily but intelligently, and said: "I am so glad. I could not think you had forgotten. And I have seen Brannan, and Brannan has not forgotten." "Now do you know," said he, "in all this railroading of mine, I have not forgotten. I have learned many things that will help. When I built the great tunnel for the Cattawissa and Opelousas, by which we got rid of the old inclined planes, there was never a stone bigger than a peach-stone within two hundred miles of us. I baked the brick of that tunnel on the line with my own kilns. Ingham, I have made more brick, I believe, than any man living in the world!"

"You are the providential man," said I.

"Am I not, Fred? More than that," said he; "I have succeeded in things the world counts worth more

* "Every man," says Dr. Peabody, "should have a vocation and an avocation." To which I add, "A third."

than brick. I have made brick, and I have made money!"

"One of us make money?" asked I, amazed.

"Even so," said dear Oructt; "one of us has made money." And he proceeded to tell me how. It was not in building tunnels, nor in making brick. No! It was by buying up the original stock of the Cattawissa and Opelousas, at a moment when that stock had hardly a nominal price in the market. There were the first mortgage bonds, and the second mortgage bonds, and the third, and I know not how much floating debt; and, worse than all, the reputation of the road lost, and deservedly lost. Every locomotive it had was asthmatic. Every car it had bore the marks of unprecedented accidents, for which no one was to blame. Rival lines, I know not how many, were cutting each other's throats for its legitimate business. At this juncture, dear George invested all his earnings as a contractor, in the despised original stock, — he actually bought it for $3\frac{1}{4}$ per cent, — good shares that had cost a round hundred to every wretch who had subscribed. Six thousand eight hundred dollars — every cent he had — did George thus invest. Then he went himself to the trustees of the first mortgage, to the trustees of the second, and to the trustees of the third, and told them what he had done.

Now it is personal presence that moves the world. Dear Orcutt has found that out since, if he did not know it before. The trustees who would have sniffed had George written to them, turned round from their desks, and begged him to take a chair, when he came to talk with them. Had he put every penny he was worth into that stock ? Then it was worth something which they did not know of, for George Orcutt was no fool about railroads. The man who bridged the Lower Rapidan when a freshet was running was no fool.

" What were his plans ?"

George did not tell — no, not to lordly trustees — what his plans were. He had plans, but he kept them to himself. All he told them was that he had plans. On those plans he had staked his all. Now would they or would they not agree to put him in charge of the running of that road, for twelve months, on a nominal salary. The superintendent they had had was a rascal. He had proved that by running away. They knew that George was not a rascal. He knew that he could make this road pay expenses, pay bondholders, and pay a dividend, — a thing no one else had dreamed of for twenty years. Could they do better than try him ?

Of course they could not, and they knew they could not. Of course, they sniffed and talked, and waited, and pretended they did not know, and that they must consult, and so forth and so on. But of course they all did try him, on his own terms. He was put in charge of the running of that road.

In one week he showed he should redeem it. In three months he did redeem it !

He advertised boldly the first day : "*Infant children at treble price.*"

The novelty attracted instant remark. And it showed many things. First, it showed he was a humane man, who wished to save human life. He would leave these innocents in their cradles, where they belonged.

Second, and chiefly, the world of travellers saw that the Crichton, the Amadis, the perfect chevalier of the future, had arisen, — a railroad manager caring for the comfort of his passengers !

The first week the number of the C. and O.'s passengers was doubled : in a week or two more freight began to come in, in driblets, on the line which its owners had gone over. As soon as the shops could turn them out, some cars were put on, with arms on which travellers could rest their elbows, with headrests where they could take naps if they were weary. These excited so much curiosity that one was exhibited in the museum at Cattawissa and another at Opelousas. It may not be generally known that the received car of the American roads was devised to secure a premium offered by the Pawtucket and Podunk Company. Their receipts were growing so large that they feared they should forfeit their charter. They advertised, therefore, for a car in which no man could sleep at night or rest by day, — in which the backs should be straight, the heads of passengers unsupported, the feet entangled in a vice, the elbows always knocked by the passing conductor. The pattern was produced which immediately came into use on all the American roads. But on the Cattawissa and Opelousas this time-honored pattern was set aside.

Of course you see the result. Men went hundreds of miles out of their way to ride on the C. and O. The third mortgage was paid off; a reserve fund was piled up for the second; the trustees of the first lived in dread of being paid; and George's stock, which he bought at $3\frac{1}{4}$, rose to 147 before two years had gone by! So was it that, as we sat together in the snuggery, George was worth wellnigh three hundred thousand dollars. Some of his eggs were in the basket where they were laid; some he had taken out and placed in other baskets; some in nests where various hens were brooding over them. Sound eggs they were, wherever placed; and such was the victory of which George had come to tell.

One of us had made money !

On his way he had seen Brannan. Brannan, the pure-minded, right-minded, shifty man of tact, man of brain, man of heart, and man of word, who held New Altona in the hollow of his hand. Brannan had made no money. Not he, nor ever will. But Brannan could do much what he pleased in this world, without money. For whenever Brannan studied the rights and the wrongs of any enterprise, all men knew that what Brannan decided about it was wellnigh the eternal truth; and therefore all men of sense were accustomed to place great confidence in his prophecies. But, more than this, and better, Brannan was an unconscious dog, who believed in the people. So, when he knew what was the right and what was the wrong, he could stand up before two or three thousand people and tell them what was right and what was wrong, and tell them with the same simplicity and freshness with which he would talk to little Horace on his knee. Of the thousands who heard him there would not be one in a hundred who knew that this was eloquence. They were fain to say, as they sat in their shops, talking, that Brannan was not eloquent. Nay, they went so far as to regret that Brannan was not eloquent! If he were only as eloquent as Carker was or as Barker was, how excellent he would be! But when, a month after, it was necessary for them to do anything about the thing he had been speaking of, they did what Brannan had told them to do; forgetting, most likely, that he had ever told them, and fancying that these were their own ideas, which, in fact, had, from his liquid, ponderous, transparent, and invisible common sense, distilled unconsciously into their being. I wonder whether Brannan ever knew that he was eloquent. What I knew, and what dear George knew, was, that he was one of the leaders of men!

Courage, my friends, we are steadily advancing to the Brick Moon!

For George had stopped, and seen Brannan; and Brannan had not forgotten. Seventeen years Brannan had remembered, and not a ship had been lost on a lee-shore because her longitude was wrong, — not a baby had wailed its last as it was ground between wrecked spar and cruel rock, — not a swollen corpse unknown had been flung up upon the sand and been buried with a nameless epitaph, — but Brannan had recollected the Brick Moon, and had, in the memory-chamber which rejected nothing, stored away the story of the horror. And now, George was ready to consecrate a round hundred thousand to the building of the Moon ; and Brannan was ready, in the thousand ways in which wise men move the people to and fro, to persuade them to give to us a hundred thousand more ; and George had come to ask me if I were not ready to undertake with them the final great effort, of which our old calculations were the embryo. For this I was now to contribute the mathematical certainty and the lore borrowed from naval science, which should blossom and bear fruit when the Brick Moon was snapped like a cherry from the ways on which it was built, was launched into the air by power gathered from a thousand freshets, and, poised at last in its own pre-calculated region of the ether, should begin its course of eternal blessings in one unchanging meridian !

Vision of Beneficence and Wonder ! Of course I consented.

O that you were not so eager for the end ! O that I might tell you, what now you will never know, — of the great campaign which we then and there inau-

gurated ! How the horrible loss of the Royal Martyr,
whose longitude was three degrees awry, startled the
whole world, and gave us a point to start from. How
I explained to George that he must not subscribe the
one hundred thousand dollars in a moment. It must
come in bits, when " the cause " needed a stimulus, or
the public needed encouragement. How we caught
neophyte editors, and explained to them enough to
make them think the Moon was wellnigh their own
invention and their own thunder. How, beginning in
Boston, we sent round to all the men of science, all
those of philanthropy, and all those of commerce,
three thousand circulars, inviting them to a private
meeting at George's parlors at the Revere. How, besides ourselves, and some nice, respectable-looking old
gentlemen Brannan had brought over from Podunk
with him, paying their fares both ways, there were
present only three men, — all adventurers whose proj-
ects had failed, — besides the representatives of the
press. How, of these representatives, some understood
the whole, and some understood nothing. How, the
next day, all gave us " first-rate notices." How, a
few days after, in the lower Horticultural Hall, we had
our first public meeting. How Haliburton brought us
fifty people who loved him, — his Bible class, most of
them, — to help fill up ; how, besides these, there were
not three persons whom we had not asked personally,
or one who could invent an excuse to stay away. How
we had hung the walls with intelligible and unin-

telligible diagrams. How I opened the meeting. Of
that meeting, indeed, I must tell something.

First, I spoke.   I did not pretend to unfold the
scheme.   I did not attempt any rhetoric.   But I did
not make any apologies.   I told them simply of the
dangers of lee-shores.   I told them when they were
most dangerous, — when seamen came upon them una-
wares.   I explained to them that, though the costly
chronometer, frequently adjusted, made a delusive
guide to the voyager who often made a harbor, still
the adjustment was treacherous, the instrument beyond the use of the poor, and that, once astray, its
error increased forever.   I said that we believed we
had a method which, if the means were supplied for
the experiment, would give the humblest fisherman
the very certainty of sunrise and of sunset in his calculations of his place upon the world.   And I said
that whenever a man knew his place in this world, it
was always likely all would go well.   Then I sat down.

Then dear George spoke, — simply, but very briefly.
He said he was a stranger to the Boston people, and
that those who knew him at all knew he was not a
talking man.   He was a civil engineer, and his business was to calculate and to build, and not to talk.
But he had come here to say that he had studied this
new plan for the longitude from the Top to the Bottom, and that he believed in it through and through.
There was his opinion, if that was worth anything to
anybody.   If that meeting resolved to go forward with

the enterprise, or if anybody proposed to, he should
offer his services in any capacity, and without any pay,
for its success.   If he might only work as a bricklayer,
he would work as a bricklayer.   For he believed, on
his soul, that the success of this enterprise promised
more for mankind than any enterprise which was ever
likely to call for the devotion of his life.   "And to the
good of mankind," he said, very simply, "my life is
devoted."   Then he sat down.

Then Brannan got up.   Up to this time, excepting
that George had dropped this hint about bricklaying,
nobody had said a word about the Moon, far less hinted
what it was to be made of.   So Ben had the whole to
open.   He did it as if he had been talking to a bright
boy of ten years old.   He made those people think
that he respected them as his equals.   But, in fact, he
chose every word, as if not one of them knew anything.
He explained, as if it were rather more simple to explain than to take for granted.   But he explained as
if, were they talking, they might be explaining to him.
He led them from point to point, — oh! so much more
clearly than I have been leading you, — till, as their
mouths dropped a little open in their eager interest,
and their lids forgot to wink in their gaze upon his
face, and so their eyebrows seemed a little lifted in
curiosity, — till, I say, each man felt as if he were himself the inventor, who had bridged difficulty after difficulty ; as if, indeed, the whole were too simple to be
called difficult or complicated.   The only wonder was

that the Board of Longitude, or the Emperor Napoleon, or the Smithsonian, or somebody, had not sent this little planet on its voyage of blessing long before. Not a syllable that you would have called rhetoric, not a word that you would have thought prepared; and then Brannan sat down.

That was Ben Brannan's way. For my part, I like it better than eloquence.

Then I got up again. We would answer any questions, I said. We represented people who were eager to go forward with this work. (Alas! except Q., all of those represented were on the stage.) We could not go forward without the general assistance of the community. It was not an enterprise which the government could be asked to favor. It was not an enterprise which would yield one penny of profit to any human being. We had therefore, purely on the ground of its benefit to mankind, brought it before an assembly of Boston men and women.

Then there was a pause, and we could hear our watches tick, and our hearts beat. Dear George asked me in a whisper if he should say anything more, but I thought not. The pause became painful, and then Tom Coram, prince of merchants, rose. Had any calculation been made of the probable cost of the experiment of one moon?

I said the calculations were on the table. The brick alone would cost $60,000. Mr. Orcutt had computed that $214,729 would complete two fly-wheels and one moon. This made no allowance for whitewashing the moon, which was not strictly necessary. The fly-wheels and water-power would be equally valuable for the succeeding moons, if any were attempted, and therefore the second moon could be turned off, it was hoped, for $159,732.

Thomas Coram had been standing all the time I spoke, and in an instant he said: "I am no mathematician. But I have had a ship ground to pieces under me on the Laccadives because our chronometer was wrong. You need $250,000 to build your first moon. I will be one of twenty men to furnish the money; or I will pay $10,000 to-morrow for this purpose, to any person who may be named as treasurer, to be repaid to me if the moon is not finished this day twenty years."

That was as long a speech as Tom Coram ever made. But it was pointed. The small audience tapped applause.

Orcutt looked at me, and I nodded. "I will be another of the twenty men," cried he. "And I another," said an old bluff Englishman, whom nobody had invited; who proved to be a Mr. Robert Boll, a Sheffield man, who came in from curiosity. He stopped after the meeting; said he should leave the country the next week, and I have never seen him since. But his bill of exchange came all the same.

That was all the public subscribing. Enough more than we had hoped for. We tried to make Coram treasurer, but he refused. We had to make Haliburton treasurer, though we should have liked a man better known than he then was. Then we adjourned. Some nice ladies then came up, and gave, one a dollar, and one five dollars, and one fifty, and so on, — and some men who have stuck by ever since. I always, in my own mind, call each of those women Damaris, and each of those men Dionysius. But those are not their real names.

How I am wasting time on an old story! Then some of these ladies came the next day and proposed a fair; and out of that, six months after, grew the great Longitude Fair, that you will all remember, if you went to it, I am sure. And the papers the next day gave us first-rate reports; and then, two by two, with our subscription-books, we went at it. But I must not tell the details of that subscription. There were two or three men who subscribed $ 5,000 each, because they were perfectly certain the amount would never be raised. They wanted, for once, to get the credit of liberality for nothing. There were many men and many women who subscribed from one dollar up to one thousand, not because they cared a straw for the longitude, nor because they believed in the least in the project; but because they believed in Brannan, in Orcutt, in Q., or in me. Love goes far in this world of ours. Some few men subscribed because others had done it: it was the thing to do, and they must not be out of fashion. And three or four, at least, subscribed because each hour of their lives there came up the memory of the day when the news came that the —— was lost, George, or Harry, or John, in the ——, and they knew that George, or Harry, or John might have been at home, had it been easier than it is to read the courses of the stars!

Fair, subscriptions, and Orcutt's reserve,— we counted up $162,000, or nearly so. There would be a little more when all was paid in.

But we could not use a cent, except Orcutt's and our own little subscriptions, till we had got the whole. And at this point it seemed as if the whole world was sick of us, and that we had gathered every penny that was in store for us. The orange was squeezed dry!

———

II. — HOW WE BUILT IT.

THE orange was squeezed dry! And how little any of us knew, — skilful George Orcutt, thoughtful Ben Brannan, loyal Haliburton, ingenious Q., or poor painstaking I, — how little we knew, or any of us, where was another orange, or how we could mix malic acid and tartaric acid, and citric acid and auric acid and sugar and water so as to imitate orange-juice, and fill up the bank-account enough to draw in the conditioned subscriptions, and so begin to build the MOON. How often, as I lay awake at night, have I added up the different subscriptions in some new order, as if that would help the matter : and how steadily they have come out one hundred and sixty-two thousand dollars, or even less, when I must needs, in my sleepiness, forget somebody's name ! So Haliburton put into railroad stocks all the money he collected, and the rest of us ground on at our mills, or flew up on our own wings towards Heaven. Thus Orcutt built more tunnels, Q. prepared for more commencements, Haliburton calculated more policies, Ben Brannan created more civilization, and I, as I could, healed the hurt of my people of Naguadavick for the months there were left to me of my stay in that thriving town.

None of us had the wit to see how the problem was to be wrought out further. No. The best things come to us when we have faithfully and well made all the preparation and done our best ; but they come in some way that is none of ours. So was it now, that to build the BRICK MOON it was necessary that I should be turned out of Naguadavick ignominiously, and that Jeff. Davis and some seven or eight other bad men should create the Great Rebellion. Hear how it happened.

Dennis Shea, my Double, — otherwise, indeed, called by my name and legally so, — undid me, as my friends supposed, one evening at a public meeting called by poor Isaacs in Naguadavick. Of that transaction I have no occasion here to tell the story. But of that transaction one consequence is that the BRICK MOON now moves in ether. I stop writing, to rest my eye upon it, through a little telescope of Alvan Clark's here, which is always trained near it. It is moving on as placidly as ever.

It came about thus. The morning after poor Dennis, whom I have long since forgiven, made his extraordinary speeches, without any authority from me, in the Town Hall at Naguadavick, I thought, and my wife agreed with me, that we had better both leave town with the children. Auchmuty, our dear friend, thought so too. We left in the ten-thirty Accommodation for Skowhegan, and so came to Township No. 9 in the 3d Range, and there for years we resided. That whole range of townships was set off under a provision admirable in its character, that the first settled minister in each town should receive one hundred acres of land as the "minister's grant," and the first settled schoolmaster eighty. To No. 9, therefore, I came. I constituted a little Sandemanian church. Auchmuty and Delafield came up and installed me, and with these hands I built the cabin in which, with Polly and the little ones, I have since spent many happy nights and days. This is not the place for me to publish a map, which I have by me, of No. 9, nor an account of its many advantages for settlers. Should I ever print my papers called "Stay-at-home Robinsons," it will be easy with them to explain its topography and geography. Suffice it now to say, that, with Alice and Bertha and Polly, I took tramps up and down through the lumbermen's

roads, and soon knew the general features of the lay
of the land. Nor was it long, of course, before we
came out one day upon the curious land-slides, which
have more than once averted the flow of the Little Carrotook River, where it has washed the rocks away so
far as to let down one section more of the overlying
yielding yellow clay.

Think how my eyes flashed, and my wife's, as, strug-
gling through a wilderness of moosewood, we came out
one afternoon on this front of yellow clay! Yellow
clay, of course, when properly treated by fire, is brick!
Here we were surrounded by forests, only waiting to
be burned; yonder was clay, only waiting to be baked.
Polly looked at me, and I looked at her, and with one
voice, we cried out, "The Moon!"

For here was this shouting river at our feet, whose
power had been running to waste since the day when
the Laurentian hills first heaved themselves above the
hot Atlantic; and that day, I am informed by Mr.
Agassiz, was the first day in the history of this solid
world. Here was water-power enough for forty fly-
wheels, were it necessary to send heavenward twenty
moons. Here was solid timber enough for a hundred
dams, yet only one was necessary to give motion to
the fly-wheels. Here was retirement, — freedom from
criticism, an escape from the journalists, who would
not embarrass us by telling of every cracked brick
which had to be rejected from the structure. We had
lived in No. 9 now for six weeks, and not an "own

correspondent" of them all had yet told what Rev.
Mr. Ingham had for dinner.

Of course I wrote to George Orcutt at once of our
great discovery, and he came up at once to examine
the situation. On the whole, it pleased him. He could
not take the site I proposed for the dam, because this
very clay there made the channel treacherous, and there
was danger that the stream would work out a new
career. But lower down we found a stony gorge with
which George was satisfied; he traced out a line for a
railway by which, of their own weight, the brick-cars
could run to the centrings; he showed us where, with
some excavations, the fly-wheels could be placed exactly above the great mill-wheels, that no power might
be wasted, and explained to us how, when the gigantic
structure was finished, the BRICK MOON would gently
roll down its ways upon the rapid wheels, to be launched
instant into the sky!

Shall I ever forget that happy October day of antici-
pation?

We spent many of those October days in tentative
surveys. Alice and Bertha were our chain-men, intelligent and obedient. I drove for George his stakes, or
I cut away his brush, or I raised and lowered the shield
at which he sighted; and at noon Polly appeared with
her baskets, and we would dine *al fresco*, on a pretty
point which, not many months after, was wholly covered by the eastern end of the dam. When the field-
work was finished we retired to the cabin for days, and

calculated and drew, and drew and calculated. Estimates for feeding Irishmen, estimates of hay for mules,
— George was sure he could work mules better than
oxen, — estimates for cement, estimates for the preliminary saw-mills, estimates for rail for the little brick-
road, for wheels, for spikes, and for cutting ties ; what
did we not estimate for — on a basis almost wholly
new, you will observe.   For here the brick would cost
us less than our old conceptions, — our water-power
cost us almost nothing, — but our stores and our wages
would cost us much more.

These estimates are now to me very curious, — a
monument, indeed, to dear George's memory, that in
the result they proved so accurate.   I would gladly
print them here at length, with some illustrative cuts,
but that I know the impatience of the public, and its
indifference to detail.   If we are ever able to print a
proper memorial of George, that, perhaps, will be the
fitter place for them.   Suffice it to say that with the
subtractions thus made from the original estimates, —
even with the additions forced upon us by working
in a wilderness, — George was satisfied that a money
charge of $197,327 would build and start THE MOON.
As soon as we had determined the site, we marked off
eighty acres, which contained all the essential local-
ities, up and down the little Carrotook River, — I
engaged George for the first schoolmaster in No. 9,
and he took these eighty acres for the schoolmaster's
reservation.   Alice and Bertha went to school to him

the next day, taking lessons in civil engineering; and I wrote to the Bingham trustees to notify them that I had engaged a teacher, and that he had selected his land.

Of course we remembered, still, that we were near forty thousand dollars short of the new estimates, and also that much of our money would not be paid us but on condition that two hundred and fifty thousand were raised. But George said that his own subscription was wholly unhampered: with that we would go to work on the preliminary work of the dam, and on the flies. Then, if the flies would hold together, — and they should hold if mortise and iron could hold them, — they might be at work summers and winters, days and nights, storing up Power for us. This would encourage the subscribers, nay, would encourage us; and all this preliminary work would be out of the way when we were really ready to begin upon the MOON.

Brannan, Haliburton, and Q. readily agreed to this when they were consulted. They were the other trustees under an instrument which we had got St. Leger to draw up. George gave up, as soon as he might, his other appointments; and taught me, meanwhile, where and how I was to rig a little saw-mill, to cut some necessary lumber. I engaged a gang of men to cut the timber for the dam, and to have it ready; and, with the next spring, we were well at work on the dam and on the flies! These needed, of course, the most solid foundation. The least irregularity of their movement might send the MOON awry.

Ah me! would I not gladly tell the history of every
bar of iron which was bent into the tires of those flies,
and of every log which was mortised into its place in
the dam, nay, of every curling mass of foam which
played in the eddies beneath, when the dam was
finished, and the waste water ran so smoothly over?
Alas! that one drop should be wasted of water that
might move a world, although a small one! I almost
dare say that I remember each and all these, — with
such hope and happiness did I lend myself, as I could,
each day to the great enterprise; lending to dear
George, who was here and there and everywhere, and
was this and that and everybody, — lending to him, I
say, such poor help as I could lend, in whatever way.
We waked, in the two cabins, in those happy days,
just before the sun came up, when the birds were in
their loudest clamor of morning joy. Wrapped each
in a blanket, George and I stepped out from our doors,
each trying to call the other, and often meeting on the
grass between. We ran to the river and plunged in,
— O, how cold it was! — laughed and screamed like
boys, rubbed ourselves aglow, and ran home to build
Polly's fire beneath the open chimney which stood
beside my cabin. The bread had risen in the night.
The water soon boiled above the logs. The children
came, laughing, out upon the grass, barefoot, and fearless of the dew. Then Polly appeared with her grid-
iron and bear-steak, or with her griddle and eggs, and,
in fewer minutes than this page has cost me, the break-

fast was ready for Alice to carry, dish by dish, to the white-clad table on the piazza. Not Raphael and Adam more enjoyed their watermelons, fox-grapes, and late blueberries! And, in the long croon of the break-fast, lingering at the board, we revenged ourselves for the haste with which it had been prepared.

When we were well at table, a horn from the cabins below sounded the reveille for the drowsier workmen. Soon above the larches rose the blue of their smokes; and when we were at last nodding to the children, to say that they might leave the table, and Polly was folding her napkin as to say she wished we were gone, we would see tall Asaph Langdon, then foreman of the carpenters, sauntering up the valley with a roll of paper, or an adze, or a shingle with some calcula-tions on it, — with something on which he wanted Mr. Orcutt's directions for the day.

An hour of nothings set the carnal machinery of the day agoing. We fed the horses, the cows, the pigs, and the hens. We collected the eggs and cleaned the hen-houses and the barns. We brought in wood enough for the day's fire, and water enough for the day's cooking and cleanliness. These heads describe what I and the children did. Polly's life during that hour was more mysterious. That great first hour of the day is devoted with women to the deepest arcana of the Eleusinian mysteries of the divine science of housekeeping. She who can meet the requisitions of that hour wisely and bravely conquers in the Day's

Battle.   But what she does in it, let no man try to
say!   It can be named, but not described, in the com-
prehensive formula, "Just stepping round."

That hour well given to chores and to digestion, the
children went to Mr. Orcutt's open-air school, and I to
my rustic study, — a separate cabin, with a rough
square table in it, and some book-boxes equally rude.
No man entered it, excepting George and me.   Here
for two hours I worked undisturbed, — how happy the
world, had it neither postman nor door-bell! — worked
upon my Traces of Sandemanianism in the Sixth and
Seventh Centuries, and then was ready to render such
service to The Cause and to George as the day might
demand.   Thus I rode to Lincoln or to Foxcroft to
order supplies; I took my gun and lay in wait on
Chairback for a bear; I transferred to the hewn lumber
the angles or bevels from the careful drawings: as best
I could, I filled an apostle's part, and became all things
to all these men around me.   Happy those days! —
and thus the dam was built; in such Arcadian simplicity was reared the mighty wheel; thus grew on
each side the towers which were to support the flies;
and thus, to our delight not unmixed with wonder, at
last we saw those mighty flies begin to turn.   Not in
one day, nor in ten; but in a year or two of happy
life, — full of the joy of joys, — the "joy of eventful
living."

Yet, for all this, $162,000 was not $197,000, far
less was it $250,000; and but for Jeff. Davis and

his crew the BRICK MOON would not have been born.

But at last Jeff. Davis was ready. "My preparations being completed," wrote General Beauregard, "I opened fire on Fort Sumter." Little did he know it, — but in that explosion the BRICK MOON also was lifted into the sky!

Little did we know it, when, four weeks after, George came up from the settlements, all excited with the news! The wheels had been turning now for four days, faster of course and faster. George had gone down for money to pay off the men, and he brought us up the news that the Rebellion had begun.

"The last of this happy life," he said; "the last, alas, of our dear MOON." How little he knew and we!

But he paid off the men, and they packed their traps and disappeared, and, before two months were over, were in the lines before the enemy. George packed up, bade us sadly good by, and before a week had offered his service to Governor Fenton in Albany. For us, it took rather longer; but we were soon packed; Polly took the children to her sister's, and I went on to the Department to offer my service there. No sign of life left in No. 9, but the two gigantic Fly-Wheels, moving faster and faster by day and by night, and accumulating Power till it was needed. If only they would hold together till the moment came!

So we all ground through the first slow year of the war. George in his place, I in mine, Brannan in his,

— we lifted as we could. But how heavy the weight seemed! It was in the second year, when the second large loan was placed, that Haliburton wrote to me, — I got the letter, I think, at Hilton Head, — that he had sold out every penny of our railroad stocks, at the high prices which railroad stocks then bore, and had invested the whole fifty-nine thousand in the new Governments. " I could not call a board meeting," said Haliburton, " for I am here only on leave of absence, and the rest are all away. But the case is clear enough. If the government goes up, the MOON will never go up; and, for one, I do not look beyond the veil." So he wrote to us all, and of course we all approved.

So it was that Jeff. Davis also served. Deep must that man go into the Pit who does not serve, though unconscious. For thus it was that, in the fourth year of the war, when gold was at 290, Haliburton was receiving on his fifty-nine thousand dollars seventeen per cent interest in currency; thus was it that, before the war was over, he had piled up, compounding his interest, more than fifty per cent addition to his capital; thus was it that, as soon as peace came, all his stocks were at a handsome percentage; thus was it that, before I returned from South America, he reported to all the subscribers that the full quarter-million was secured; thus was it that, when I returned after that long cruise of mine in the Florida, I found Polly and the children again at No. 9, George there also, directing a working party of nearly eighty bricklayers and hodmen, the lower centrings wellnigh filled to their diameter, and the BRICK MOON, to the eye, seeming almost half completed.

Here it is that I regret most of all that I cannot print the working-drawings with this paper. If you will cut open the seed-vessel of Spergularia Rubra, or any other carpel that has a free central placenta, and observe how the circular seeds cling around the circular centre, you will have some idea of the arrangement of a transverse horizontal section of the completed MOON. Lay three croquet-balls on the piazza, and call one or two of the children to help you poise seven in one plane above the three; then let another child place three more above the seven, and you have the *core* of the MOON completely. If you want a more poetical illustration, it was what Mr. Wordsworth calls a mass

"Of conglobated bubbles undissolved."

Any section through any diameter looked like an immense rose-window, of six circles grouped round a seventh. In truth, each of these sections would reveal the existence of seven chambers in the moon, — each a sphere itself, — whose arches gave solidity to the whole; while yet, of the whole moon, the greater part was air. In all there were thirteen of these moonlets, if I am so to call them; though no one section, of course, would reveal so many. Sustained on each side by their groined arches, the surface of the whole moon was built over them and under them, — simply two domes connected at the bases. The chambers themselves were made lighter by leaving large, round windows or open circles in the parts of their vaults farthest from their points of contact, so that each of them looked not unlike the outer sphere of a Japanese ivory nest of concentric balls. You see the object was to make a moon, which, when left to its own gravity, should be fitly supported or braced within. Dear George was sure that, by this constant repetition of arches, we should with the least weight unite the greatest strength. I believe it still, and experience has proved that there is strength enough.

When I went up to No. 9, on my return from South America, I found the lower centring up, and half full of the working-bees, — who were really Keltic laborers, — all busy in bringing up the lower half-dome of the shell. This lower centring was of wood, in form exactly like a Roman amphitheatre if the seats of it be circular; on this the lower or inverted brick dome was laid. The whole fabric was on one of the terraces which were heaved up in some old geological cataclysm, when some lake gave way, and the Carrotook River was born. The level was higher than that of the top of the fly-wheels, which, with an awful velocity now, were circling in their wild career in the ravine below. Three of the lowest moonlets, as I have called them, — separate croquet-balls, if you take my other illustration, — had been completed; their centrings had been taken to pieces and drawn out through the holes, and were now set up again with other new centrings for the second story of cells.

I was received with wonder and delight. I had telegraphed my arrival, but the despatches had never been forwarded from Skowhegan. Of course, we all had a deal to tell; and, for me, there was no end to inquiries which I had to make in turn. I was never tired of exploring the various spheres, and the nameless spaces between them. I was never tired of talking with the laborers. All of us, indeed, became skilful bricklayers; and on a pleasant afternoon you might see Alice and Bertha, and George and me, all laying brick together, — Polly sitting in the shade of some wall which had been built high enough, and reading to us from Jean Ingelow or Monte-Cristo or Jane Austen, while little Clara brought to us our mortar. Happily and lightly went by that summer. Haliburton and his wife made us a visit; Ben Brannan brought up his wife and children; Mrs. Haliburton herself put in the keystone to the central chamber, which had always been named G. on the plans; and at her suggestion, it was named Grace now, because her mother's name was Hannah. Before winter we had passed the diameter of I, J, and K, the three uppermost cells of all; and the surrounding shell was closing in upon them. On the whole, the funds had held out amazingly well. The wages had been rather higher than we meant; but the men had no chances at liquor or dissipation, and

had worked faster than we expected; and, with our
new brick-machines, we made brick inconceivably
fast, while their quality was so good that dear George
said there was never so little waste. We celebrated
Thanksgiving of that year together, — my family and
his family. We had paid off all the laborers; and
there were left, of that busy village, only Asaph Langdon and his family, Levi Jordan and Levi Ross, Horace
Leonard and Seth Whitman with theirs. "Theirs," I
say, but Ross had no family. He was a nice young
fellow who was there as Haliburton's representative,
to take care of the accounts and the pay-roll; Jordan
was the head of the brick-kilns; Leonard, of the carpenters; and Whitman, of the commissariat, — and a
good commissary Whitman was.

We celebrated Thanksgiving together! Ah me!
what a cheerful, pleasant time we had; how happy
the children were together! Polly and I and our
bairns were to go to Boston the next day. I was to
spend the winter in one final effort to get twenty-five
thousand dollars more if I could, with which we might
paint the MOON, or put on some ground felspathic
granite dust, in a sort of paste, which in its hot flight
through the air might fuse into a white enamel. All
of us who saw the MOON were so delighted with its
success that we felt sure "the friends" would not
pause about this trifle. The rest of them were to stay
there to watch the winter, and to be ready to begin
work the moment the snow had gone. Thanksgiving

afternoon, — how well I remember it, — that good fellow, Whitman, came and asked Polly and me to visit his family in their new quarters. They had moved for the winter into cells B and E, so lofty, spacious, and warm, and so much drier than their log cabins. Mrs. Whitman, I remember, was very cheerful and jolly; made my children eat another piece of pie, and stuffed their pockets with raisins; and then with great ceremony and fun we christened room B by the name of Bertha, and E, Ellen, which was Mrs. Whitman's name. And the next day we bade them all good by, little thinking what we said, and with endless promises of what we would send and bring them in the spring.

Here are the scraps of letters from Orcutt, dear fellow, which tell what more there is left to tell : —

"December 10th.

". . . . After you left we were a little blue, and hung round loose for a day or two. Sunday we missed you especially, but Asaph made a good substitute, and Mrs. Leonard led the singing. The next day we moved the Leonards into L and M, which we christened Leonard and Mary (Mary is for your wife). They are pretty dark, but very dry. Leonard has swung hammocks, as Whitman did.

"Asaph came to me Tuesday and said he thought they had better turn to and put a shed over the unfinished circle, and so take occasion of warm days for dry

work there.   This we have done, and the occupation
is good for us. . . . ."

" December 25th.

" I have had no chance to write for a fortnight.   The
truth is, that the weather has been so open that I let
Asaph go down to No. 7 and to Wilder's, and engage
five-and-twenty of the best of the men, who, we knew,
were hanging round there.   We have all been at work
most of the time since, with very good success.   H is
now wholly covered in, and the centring is out.   The
men have named it Haliburton.   I is well advanced.
J is as you left it.   The work has been good for us all,
morally."

" February 11th.

" . . . . We got your mail unexpectedly by some lumbermen on their way to the 9th Range.   One of them
has cut himself, and takes this down.

" You will be amazed to hear that I and K are both
done.   We have had splendid weather, and have worked
half the time.   We had a great jollification when K
was closed in, — called it Kilpatrick, for Seth's old
general.   I wish you could just run up and see us.
You must be quick, if you want to put in any of the
last licks. . . . ."

" March 12th.

" DEAR FRED, — I have but an instant.   By all
means make your preparations to be here by the end
of the month or early in next month.   The weather
has been faultless, you know.   Asaph got in a dozen

more men, and we have brought up the surface farther than you could dream. The ways are well forward, and I cannot see why, if the freshet hold off a little, we should not launch her by the 10th or 12th. I do not think it worth while to wait for paint or enamel. Telegraph Brannan that he must be here. You will be amused by our quarters. We, who were the last outsiders, move into A and D to-morrow, for a few weeks. It is much warmer there.

"Ever yours,

"G. O."

I telegraphed Brannan, and in reply he came with his wife and his children to Boston. I told him that he could not possibly get up there, as the roads then were; but Ben said he would go to Skowhegan, and take his chance there. He would, of course, communicate with me as soon as he got there. Accordingly I got a note from him at Skowhegan, saying he had hired a sleigh to go over to No. 9 ; and in four days more I got this letter : —

"March 27th.

"DEAR FRED, — I am most glad I came, and I beg you to bring your wife as soon as possible. The river is very full, the wheels, to which Leonard has added two auxiliaries, are moving as if they could not hold out long, the ways are all but ready, and we think we must not wait. Start with all hands as soon as you can. I had no difficulty in coming over from Skowhegan. We did it in two days."

This note I sent at once to Haliburton ; and we got
all the children ready for a winter journey, as the spec-
tacle of the launch of the MOON was one to be remembered their life long. But it was clearly impossible to
attempt, at that season, to get the subscribers together.
Just as we started, this despatch from Skowhegan was
brought me, — the last word I got from them : —

" Stop for nothing. There is a jam below us in the
stream, and we fear back-water.

"ORCUTT."

Of course we could not go faster than we could. We
missed no connection. At Skowhegan, Haliburton and
I took a cutter, leaving the ladies and children to follow at once in larger sleighs. We drove all night,
changed horses at Prospect, and kept on all the next
day. At No. 7 we had to wait over night. We started
early in the morning, and came down the Spoonwood
Hill at four in the afternoon, in full sight of our little
village.

It was quiet as the grave ! Not a smoke, not a man,
not an adze-blow, nor the tick of a trowel. Only the
gigantic fly-wheels were whirling as I saw them last.

There was the lower Coliseum-like centring, somewhat as I first saw it.

But where was the Brick Dome of the MOON ?

" Good Heavens ! has it fallen on them all ? " cried I.

Haliburton lashed the beast till he fairly ran down
that steep hill. We turned a little point, and came

out in front of the centring. There was no Moon
there ! An empty amphitheatre, with not a brick nor
a splinter within !

We were speechless. We left the cutter. We ran
up the stairways to the terrace. We ran by the familiar paths into the centring. We came out upon the
ways, which we had never seen before. These told
the story too well ! The ground and crushed surface
of the timbers, scorched by the rapidity with which
THE Moon had slid down, told that they had done the
duty for which they were built.

It was too clear that in some wild rush of the waters
the ground had yielded a trifle. We could not find
that the foundations had sunk more than six inches,
but that was enough. In that fatal six inches' decline
of the centring, the Moon had been launched upon the
ways just as George had intended that it should be
when he was ready. But it had slid, not rolled, down
upon these angry fly-wheels, and in an instant, with
all our friends, it had been hurled into the sky !

" They have gone up ! " said Haliburton ; " She has
gone up ! " said I ; — both in one breath. And with
a common instinct, we looked up into the blue.

But of course she was not there.

Not a shred of letter or any other tidings could we
find in any of the shanties. It was indeed six weeks
since George and Fanny and their children had moved
into Annie and Diamond, — two unoccupied cells of

the MOON, — so much more comfortable had the cells
proved than the cabins, for winter life. Returning to
No. 7, we found there many of the laborers, who were
astonished at what we told them. They had been paid
off on the 30th, and told to come up again on the 15th
of April, to see the launch. One of them, a man named
Rob Shea, told me that George kept his cousin Peter
to help him move back into his house the beginning
of the next week.

And that was the last I knew of any of them for
more than a year. At first I expected, each hour, to
hear that they had fallen somewhere. But time passed
by, and of such a fall, where man knows the world's
surface, there was no tale. I answered, as best I could,
the letters of their friends, by saying I did not know
where they were, and had not heard from them. My
real thought was, that if this fatal MOON did indeed
pass our atmosphere, all in it must have been burned
to death in the transit. But this I whispered to no
one save to Polly and Annie and Haliburton. In this
terrible doubt I remained, till I noticed one day in the
"Astronomical Record" the memorandum, which you
perhaps remember, of the observation, by Dr. Zitta, of
a new asteroid, with an enormous movement in declination.

III. — FULFILMENT.

LOOKING back upon it now, it seems inconceivable that we said as little to each other as we did, of this horrible catastrophe. That night we did not pretend to sleep. We sat in one of the deserted cabins, now talking fast, now sitting and brooding, without speaking, perhaps, for hours. Riding back the next day to meet the women and children, we still brooded, or we discussed this " if," that " if," and yet others. But after we had once opened it all to them, — and when we had once answered the children's horribly naïve questions as best we could, — we very seldom spoke to each other of it again. It was too hateful, all of it, to talk about. I went round to Tom Coram's office one day, and told him all I knew. He saw it was dreadful to me, and, with his eyes full, just squeezed my hand, and never said one word more. We lay awake nights, pondering and wondering, but hardly ever did I to Haliburton or he to me explain our respective notions as they came and went. I believe my general impression was that of which I have spoken, that they were all burned to death on the instant, as the little aerolite fused in its passage through our atmosphere. I believe Haliburton's thought more often was that they were conscious of what had happened, and gasped out their lives in one or two breathless minutes, — so horribly long ! — as they shot outside of our atmosphere. But it was all too terrible for words. And that which we could not but think upon, in those dreadful waking nights, we scarcely whispered even to our wives.

Of course I looked and he looked for the miserable thing. But we looked in vain. I returned to the few subscribers the money which I had scraped together towards whitewashing the moon, — "shrouding its guilty face with innocent white" indeed! But we agreed to spend the wretched trifle of the other money, left in the treasury after paying the last bills, for the largest Alvan Clark telescope that we could buy; and we were fortunate in obtaining cheap a second-hand one which came to the hammer when the property of the Shubael Academy was sold by the mortgagees. But we had, of course, scarce a hint whatever as to where the miserable object was to be found. All we could do was to carry the glass to No. 9, to train it there on the meridian of No. 9, and take turns every night in watching the field, in the hope that this child of sorrow might drift across it in its path of ruin. But, though everything else seemed to drift by, from east to west, nothing came from south to north, as we expected. For a whole month of spring, another of autumn, another of summer, and another of winter, did Haliburton and his wife and Polly and I glue our eyes to that eye-glass, from the twilight of evening to the twilight of morning, and the dead hulk never hove in sight. Wherever else it was, it seemed not to be on that meridian, which was where it ought to be and was made to be ! Had ever any dead mass of matter wrought such ruin to its makers, and, of its own stupid inertia, so falsified all the prophecies of its birth ! O, the total depravity of things !

It was more than a year after the fatal night, — if it all happened in the night, as I suppose, — that, as I dreamily read through the " Astronomical Record " in the new reading-room of the College Library at Cambridge, I lighted on this scrap : —

" Professor Karl Zitta of Breslau writes to the *Astronomische Nachrichten* to claim the discovery of a new asteroid observed by him on the night of March 31st.

(92)

Bresl. M. T.	App. A. R.	App. Decl.	
	h. m. s.	h. m. s.	° ′ ″ Size.
March 31	12 53 51.9	15 39 52.32	—23 50 26.1 12.9
April 1	1 3 2.1	15 39 52.32	—23 9 1.9 12.9

He proposes for the asteroid the name of Phœbe. Dr. Zitta states that in the short period which he had for observing Phœbe, for an hour after midnight, her motion in R. A. seemed slight and her motion in declination very rapid."

After this, however, for months, nay even to this moment, nothing more was heard of Dr. Zitta of Breslau.

But, one morning, before I was up, Haliburton came banging at my door on D Street. The mood had taken him, as he returned from some private theatricals at Cambridge, to take the comfort of the new reading-room at night, and thus express in practice his gratitude to the overseers of the college for keeping it open through all the twenty-four hours. Poor Haliburton, he did not sleep well in those times ! Well, as he read away on the *Astronomische Nachrichten* itself, what should he find but this in German, which he copied for me, and then, all on foot in the rain and darkness, tramped over with, to South Boston : —

" The most enlightened head professor Dr. Gmelin writes to the director of the Porpol Astronomik at St. Petersburg, to claim the discovery of an asteroid in a very high southern latitude, of a wider inclination of the orbit, as will be noticed, than any asteroid yet observed.

" Planet's apparent a 21^h 20^m 51^s.40. Planet's apparent δ —39° 31′ 11″.9. Comparison star a.

" Dr. Gmelin publishes no separate second observation, but is confident that the declination is diminishing. Dr. Gmelin suggests for the name of this extra-zodiacal planet " Io," as appropriate to its wanderings from the accustomed ways of planetary life, and trusts that the very distinguished Herr Peters, the godfather of so many planets, will relinquish this name, already claimed for the asteroid (85) observed by him, September 15, 1865."

I had run down stairs almost as I was, slippers and dressing-gown being the only claims I had on society.

But to me, as to Haliburton, this stuff about "extra-zodiacal wandering" blazed out upon the page, and though there was no evidence that the "most enlightened" Gmelin found anything the next night, yet, if his "diminishing" meant anything, there was, with Zitta's observation, — whoever Zitta might be, — something to start upon. We rushed upon some old bound volumes of the Record and spotted the "enlightened Gmelin." He was chief of a college at Taganrog, where perhaps they had a spyglass. This gave us the parallax of his observation. Breslau, of course, we knew, and so we could place Zitta's, and with these poor data I went to work to construct, if I could, an orbit for this Io-Phœbe mass of brick and mortar. Haliburton, not strong in spherical trigonometry, looked out logarithms for me till breakfast, and, as soon as it would do, went over to Mrs. Bowdoin, to borrow her telescope, ours being left at No. 9.

Mrs. Bowdoin was kind, as she always was, and at noon Haliburton appeared in triumph with the boxes on P. Nolan's job-wagon. We always employ P., in memory of dear old Phil. We got the telescope rigged, and waited for night, only, alas! to be disappointed again. Io had wandered somewhere else, and, with all our sweeping back and forth on the tentative curve I had laid out, Io would not appear. We spent that night in vain.

But we were not going to give it up so. Phœbe might have gone round the world twice before she

became Io; might have gone three times, four, five, six,
— nay, six hundred, — who knew ? Nay, who knew
how far off Phœb-Io was or Io-Phœbe ? We sent over
for Annie, and she and Polly and George and I went
to work again. We calculated in the next week sixty-
seven orbits on the supposition of so many different
distances from our surface. I laid out on a paper,
which we stuck up on the wall opposite, the formula,
and then one woman and one man attacked each set
of elements, each having the Logarithmic Tables, and
so in a week's working-time, the sixty-seven orbits
were completed. Sixty-seven possible places for Io-
Phœbe to be in on the forthcoming Friday evening.
Of these sixty-seven, forty-one were observable above
our horizon that night.

She was not in one of the forty-one, nor near it.

But Despair, if Giotto be correct, is the chief of
sins. So has he depicted her in the fresco of the
Arena in Padua. No sin, that, of ours ! After searching all that Friday night, we slept all Saturday (sleeping after sweeping). We all came to the Chapel,
Sunday, kept awake there, and taught our Sunday
classes special lessons on Perseverance. On Monday
we began again, and that week we calculated sixty-
seven more orbits. I am sure I do not know why we
stopped at sixty-seven. All of these were on the supposition that the revolution of the Brick Moon, or
Io-Phœbe, was so fast that it would require either
fifteen days to complete its orbit, or sixteen days, or

seventeen days, and so on up to eighty-one days.
And, with these orbits, on the next Friday we waited
for the darkness. As we sat at tea, I asked if I
should begin observing at the smallest or at the largest
orbit. And there was a great clamor of diverse opinions. But little Bertha said, "Begin in the middle."

"And what is the middle?" said George, chaffing
the little girl.

But she was not to be dismayed. She had been in
and out all the week, and knew that the first orbit
was of fifteen days and the last of eighty-one; and,
with true Lincoln School precision, she said, "The
mean of the smallest orbit and the largest orbit is
forty-eight days."

"Amen!" said I, as we all laughed. "On forty-
eight days we will begin."

Alice ran to the sheets, turned up that number, and
read, "R. A. 27° 11'. South declination 34° 49'."

"Convenient place," said George; "good omen, Bertha, my darling! If we find her there, Alice and
Bertha and Clara shall all have new dolls."

It was the first word of pleasantry that had been
spoken about the horrid thing since Spoonwood
Hill!

Night came at last. We trained the glass on the
fated spot. I bade Polly take the eye-glass. She did
so, shook her head uneasily, screwed the tube northward herself a moment, and then screamed, "It is
there! it is there, — a clear disk, — gibbous shape, —

and very sharp on the upper edge. Look! look! as
big again as Jupiter!"

Polly was right! The Brick Moon was found!

Now we had found it, we never lost it. Zitta and
Gmelin, I suppose, had had foggy nights and stormy
weather often. But we had some one at the eye-glass
all that night, and before morning had very respectable
elements, good measurements of angular distance when
we got one, and another star in the field of our lowest
power. For we could see her even with a good French
opera-glass I had, and with a night-glass which I used
to carry on the South Atlantic Station. It certainly
was an extraordinary illustration of Orcutt's engineering ability, that, flying off as she did, without leave or
license, she should have gained so nearly the orbit
of our original plan,—nine thousand miles from the
earth's centre, five thousand from the surface. He
had always stuck to the hope of this, and on his very
last tests of the Flies he had said they were almost up
to it. But for this accuracy of his, I can hardly suppose we should have found her to this hour, since she
had failed, by what cause I then did not know, to take
her intended place on the meridian of No. 9. At five
thousand miles the MOON appeared as large as the
largest satellite of Jupiter appears. And Polly was
right in that first observation, when she said she
got a good disk with that admirable glass of Mrs.
Bowdoin.

The orbit was not on the meridian of No. 9, nor did

it remain on any meridian. But it was very nearly
South and North, — an enormous motion in declination
with a very slight *retrograde* motion in Right Ascen-
sion. At five thousand miles the MOON showed as
large as a circle two miles and a third in diameter
would have shown on old Thornbush, as we always
called her older sister. We longed for an eclipse of
Thornbush by B. M., but no such lucky chance is on
the cards in any place accessible to us for many years.
Of course, with a MOON so near us the terrestrial parallax is enormous.

Now, you know, dear reader, that the gigantic reflector of Lord Rosse, and the exquisite fifteen-inch
refractors of the modern observatories, eliminate from
the chaotic rubbish-heap of the surface of old Thornbush much smaller objects than such a circle as I have
named. If you have read Mr. Locke's amusing Moon
Hoax as often as I have, you have those details fresh
in your memory. As John Farrar taught us when all
this began, — and as I have said already, — if there
were a State House in Thornbush two hundred feet
long, the first Herschel would have seen it. His mag-
nifying power was 6450 ; that would have brought this
deaf and dumb State House within some forty miles.
Go up on Mt. Washington and see white sails eighty
miles away, beyond Portland, with your naked eye,
and you will find how well he would have seen that
State House with his reflector. Lord Rosse's statement is, that with his reflector he can see objects on

old Thornbush two hundred and fifty-two feet long.
If he can do that he can see on our B. M. objects
which are five feet long; and, of course, we were
beside ourselves to get control of some instrument
which had some approach to such power. Haliburton
was for at once building a reflector at No. 9; and perhaps he will do it yet, for Haliburton has been successful in his paper-making and lumbering. But I
went to work more promptly.

I remembered, not an apothecary, but an observatory, which had been dormant, as we say of volcanoes,
now for ten or a dozen years, — no matter why! The
trustees had quarrelled with the director, or the funds
had given out, or the director had been shot at the
head of his division, — one of those accidents had
happened which will happen even in observatories
which have fifteen-inch equatorials; and so the equatorial here had been left as useless as a cannon whose
metal has been strained or its reputation stained in an
experiment. The observatory at Tamworth, dedicated
with such enthusiasm, — "another light-house in the
skies," — had been, so long as I have said, worthless
to the world. To Tamworth, therefore, I travelled. In
the neighborhood of the observatory I took lodgings. To
the church where worshipped the family which lived in
the observatory buildings I repaired; after two Sundays
I established acquaintance with John Donald, the head
of this family. On the evening of the third, I made
acquaintance with his wife in a visit to them. Before

three Sundays more he had recommended me to the surviving trustees as his successor as janitor to the buildings. He himself had accepted promotion, and gone, with his household, to keep a store for Haliburton in North Ovid. I sent for Polly and the children, to establish them in the janitor's rooms; and, after writing to her, with trembling eye I waited for the Brick Moon to pass over the field of the fifteen-inch equatorial.

Night came. I was "sole alone!" B. M. came, more than filled the field of vision, of course! but for that I was ready. Heavens! how changed. Red no longer, but green as a meadow in the spring. Still I could see — black on the green — the large twenty-foot circles which I remembered so well, which broke the concave of the dome; and, on the upper edge — were these palm-trees? They were. No, they were hemlocks by their shape, and among them were moving to and fro — — — — — flies? Of course, I cannot see flies! But something is moving, — coming, going. One, two, three, ten; there are more than thirty in all! They are men and women and their children!

Could it be possible? It was possible! Orcutt and Brannan and the rest of them had survived that giddy flight through the ether, and were going and coming on the surface of their own little world, bound to it by its own attraction and living by its own laws!

As I watched, I saw one of them leap from that surface. He passed wholly out of my field of vision, but

in a minute, more or less, returned. Why not! Of
course, the attraction of his world must be very small,
while he retained the same power of muscle he had
when he was here. They must be horribly crowded,
I thought. No. They had three acres of surface, and
there were but thirty-seven of them. Not so much
crowded as people are in Roxbury, not nearly so
much as in Boston; and, besides, these people are
living underground, and have the whole of their surface for their exercise.

I watched their every movement as they approached
the edge and as they left it. Often they passed beyond it, so that I could see them no more. Often they
sheltered themselves from that tropical sun beneath
the trees. Think of living on a world where from the
vertical heat of the hottest noon of the equator to the
twilight of the poles is a walk of only fifty paces!
What atmosphere they had, to temper and diffuse
those rays, I could not then conjecture.

I knew that at half past ten they would pass into
the inevitable eclipse which struck them every night
at this period of their orbit, and must, I thought, be a
luxury to them, as recalling old memories of night
when they were on this world. As they approached
the line of shadow, some fifteen minutes before it was
due, I counted on the edge thirty-seven specks arranged
evidently in order; and, at one moment, as by one signal, all thirty-seven jumped into the air, — high jumps.

Again they did it, and again. Then a low jump; then a high one. I caught the idea in a moment. They were telegraphing to our world, in the hope of an observer. Long leaps and short leaps, — the long and short of Morse's Telegraph Alphabet, — were communicating ideas. My paper and pencil had been of course before me. I jotted down the despatch, whose language I knew perfectly: —

" Show ' I understand ' on the Saw-Mill Flat."
" Show ' I understand ' on the Saw-Mill Flat."
" Show ' I understand ' on the Saw-Mill Flat."

By " I understand " they meant the responsive signal given, in all telegraphy, by an operator who has received and understood a message.

As soon as this exercise had been three times repeated, they proceeded in a solid body — much the most apparent object I had had until now — to Circle No. 3, and then evidently descended into the MOON.

The eclipse soon began, but I knew the MOON's path now, and followed the dusky, coppery spot without difficulty. At 1.33 it emerged, and in a very few moments I saw the solid column pass from Circle No. 3 again, deploy on the edge again, and repeat three times the signal: —

" Show ' I understand ' on the Saw-Mill Flat."
" Show ' I understand ' on the Saw-Mill Flat."
" Show ' I understand ' on the Saw-Mill Flat."

It was clear that Orcutt had known that the edge of his little world would be most easy of observation, and that he had guessed that the moments of obscuration and of emersion were the moments when observers would be most careful. After this signal they broke up again, and I could not follow them. With daylight I sent off a despatch to Haliburton, and, grateful and happy in comparison, sank into the first sleep not haunted by horrid dreams, which I had known for years.

Haliburton knew that George Orcutt had taken with him a good Dolland's refractor, which he had bought in London, of a two-inch glass. He knew that this would give Orcutt a very considerable power, if he could only adjust it accurately enough to find No. 9 in the 3d Range. Orcutt had chosen well in selecting the "Saw-Mill Flat," a large meadow, easily distinguished by the peculiar shape of the mill-pond which we had made. Eager though Haliburton was, to join me, he loyally took moneys, caught the first train to Skowhegan, and, travelling thence, in thirty-six hours more was again descending Spoonwood Hill, for the first time since our futile observations. The snow lay white upon the Flat. With Rob. Shea's help, he rapidly unrolled a piece of black cambric twenty yards long, and pinned it to the crust upon the snow ; another by its side, and another. Much cambric had he left. They had carried down with them enough for the funerals of two Presidents. Haliburton showed the symbols for " I understand," but he could not resist also displaying $\cdot\,\cdot$ — $\cdot$ —, which are the dots and lines to represent O. K., which, he says, is the shortest message of comfort. And not having exhausted the space on the Flat, he and Robert, before night closed in, made a gigantic **O. K.,** fifteen yards from top to bottom, and in marks that were fifteen feet through.

I had telegraphed my great news to Haliburton on Monday night. Tuesday night he was at Skowhegan. Thursday night he was at No. 9. Friday he and Rob. stretched their cambric. Meanwhile, every day I slept. Every night I was glued to the eye-piece. Fifteen minutes before the eclipse every night this weird dance of leaps two hundred feet high, followed by hops of twenty feet high, mingled always in the steady order I have described, spelt out the ghastly message : —

" Show ' I understand ' on the Saw-Mill Flat."

And every morning, as the eclipse ended, I saw the column creep along to the horizon, and again, as the duty of opening day, spell out the same : —

" Show ' I understand ' on the Saw-Mill Flat."

They had done this twice in every twenty-four hours for nearly two years. For three nights steadily, I read these signals twice each night; only these, and nothing more.

But Friday night all was changed. After " Attention," that dreadful " Show " did not come, but this cheerful signal : —

" Hurrah. All well. Air, food, and friends ! what more can man require ? Hurrah."

How like George ! How like Ben Brannan ! How like George's wife ! How like them all ! And they were all well ! Yet poor *I* could not answer. Nay, I could only guess what Haliburton had done. But I have never, I believe, been so grateful since I was born !

After a pause, the united line of leapers resumed their jumps and hops. Long and short spelled out : —

" Your O. K. is twice as large as it need be."

Of the meaning of this, lonely *I* had, of course, no idea.

" I have a power of seven hundred," continued George. How did he get that ? He has never told us. But this I can see, that all our analogies deceive us, — of views of the sea from Mt. Washington, or of the Boston State House from Wachusett. For in these views we look through forty or eighty miles of dense terrestrial atmosphere. But Orcutt was looking nearly vertically through an atmosphere which was, most of it, rare indeed, and pure indeed, compared with its lowest stratum.

In the record-book of my observations these despatches are entered as 12 and 13. Of course it was impossible for me to reply. All I could do was to telegraph these in the morning to Skowhegan, sending them to the care of the Moores, that they might forward them. But the next night showed that this had not been necessary.

Friday night George and the others went on for a

quarter of an hour. Then they would rest, saying, "two," "three," or whatever their next signal time would be. Before morning I had these despatches : —

14. "Write to all hands that we are doing well. Langdon's baby is named Io, and Leonard's is named Phœbe."

How queer that was ! What a coincidence ! And they had some humor there.

15 was : "Our atmosphere stuck to us. It weighs three tenths of an inch — our weight."

16. "Our rain-fall is regular as the clock. We have made a cistern of Kilpatrick."

This meant the spherical chamber of that name.

17. "Write to Darwin that he is all right. We began with lichens and have come as far as palms and hemlocks."

These were the first night's messages. I had scarcely covered the eye-glasses, and adjusted the equatorial for the day, when the bell announced the carriage in which Polly and the children came from the station to relieve me in my solitary service as janitor. I had the joy of showing her the good news. This night's work seemed to fill our cup. For all the day before, when I was awake, I had been haunted by the fear of famine for them. True, I knew that they had stored away in chambers H, I, and J the pork and flour which we had sent up for the workmen through the summer, and the corn and oats for the horses. But this could not last forever.

Now, however, that it proved that in a tropical climate they were forming their own soil, developing their own palms, and eventually even their bread-fruit and bananas, planting their own oats and maize, and developing rice, wheat, and all other cereals, harvesting these six, eight, or ten times — for aught I could see — in one of our years, — why then, there was no danger of famine for them. If, as I thought, they carried up with them heavy drifts of ice and snow in the two chambers which were not covered in when they started, why, they had waters in their firmament quite sufficient for all purposes of thirst and of ablution. And what I had seen of their exercise showed that they were in strength sufficient for the proper development of their little world.

Polly had the messages by heart before an hour was over, and the little girls, of course, knew them sooner than she.

Haliburton, meanwhile, had brought out the Shubael refractor (Alvan Clark), and by night of Friday was in readiness to see what he could see. Shubael of course gave him no such luxury of detail as did my fifteen-inch equatorial. But still he had no difficulty in making out groves of hemlock, and the circular openings. And although he could not make out my thirty-seven flies, still when 10.15 came he saw distinctly the black square crossing from hole Mary to the edge, and begin its Dervish dances. They were on his edge

more precisely than on mine. For Orcutt knew nothing of Tamworth, and had thought his best chance was
to display for No. 9. So was it that, at the same
moment with me, Haliburton also was spelling out
Orcutt & Co.'s joyous " Hurrah ! "

" Thtephen," lisps Celia, " promith that you will
look at yon moon [old Thornbush] at the inthtant I
do." So was it with me and Haliburton.

He was of course informed long before the Moores'
messenger came, that, in Orcutt's judgment, twenty
feet of length were sufficient for his signals. Orcutt's
atmosphere, of course, must be exquisitely clear.

So, on Saturday, Rob. and Haliburton pulled up all
their cambric and arranged it on the Flat again, in
letters of twenty feet, in this legend : —

RAH. AL WEL.

Haliburton said he could not waste flat or cambric on
spelling.

He had had all night since half past ten to consider
what next was most important for them to know ; and
a very difficult question it was, you will observe.
They had been gone nearly two years, and much had
happened. Which thing was, on the whole, the most
interesting and important ? He had said we were
all well. What then ?

Did you never find yourself in the same difficulty ?
When your husband had come home from sea, and
kissed you and the children, and wondered at their

size, did you never sit silent, and have to think what you should say? Were you never fairly relieved when little Phil said, blustering, " I got three eggs to-day." The truth is, that silence is very satisfactory intercourse, if we only know all is well. When De Sauty got his original cable going, he had not much to tell after all; only that consols were a quarter per cent higher than they were the day before. "Send me news," lisped he — poor lonely myth! — from Bull's Bay to Valentia, — " send me news; they are mad for news." But how if there be no news worth sending? What do I read in my cable despatch to-day? Only that the Harvard crew pulled at Putney yesterday, which I knew before I opened the paper, and that there had been a riot in Spain, which I also knew. Here is a letter just brought me by the mail from Moreau, Tazewell County, Iowa. It is written by Follansbee, in a good cheerful hand. How glad I am to hear from Follansbee! Yes; but do I care one straw whether Follansbee planted spring wheat or winter wheat? Not I. All I care for is Follansbee's way of telling it. All these are the remarks by which Haliburton explains the character of the messages he sent in reply to George Orcutt's autographs, which were so thoroughly satisfactory.

Should he say Mr. Borie had left the Navy Department, and Mr. Robeson come in? Should he say the Lords had backed down on the Disendowment Bill? Should he say the telegraph had been landed at Dux-

bury ? Should he say Ingham had removed to Tamworth ? What did they care for this ? What does
anybody ever care for facts ? Should he say that the
State Constable was enforcing the liquor law on whis-
key, but was winking at lager ? All this would take
him a week, in the most severe condensation, — and
for what good ? as Haliburton asked. Yet these were
the things that the newspapers told, and they told
nothing else. There was a nice little poem of Jean
Ingelow's in a Transcript Haliburton had with him.
He said he was really tempted to spell that out. It
was better worth it than all the rest of the newspaper
stuff, and would be remembered a thousand years after
that was forgotten. "What they wanted," says Haliburton, " was sentiment. That is all that survives and
is eternal." So he and Rob. laid out their cambric
thus : —

RAH. AL WEL. SO GLAD.

Haliburton hesitated whether he would not add,
" Power 5000," to indicate the full power I was using
at Tamworth. But he determined not to, and, I
think, wisely. The convenience was so great, of receiving the signal at the spot where it could be
answered, that for the present he thought it best that
they should go on as they did. That night, however,
to his dismay, clouds gathered and a grim snow-storm
began. He .got no observations ; and the next day it
stormed so heavily that he could not lay his signals

out. For me at Tamworth, I had a heavy storm all day, but at midnight it was clear; and as soon as the regular eclipse was past George began with what we saw was an account of the great anaclysm which sent them there. You observe that Orcutt had far greater power of communicating with us than we had with him. He knew this. And it was fortunate he had. For he had, on his little world, much more of interest to tell than we had, on our large one.

18. "It stormed hard. We were all asleep, and knew nothing till morning; the hammocks turned so slowly."

Here was another revelation and relief. I had always supposed that, if they knew anything before they were roasted to death, they had had one wild moment of horror. Instead of this, the gentle slide of the MOON had not wakened them, the flight upward had been as easy as it was rapid, the change from one centre of gravity to another had of course been slow, — and they had actually slept through the whole. After the dancers had rested once, Orcutt continued : —

19. "We cleared E. A. in two seconds, I think. Our outer surface fused and cracked somewhat. So much the better for us."

They moved so fast that the heat of their friction through the air could not propagate itself through the whole brick surface. Indeed, there could have been but little friction after the first five or ten miles. By E. A. he means earth's atmosphere.

His 20th despatch is: " I have no observations of
ascent. But by theory our positive ascent ceased in
two minutes five seconds, when we fell into our proper
orbit, which, as I calculate, is 5,109 miles from your
mean surface."

In all this, observe, George dropped no word of regret through these five thousand miles.

His 21st despatch is : " Our rotation on our axis is
made once in seven hours, our axis being exactly vertical to the plane of our own orbit. But in each of
your daily rotations we get sunned all round."

Of course, they never had lost their identity with us,
so far as our rotation and revolution went : our inertia
was theirs ; all the fatal Fly-Wheels had given them
was an additional motion in space of their own.

This was the last despatch before daylight of Sunday
morning ; and the terrible snow-storm of March, sweeping our hemisphere, cut off our communication with
them, both at Tamworth and No. 9, for several days.

But here was ample food for reflection. Our friends
were in a world of their own, all thirty-seven of them
well, and it seemed they had two more little girls
added to their number since they started. They had
plenty of vegetables to eat, with prospect of new tropical varieties according to Dr. Darwin. Rob. Shea was
sure that they carried up hens ; he said he knew Mrs.
Whitman had several Middlesexes and Mrs. Leonard
two or three Black Spanish fowls, which had been
given her by some friends in Foxcroft. Even if they

had not yet had time enough for these to develop into Alderneys and venison, they would not be without animal food.

When at last it cleared off, Haliburton had to telegraph: "Repeat from 21"; and this took all his cambric, though he had doubled his stock. Orcutt replied the next night: —

22. "I can see your storms. We have none. When we want to change climate we can walk in less than a minute from midsummer to the depth of winter. But in the inside we have eleven different temperatures, which do not change."

On the whole there is a certain convenience in such an arrangement. With No. 23 he went back to his story: —

"It took us many days, one or two of our months, to adjust ourselves to our new condition. Our greatest grief is that we are not on the meridian. Do you know why?"

Loyal George! He was willing to exile himself and his race from the most of mankind, if only the great purpose of his life could be fulfilled. But his great regret was that it was not fulfilled. He was not on the meridian. I did not know why. But Haliburton, with infinite labor, spelt out on the Flat,

CYC. PROJECT. AD FIN.,

by which he meant, "See article Projectiles in the Cyclopædia at the end"; and there indeed is the only explanation to be given. When you fire a shot, why does it ever go to the right or left of the plane in which it is projected? Dr. Hutton ascribes it to a whirling motion acquired by the bullet by friction with the gun. Euler thinks it due chiefly to the irregularity of the shape of the ball. In our case the B. M. was regular enough. But on one side, being wholly unprepared for flight, she was heavily stored with pork and corn, while her other chambers had in some of them heavy drifts of snow, and some only a few men and women and hens.

Before Orcutt saw Haliburton's advice, he had sent us 24 and 25.

24. "We have established a Sandemanian church, and Brannan preaches. My son Edward and Alice Whitman are to be married this evening."

This despatch unfortunately did not reach Haliburton, though I got it. So, all the happy pair received for our wedding-present was the advice to look in the Cyclopædia at article Projectiles near the end.

25 was : —

"We shall act 'As You Like It' after the wedding. Dead-head tickets for all of the old set who will come."

Actually, in one week's reunion we had come to joking.

The next night we got 26 : —

"Alice says she will not read the Cyclopædia in the honeymoon, but is much obliged to Mr. Haliburton for his advice."

" How did she ever know it was I ? " wrote the matter-of-fact Haliburton to me.

27. " Alice wants to know if Mr. Haliburton will not send here for some rags ; says we have plenty, with little need for clothes."

And then despatches began to be more serious again. Brannan and Orcutt had failed in the great scheme for the longitude, to which they had sacrificed their lives, — if, indeed, it were a sacrifice to retire with those they love best to a world of their own. But none the less did they devote themselves, with the rare power of observation they had, to the benefit of our world. Thus, in 28 : —

" Your North Pole is an open ocean. It was black, which we think means water, from August 1st to September 29th. Your South Pole is on an island bigger than New Holland. Your Antarctic Continent is a great cluster of islands."

29. " Your Nyanzas are only two of a large group of African lakes. The green of Africa, where there is no water, is wonderful at our distance."

30. " We have not the last numbers of ' Foul Play.' Tell us, in a word or two, how they got home. We can see what we suppose their island was."

31. " We should like to know who proved Right in ' He Knew He was Right.' "

This was a good night's work, as they were then telegraphing. As soon as it cleared, Haliburton displayed, —

BEST HOPES. CARRIER DUCKS.

This was Haliburton's masterpiece. He had no room for more, however, and was obliged to reserve for the next day his answer to No. 31, which was simply,

SHE.

A real equinoctial now parted us for nearly a week, and at the end of that time they were so low in our northern horizon that we could not make out their signals; we and they were obliged to wait till they had passed through two thirds of their month before we could communicate again. I used the time in speeding to No. 9. We got a few carpenters together, and arranged on the Flat two long movable black platforms, which ran in and out on railroad-wheels on tracks, from under green platforms ; so that we could display one or both as we chose, and then withdraw them. With this apparatus we could give forty-five signals in a minute, corresponding to the line and dot of the telegraph ; and thus could compass some twenty letters in that time, and make out perhaps two hundred and fifty words in an hour. Haliburton thought that, with some improvements, he could send one of Mr. Buchanan's messages up in thirty-seven working-nights.

IV. — INDEPENDENCE.

I own to a certain mortification in confessing that after this interregnum, forced upon us by so long a period of non-intercourse, we never resumed precisely the same constancy of communication as that which I have tried to describe at the beginning. The apology for this benumbment, if I may so call it, will suggest itself to the thoughtful reader.

It is indeed astonishing to think that we so readily accept a position when we once understand it. You buy a new house. You are fool enough to take out a staircase that you may put in a bathing-room. This will be done in a fortnight, everybody tells you, and then everybody begins. Plumbers, masons, carpenters, plasterers, skimmers, bell-hangers, speaking-tube men, men who make furnace-pipe, paper-hangers, men who scrape off the old paper, and other men who take off the old paint with alkali, gas men, city water men, and painters begin. To them are joined a considerable number of furnace-men's assistants, stovepipe-men's assistants, mason's assistants, and hodmen who assist the assistants of the masons, the furnace-men, and the pipe-men. For a day or two these all take possession of the house and reduce it to chaos. In the language of Scripture, they enter in and dwell there. Compare, for the details, Matt. xii. 45. Then you revisit it at the end of the fortnight, and find it in chaos, with the woman whom you employed to wash the attics the only person on the scene. You ask her where the paper-hanger is ; and she says he can do nothing because the plaster is not dry. You ask why the plaster is not dry, and are told it is because the furnace-man has not come. You send for him, and he says he did come, but the stove-pipe man was away. You send for him, and he says he lost a day in coming, but that the mason had not cut the right hole in the chimney. You go and find the mason, and he says they are all fools, and that there is nothing in the house that need take two days to finish.

Then you curse, not the day in which you were born, but the day in which bath-rooms were invented. You say, truly, that your father and mother, from whom you inherit every moral and physical faculty you prize, never had a bath-room till they were past sixty, yet they thrived, and their children. You sneak through back streets, fearful lest your friends shall ask you when your house will be finished. You are sunk in wretchedness, unable even to read your proofs accurately, far less able to attend the primary meetings of the party with which you vote, or to discharge any of the duties of a good citizen. Life is wholly embittered to you.

Yet, six weeks after, you sit before a soft-coal fire, in your new house, with the feeling that you have always lived there. You are not even grateful that you are there. You have forgotten the plumber's name ;

and if you met in the street that nice carpenter that drove things through, you would just nod to him, and would not think of kissing him or embracing him.

Thus completely have you accepted the situation.

Let me confess that the same experience is that with which, at this writing, I regard the BRICK MOON. It is there in ether. I cannot keep it. I cannot get it down. I cannot well go to it, — though possibly that might be done, as you will see. They are all very happy there, — much happier, as far as I can see, than if they lived in sixth floors in Paris, in lodgings in London, or even in tenement-houses in Phœnix Place, Boston. There are disadvantages attached to their position; but there are also advantages. And what most of all tends to our accepting the situation is, that there is " nothing that we can do about it," as Q. says, but to keep up our correspondence with them, and to express our sympathies.

For them, their responsibilities are reduced, in somewhat the same proportion as the gravitation which binds them down, — I had almost said to earth, — which binds them down to brick, I mean. This decrease of responsibility must make them as light-hearted as the loss of gravitation makes them light-bodied.

On which point I ask for a moment's attention. And as these sheets leave my hand, an illustration turns up, which well serves me. It is the 23d of October. Yesterday morning all wakeful women in New England were sure there was some one under the bed. This is a certain sign of an earthquake. And when we read the evening newspapers we were made sure there had been an earthquake. What blessings the newspapers are, — and how much information they give us! Well, they said it was not very severe here, but perhaps it was more severe elsewhere; hopes really arising in the editorial mind, that in some Caraccas or Lisbon all churches and the cathedral might have fallen. I did not hope for that. But I did have just the faintest feeling, that *if* — if — if — it should prove that the world had blown up into six or eight pieces, and they had gone off into separate orbits, life would be vastly easier for all of us, on whichever bit we happened to be.

That thing has happened, they say, once. Whenever the big planet between Mars and Jupiter blew up, and divided himself into one hundred and two or more asteroids, the people on each one only knew there had been an earthquake, until they read their morning journals. And then, all that they knew at first was that telegraphic communication had ceased beyond — say two hundred miles. Gradually people and despatches came in, who said that they had parted company with some of the other islands and continents. But, as I say, on each piece the people not only weighed much less, but were much lighter-hearted, had less responsibility.

Now will you imagine the enthusiasm here, at Miss Hale's school, when it should be announced that geography, in future, would be confined to the study of

the region east of the Mississippi and west of the
Atlantic, — the earth having parted at the seams so
named. No more study of Italian, German, French,
or Sclavonic, — the people speaking those languages
being now in different orbits or other worlds. Imagine also the superior ease of the office-work of the A.
B. C. F. M. and kindred societies, the duties of instruc-
tion and civilizing, of evangelizing in general, being
reduced within so much narrower bounds. For you
and me also, who cannot decide what Mr. Gladstone
ought to do with the land tenure in Ireland, and who
distress ourselves so much about it in conversation,
what a satisfaction to know that Great Britain is flung
off with one rate of movement, Ireland with another,
and the Isle of Man with another, into space, with no
more chance of meeting again than there is that you
shall have the same hand at whist to-night that you
had last night! Even Victoria would sleep easier,
and I am sure Mr. Gladstone would.

Thus, I say, were Orcutt's and Brannan's responsibilities so diminished, that after the first I began to
see that their contracted position had its decided com-
pensating ameliorations.

In these views, I need not say, the women of our
little circle never shared. After we got the new telegraph arrangement in good running-order, I observed
that Polly and Annie Haliburton had many private
conversations, and the secret came out one morning,
when, rising early in the cabins, we men found they

had deserted us; and then, going in search of them, found them running the signal boards in and out as rapidly as they could, to tell Mrs. Brannan and the bride Alice Orcutt that flounces were worn an inch and a half deeper, and that people trimmed now with harmonizing colors and not with contrasts. I did not say that I believed they wore fig-leaves in B. M., but that was my private impression.

After all, it was hard to laugh at the girls, as these ladies will be called, should they live to be as old as Helen was when she charmed the Trojan senate (that was ninety-three, if Heyne be right in his calculations). It was hard to laugh at them, because this was simple benevolence, and the same benevolence led to a much more practical suggestion, when Polly came to me and told me she had been putting up some baby things for little Io and Phœbe, and some playthings for the older children, and she thought we might " send up a bundle."

Of course we could. There were the Flies still moving ! or we might go ourselves !

[And here the reader must indulge me in a long parenthesis. I beg him to bear me witness that I never made one before. This parenthesis is on the tense that I am obliged to use in sending to the press these minutes. The reader observes that the last transactions mentioned happen in April and May, 1871. Those to be narrated are the sequence of those already told. Speaking of them in 1870 with the coarse tenses of the English language is very difficult. One needs, for accuracy, a pure future, a second future, a paulo-post future, and a paulum-

ante future, none of which does this language have.   Failing
this, one would be glad of an a-orist, — tense without time, —
if the grammarians will not swoon at hearing such language.
But the English tongue hath not that either.   Doth the learned
reader remember that the Hebrew, — language of history and
prophecy, — hath only a past and a future tense, but hath no
present?   Yet that language succeeded tolerably in expressing
the present griefs or joys of David and of Solomon.   Bear with
me, then, O critic! if even in 1870 I use the so-called past
tenses in narrating what remaineth of this history up to the
summer of 1872.   End of the parenthesis.]

On careful consideration, however, no one volunteers
to go.   To go, if you observe, would require that a man
envelope himself thickly in asbestos or some similar
non-conducting substance, leap boldly on the rapid
Flies, and so be shot through the earth's atmosphere
in two seconds and a fraction, carrying with him all
the time in a non-conducting receiver the condensed
air he needed, and landing quietly on B. M. by a pre-
calculated orbit.   At the bottom of our hearts I think
we were all afraid.   Some of us confessed to fear;
others said, and said truly, that the population of the
Moon was already dense, and that it did not seem
reasonable or worth while, on any account, to make it
denser.   Nor has any movement been renewed for
going.   But the plan of the bundle of "things"
seemed more feasible, as the things would not require
oxygen.   The only precaution seemed to be that
which was necessary for protecting the parcel against
combustion as it shot through the earth's atmosphere.

We had not asbestos enough. It was at first proposed to pack them all in one of Professor Horsford's
safes. But when I telegraphed this plan to Orcutt,
he demurred. Their atmosphere was but shallow, and
with a little too much force the corner of the safe
might knock a very bad hole in the surface of his
world. He said if we would send up first a collection
of things of no great weight, but of considerable bulk,
he would risk that, but he would rather have no compact metals.

I satisfied myself, therefore, with a plan which I
still think good. Making the parcel up in heavy old
woollen carpets, and cording it with worsted cords, we
would case it in a carpet-bag larger than itself, and
fill in the interstice with dry sand, as our best non-
conductor; cording this tightly again, we would renew
the same casing, with more sand; and so continually
offer surfaces of sand and woollen, till we had five
separate layers between the parcel and the air. Our
calculation was that a perceptible time would be
necessary for the burning and disintegrating of each
sand-bag. If each one, on the average, would stand
two fifths of a second, the inner parcel would get
through the earth's atmosphere unconsumed. If, on
the other hand, they lasted a little longer, the bag, as
it fell on B. M., would not be unduly heavy. Of
course we could take their night for the experiment,
so that we might be sure they should all be in bed
and out of the way.

We had very funny and very merry times in selecting things important enough and at the same time
bulky and light enough to be safe. Alice and Bertha
at once insisted that there must be room for the
children's playthings. They wanted to send the most
approved of the old ones, and to add some new
presents. There was a woolly sheep in particular,
and a watering-pot that Rose had given Fanny, about
which there was some sentiment ; boxes of dominos,
packs of cards, magnetic fishes, bows and arrows,
checker-boards and croquet sets. Polly and Annie
were more considerate. Down to Coleman and Company they sent an order for pins, needles, hooks and
eyes, buttons, tapes, and I know not what essentials.
India-rubber shoes for the children Mrs. Haliburton
insisted on sending. Haliburton himself bought open-
eye-shut-eye dolls, though I felt that wax had been,
since Icarus's days, the worst article in such an adventure. For the babies he had india-rubber rings :
he had tin cows and carved wooden lions for the
bigger children, drawing-tools for those older yet, and
a box of crochet tools for the ladies. For my part I
piled in literature, — a set of my own works, the Legislative Reports of the State of Maine, Jean Ingelow,
as I said or intimated, and both volumes of the Earthly
Paradise. All these were packed in sand, bagged, and
corded, — bagged, sanded, and corded again, — yet
again and again, — five times. Then the whole
awaited Orcutt's orders and our calculations.

At last the moment came. We had, at Orcutt's order, reduced the revolutions of the Flies to 7230, which was, as nearly as he knew, the speed on the fatal night. We had soaked the bag for near twelve hours, and, at the moment agreed upon, rolled it on the Flies, and saw it shot into the air. It was so small that it went out of sight too soon for us to see it take fire.

Of course we watched eagerly for signal time. They were all in bed on B. M. when we let fly. But the despatch was a sad disappointment.

107. "Nothing has come through but two croquet balls and a china horse. But we shall send the boys hunting in the bushes, and we may find more."

108. "Two Harpers and an Atlantic, badly singed. But we can read all but the parts which were most dry."

109. "We see many small articles revolving round us which may perhaps fall in."

They never did fall in, however. The truth was, that all the bags had burned through. The sand, I suppose, went to its own place, wherever that was. And all the other things in our bundle became little asteroids or aerolites in orbits of their own, except a well-disposed score or two, which persevered far enough to get within the attraction of Brick Moon, and to take to revolving there, not having hit quite square, as the croquet balls did. They had five volumes of the Congressional Globe whirling round like bats within a hundred feet of their heads. Another body, which I am afraid was "The Ingham Papers," flew a little higher, not quite so heavy. Then there was an absurd procession of the woolly sheep, a china cow, a pair of india-rubbers, a lobster Haliburton had chosen to send, a wooden lion, the wax doll, a Salter's balance, the New York Observer, the bow and arrows, a Nuremberg nanny-goat, Rose's watering-pot, and the magnetic fishes, which gravely circled round and round them slowly, and made the petty zodiac of their petty world.

We have never sent another parcel since, but we probably shall at Christmas, gauging the Flies perhaps to one revolution more. The truth is, that although we have never stated to each other in words our difference of opinion or feeling, there is a difference of habit of thought in our little circle as to the position which the B. M. holds. Somewhat similar is the difference of habit of thought in which different statesmen of England regard their colonies.

Is B. M. a part of our world, or is it not? Should its inhabitants be encouraged to maintain their connections with us, or is it better for them to "accept the situation" and gradually wean themselves from us and from our affairs? It would be idle to determine this question in the abstract: it is perhaps idle to decide any question of casuistry in the abstract. But, in practice, there are constantly arising questions which really require some decision of this abstract problem for their solution.

For instance, when that terrible breach occurred in the Sandemanian church, which parted it into the Old School and New School parties, Haliburton thought it very important that Brannan and Orcutt and the church in B. M. under Brannan's ministry should give in their adhesion to our side. Their church would count one more in our registry, and the weight of its influence would not be lost. He therefore spent eight or nine days in telegraphing, from the early proofs, a copy of the address of the Chatauque Synod to Brannan, and asked Brannan if he were not willing to have his name signed to it when it was printed. And the only thing which Haliburton takes sorely in the whole experience of the Brick Moon, from the beginning, is that neither Orcutt nor Brannan has ever sent one word of acknowledgment of the despatch. Once, when Haliburton was very low-spirited, I heard him even say that he believed they had never read a word of it, and that he thought he and Rob. Shea had had their labor for their pains in running the signals out and in.

Then he felt quite sure that they would have to establish civil government there. So he made up an excellent collection of books, — De Lolme on the British Constitution ; Montesquieu on Laws ; Story, Kent, John Adams, and all the authorities here ; with ten copies of his own address delivered before the Young Men's Mutual Improvement Society of Podunk, on the " Abnormal Truths of Social Order." He tele-

graphed to know what night he should send them, and
Orcutt replied : —

129. " Go to thunder with your old law-books. We
have not had a primary meeting nor a justice court
since we have been here, and, D. V., we never will
have."

Haliburton says this is as bad as the state of things
in Kansas, when, because Frank Pierce would not give
them any judges or laws to their mind, they lived a
year or so without any. Orcutt added in his next
despatch : —

130. " Have not you any new novels ? Send up
Scribe and the Arabian Nights and Robinson Crusoe
and the Three Guardsmen, and Mrs. Whitney's books.
We have Thackeray and Miss Austen."

When he read this, Haliburton felt as if they
were not only light-footed, but light-headed. And he
consulted me quite seriously as to telegraphing to
them " Pycroft's Course of Reading." I coaxed him
out of that, and he satisfied himself with a serious ex-
postulation with George as to the way in which their
young folks would grow up. George replied by telegraphing Brannan's last sermon, 1 Thessalonians iv. 11.
The sermon had four heads, must have occupied an
hour and a half in delivery, and took five nights to
telegraph. I had another engagement, so that Haliburton had to sit it all out with his eye to Shubael:
and he has never entered on that line of discussion
again. It was as well, perhaps, that he got enough
of it.

The women have never had any misunderstandings. When we had received two or three hundred despatches from B. M., Annie Haliburton came to me and said, in that pretty way of hers, that she thought they had a right to their turn again. She said this lore about the Albert Nyanza and the North Pole was all very well, but, for her part, she wanted to know how they lived, what they did, and what they talked about, whether they took summer journeys, and how and what was the form of society where thirty-seven people lived in such close quarters. This about "the form of society" was merely wool pulled over my eyes. So she said she thought her husband and I had better go off to the Biennial Convention at Assampink, as she knew we wanted to do, and she and Bridget and Polly and Cordelia would watch for the signals, and would make the replies. She thought they would get on better if we were out of the way.

So we went to the convention, as she called it, which was really not properly a convention, but the Forty-fifth Biennial General Synod, and we left the girls to their own sweet way.

Shall I confess that they kept no record of their own signals, and did not remember very accurately what they were ? " I was not going to keep a string of ' says I's ' and ' says she's,' " said Polly, boldly. " It shall not be written on my tomb that I have left more annals for people to file or study or bind or dust or catalogue." But they told us that they had begun

by asking the "bricks" if they remembered what
Maria Theresa said to her ladies-in-waiting.* Quicker
than any signal had ever been answered, George Orcutt's party replied from the moon, "We hear, and we
obey." Then the women-kind had it all to themselves. The brick-women explained at once to our
girls that they had sent their men round to the other
side to cut ice, and that they were manning the telescope, and running the signals for themselves, and
that they could have a nice talk without any bother
about the law-books or the magnetic pole. As I say,
I do not know what questions Polly and Annie put;
but, — to give them their due, — they had put on
paper a coherent record of the results arrived at in
the answers; though, what were the numbers of the
despatches, or in what order they came, I do not
know; for the session of the synod kept us at Assampink for two or three weeks.

Mrs. Brannan was the spokesman. "We tried a
good many experiments about day and night. It was
very funny at first, not to know when it would be
light and when dark, for really the names day and
night do not express a great deal for us. Of course
the pendulum clocks all went wrong till the men got

---

* Maria Theresa's husband, Francis, Duke of Tuscany, was hanging about loose one day, and the Empress, who had got a little tired,
said to the maids of honor, "Girls, whenever you marry, take care
and choose a husband who has something to do outside of the
house."

them overhauled, and I think watches and clocks both will soon go out of fashion. But we have settled down on much the old hours, getting up, without reference to daylight, by our great gong, at your eight o'clock. But when the eclipse season comes, we vary from that for signalling.

"We still make separate families, and Alice's is the seventh. We tried hotel life, and we liked it, for there has never been the first quarrel here. You can't quarrel here, where you are never sick, never tired, and need not be ever hungry. But we were satisfied that it was nicer for the children, and for all round, to live separately, and come together at parties, to church, at signal time, and so on. We had something to say then, something to teach, and something to learn.

"Since the carices developed so nicely into flax, we have had one great comfort, which we had lost before, in being able to make and use paper. We have had great fun, and we think the children have made great improvement in writing novels for the Union. The Union is the old Union for Christian work that we had in dear old No. 9. We have two serial novels going on, one called 'Diana of Carrotook,' and the other called 'Ups and Downs'; the first by Levi Ross, and the other by my Blanche. They are really very good, and I wish we could send them to you. But they would not be worth despatching.

"We get up at eight; dress, and fix up at home; a sniff of air, as people choose; breakfast; and then we meet for prayers outside. Where we meet depends on the temperature; for we can choose any temperature we want, from boiling water down, which is convenient. After prayers an hour's talk, lounging, walking, and so on; no flirting, but a favorite time with the young folks.

"Then comes work. Three hours' head-work is the maximum in that line. Of women's work, as in all worlds, there are twenty-four in one of your days, but for my part I like it. Farmers and carpenters have their own laws, as the light serves and the seasons. Dinner is seven hours after breakfast began; always an hour long, as breakfast was. Then every human being sleeps for an hour. Big gong again, and we ride, walk, swim, telegraph, or what not, as the case may be. We have no horses yet, but the Shanghaes are coming up into very good dodos and ostriches, quite big enough for a trot for the children.

"Only two persons of a family take tea at home. The rest always go out to tea without invitation. At 8 P. M. big gong again, and we meet in 'Grace,' which is the prettiest hall, church, concert-room, that you ever saw. We have singing, lectures, theatre, dancing, talk, or what the mistress of the night determines, till the curfew sounds at ten, and then we all go home. Evening prayers are in the separate households, and every one is in bed by midnight. The only law on the statute-book is that every one shall sleep nine hours out of every twenty-four.

"Only one thing interrupts this general order. Three taps on the gong means 'telegraph,' and then, I tell you, we are all on hand.

"You cannot think how quickly the days and years go by!"

Of course, however, as I said, this could not last. We could not subdue our world, and be spending all our time in telegraphing our dear B. M. Could it be possible? — perhaps it was possible, — that they there had something else to think of and to do, besides attending to our affairs. Certainly their indifference to Grant's fourth Proclamation, and to Mr. Fish's celebrated protocol in the Tahiti business, looked that way. Could it be that that little witch of a Belle Brannan really cared more for their performance of Midsummer Night's Dream, or her father's birthday, than she cared for that pleasant little account I telegraphed up to all the children, of the way we went to muster when we were boys together? Ah well! I ought not to have supposed that all worlds were like this old world. Indeed, I often say this is the queerest world I ever knew. Perhaps theirs is not so queer, and it is I who am the oddity.

Of course it could not last. We just arranged correspondence days, when we would send to them, and they to us. I was meanwhile turned out from my place at Tamworth Observatory. Not but I did my work well, and Polly hers. The observer's room was a miracle of neatness. The children were kept in the basement. Visitors were received with great courtesy; and all the fees were sent to the treasurer; he got three dollars and eleven cents one summer, — that was the year General Grant came there; and that was the largest amount that they ever received from any source but begging. I was not unfaithful to my trust. Nor was it for such infidelity that I was removed. No! But it was discovered that I was a Sandemanian; a Glassite, as in derision I was called. The annual meeting of the trustees came round. There was a large Mechanics' Fair in Tamworth at the time, and an Agricultural Convention. There was no horse-race at the convention, but there were two competitive examinations in which running horses competed with each other, and trotting horses competed with each other, and five thousand dollars was given to the best runner and the best trotter. These causes drew all the trustees together. The Rev. Cephas Philpotts presided. His doctrines with regard to free agency were considered much more sound than mine. He took the chair, — in that pretty observatory parlor, which Polly had made so bright with smilax and ivy. Of course I took no chair; I waited, as a janitor should, at the door. Then a brief address. Dr. Philpotts trusted that the observatory might always be administered in the interests of science, of true science; of that science which rightly distinguishes between unlicensed liberty and true freedom; between the unrestrained volition and the freedom of the will.

He became eloquent, he became noisy. He sat down. Then three other men spoke, on similar subjects. Then the executive committee which had appointed me was dismissed with thanks. Then a new executive committee was chosen, with Dr. Philpotts at the head. The next day I was discharged. And the next week the Philpotts family moved into the observatory, and their second girl now takes care of the instruments.

I returned to the cure of souls and to healing the hurt of my people. On observation days somebody runs down to No. 9, and by means of Shubael communicates with B. M. We love them, and they love us all the same.

Nor do we grieve for them as we did. Coming home from Pigeon Cove in October, with those nice Wadsworth people, we fell to talking as to the why and wherefore of the summer life we had led. How was it that it was so charming ? And why were we a little loath to come back to more comfortable surroundings ? " I hate the school," said George Wadsworth. " I hate the making calls," said his mother. " I hate the office hour," said her poor husband ; " if there were only a dozen I would not mind, but seventeen hundred thousand in sixty minutes is too many." So that led to asking how many of us there had been at Pigeon Cove. The children counted up all the six families, — the Haliburtons, the Wadsworths, the Pontefracts, the Midges, the Hayeses, and the Inghams, and the two good-natured girls, — thirty-seven in all, — and the two babies born this summer. "Really," said Mrs. Wadsworth, "I have not spoken to a human being besides these since June; and what is more, Mrs. Ingham, I have not wanted to. We have really lived in a little world of our own."

"World of our own!" Polly fairly jumped from her seat, to Mrs. Wadsworth's wonder. So we had — lived in a world of our own. Polly reads no newspaper since the "Sandemanian" was merged. She has a letter or two tumble in sometimes, but not many; and the truth was that she had been more secluded from General Grant and Mr. Gladstone and the Khedive, and the rest of the important people, than had Brannan or Ross or any of them!

And it had been the happiest summer she had ever known.

Can it be possible that all human sympathies can thrive, and all human powers be exercised, and all human joys increase, if we live with all our might with the thirty or forty people next to us, telegraphing kindly to all other people, to be sure? Can it be possible that our passion for large cities, and large parties, and large theatres, and large churches, develops no faith nor hope nor love which would not find aliment and exercise in a little "world of our own"?

WATER TALK.

A True Story.

I.

ASAPH FERGUSON and I were in the sea just out-side the breakers on Matoonoc Beach in Rhode Island. I take it this is just the finest bath possible in New England, which is to say, of course, in the United States, which is, I suppose, in the world, though I am not perfectly sure about the surf south of the La Plata River.

Ferguson thought we had had enough fooling in the breakers, — said he had come into the water for exer-cise, — and proposed a pull along the shore, outside the white crests, toward Stony Point, to which I agreed. And he fell to talking about the disappear-ance of a Creole girl from the pier; she had been advertised as kidnapped, in the papers.

"Did I ever tell you my story of the disappearance of that Boothby child — English child ?" said I. No — Ferguson said — not if he remembered the name. So as we swam on I told him just as I tell it to you.

"These Boothbys were English spinners, of the better sort, from Manchester. They came over in the midst of that awful strike which Mrs. Gaskell immortalized in 'Mary Barton.' I have talked with them about that very strike. Well, the strike did not improve their fortunes much, but some committee of workmen, or employers, poor-boards, landlords, or somebody, sent them all, bag and baggage, paralytic mother, half-witted father, and deaf-and-dumb niece, over to America. That is a convenience of an old country, that you have a new one under your lee. Well, they landed at Boston, and at Boston the philanthropists thought they must be sent to the West. 'Great country, the West!' So they were sent to the West. But in those days, sending them to the West, when the Boston philanthropists did it, meant giving them all second-class tickets to Worcester, forty miles away. The Boston philanthropists are not apt now to get them so far. I was a minister in Worcester then, so before a year was over somebody reported the Boothbys to me.

"They had got along, at first, sufficiently well. I don't remember where the half-witted father was, nor the deaf-and-dumb niece; somewhere or other at the public charge I suppose. The man and his wife had some sort of work in some sort of mill, when there came a drought and everybody shut off work, — as bad as the Manchester strike. Then he got discouraged and half starved, and they all were half starved, and they had in the house with them a bad case of typhus, and they all got frightened about that; all this, mark

you, before they consulted any people of sense, or not
a word of this that I am going to tell you need have
happened."

"O, need not it?" asked Ferguson, rather indif-
ferently, as if he did not much care whether it happened or not. But he turned over on his right side,
and began swimming with the hand-over-hand stroke.
So did I. And as I had got started, I went on. I
knew he would be interested before I was done.

"They took bad advice, or rather they took none at
all. They agreed that the sick father should go to the
town poor-house; and he was so sick that he could
not be sent far away. So the people there had to take
care of him till he mended. He saw that things
looked comfortably there, — there were some children
he got fond of, — and when he came back he per-
suaded his wife to send their little Bessy there till
the man who had the fever was well. And my story
is about Bessy."

"O, is it?" said Ferguson, rather lazily. "I
thought it was about Boothby. I think we had better go home."

"It is about Bessy Boothby; her first name is Bessy,
and her last name is Boothby. They were more used
to workhouse life in England than our laboring people
are here, and they thought no shame to have the child
at the poor-house for a few weeks, pretty much as the
grandfather was at one asylum and the niece, if she
was a niece, at another. So Bessy was sent to the

town poor-house also. This, you see, was before any
of us knew them, or no such blunder would have been
made."

"Blunder?" said Ferguson; "I see no blunder.
They all appear to have been poor. What is a poor-
house for but for poor people?" And Ferguson lay
over on his breast again, and began swimming with
General Kraströmm's stroke. So did I.

"A poor-house for poor people? My dear Asaph,
that shows you do not understand the law of settlements, — as how should you, being only an attorney-
at-law. There never were but three men in Massachusetts who understood it. Governor Andrew was
one, and he is dead. Another of the three is in London. And the third is — not in Massachusetts at this
moment. She should not have gone to the poor-
house, because she had no settlement in Worcester."

"I thought you said they had settled there."

"So I did. But that has nothing to do with it; and
if you keep interrupting me, you will never hear your
story."

Asaph muttered that he thought it was my story.
But I did not mind him, but lay over on my back,
and struck into the Deuteron-proteron stroke while he
went on with the Baron.

"No! she had no settlement. And so, before she
had been at the poor-house a week, she was sent to
the State Poor-house in Monson."

"Why, had she a settlement in Monson?"

"You must not interrupt! She had no settlement at all. That was the reason she went to Monson. Boothby and his wife knew she was there, but they were lied to; and they supposed Monson was just out of sight, the other side of Chandler Hill, so they stuck to their business. The mills got open again, they moved into a new tenement, they whitewashed it nicely, and then, of a Sunday morning, Boothby inquired his way to Monson, to find that it was thirty miles away.

"Boothby did not like this; he had to lose a day going there. But he bought his ticket and went. He found three hundred children, and found a master and staff, but he found no Bessy Boothby."

"Blown up in the cars?" asked Asaph, beginning to be just a little interested.

"Wait, and you shall know; that is the end of the story. She was not blown up in the cars. She had been there, and was on the books. But she was not there now."

"Dead?"

"You must not interrupt. She was not dead."

"Run away?"

"You must not interrupt. She had not run away."

"Small-pox, and off at the infirmary?"

"She had been vaccinated in her youth. No, sir. She had been kidnapped, and kidnapped under the eyes of the authorities. Very cheap they were. And although Thomas Boothby was rather a seedy-looking

man, and as stupid as some other Englishmen I have
known, the authorities did not dare to bully him.
Massachusetts had some stiff statutes just then about
kidnapping and the accessories to kidnapping. Are
you aware, by the way, that 'kid' in the vernacular
means 'child,' and to 'nap' is to 'nab' in the San-
skrit ? This child had been nabbed under their eyes.

"All they could say was that some very nice people
took her. 'Indeed they were nice. They were ex-
traordinarily nice. And they had a very nice team.
The kerridge, you can't think, Mr. Boothby, what a
nice kerridge it was, and the horses, two Morgan bays.
If you had seen the kerridge, Mr. Boothby, I am quite
sure you would be pleased.'

"But poor Boothby had not seen the carriage, and
he was not pleased at all. He stormed and he swore,
and he swore and he stormed. But swearing and
storming did no good. How could it ? These people
had let the child go to some blackguards who had
given them false names. How could they tell what
they did not know ?"

"I say," said Asaph, "the women are waving their
towels. They want us to come in. Let's pull ashore."

So we pulled ashore through the breakers again,
and the women had many tales to tell us. How
Mabel had been thrown over by the breakers. How
Grace had swum ten strokes without putting her feet
to the ground, and how Abigail had been looking on,
and had not noticed a great tall rounder from the sea,

and had got her mouth full in consequence. And in the midst of these interruptions I had no chance to finish the story of Bessy Boothby.

II.

I WAS a little annoyed, to tell the truth, that Asaph Ferguson asked me no further question about Bessy Boothby. We led the ladies up the beach, filled their pails with salt water, carried the pails across to the bathing-house, wiped and dressed. All through this process Asaph was talking about the circulation, and the reaction, and the qualities of crash towels, and a bathing burnouse he had from Egypt. And he seemed to have forgotten that I had left my little heroine in a very unaccounted-for condition. When we got up to Willowdell, where we were staying, he found a despatch summoning him to sit on a reference in Washington. A nice place, that, in August! and good enough for him! For if he had not interrupted he would have heard all the story; or if he had asked me, I could have told him as we rode home.

It happened, however, ten days after, that we were both of us at York Harbor, in Maine. It is a nice place; it was better known in Fernando Gorges's time than it is now, under the title of the city of Gorgiana. This city, in fact, still remains, in the guise of three or four almost deserted houses and a grass-grown Main

Street. Well, the ocean is as near as it was in Gorges's day, if there are not so many ships in the bay as he hoped there would be. Within an arrow-shot of the Marshall House, where we were staying, is an excellent beach; and as I undressed, I was not surprised to see Ferguson come down and join me. We played in the breakers a little while, then swam out beyond them; and I proposed to him to swim across to a little point which makes out at the farther end of the beach, which we did. The water is a great deal colder on that shore than at Newport or Matoonoc, so that you need a steady, long pull to keep you warm.

We had just started, when Asaph soothed my wounded pride a little, by saying, "What did you tell me happened to that English child you were talking about at Matoonoc?"

I was a little grim, and I said, "I did not tell you what happened to her."

"Well, I am glad to hear you say so. I know I did not remember. What did happen to her, and how came she to be kidnapped?"

So I got my revenge, though I got no apology; and I resumed my little story. I will tell it to you more briefly than I did to him, for we have not twenty minutes of salt-water before us.

Boothby came back to Worcester enraged. He told his story to foreman, superintendent, and finally to the owner of the mills. They were all stiff Free-Soilers, and they did not mean to have such things

happen in Massachusetts; and Mr. Slater, the manu-
facturer, told the story at the next meeting of the
bank directors, and then he and Mr. Stephens, President of the bank, took up poor Boothby's case as if it
had been their own, and they then sent for me. You
see they wanted somebody who knew something about
the law of settlement. This was the first time I ever
heard of Boothby.

Well, we wrote a stiff letter to the Master of the
house at Monson. And we got a pretty meek one
from him. But he knew nothing, and so he could not
tell much, not being a regular correspondent of a daily
journal. Then we sent up a young lawyer there; but
he learned nothing, because there was nothing to learn.
Then we wrote a thundering letter to the Master, and
threatened a complaint to the governor and Council,
which at that moment we meant to make. This time
the Master came down to see, well frightened, — for
Stephens and Slater were men as good as their word,
to say nothing of me; and, whatever else happened,
this Master did not want to be dismissed in disgrace.

To tell the truth, his story was not a bad one. He
was green in his place, and not used to the ways of
the people who came to inspect his children and
wanted to take them away. Nothing was clearer or
more guarded than the law of Massachusetts, by which
he was bound. He had no right to put the child into
the hands of any person outside the State; no right to
intrust her to persons not known to him, unless they

brought testimonials from satisfactory persons, properly approved by official persons. But this Mr. and Mrs. Pendleton, as the nabbers called themselves, affected high and mighty ways. They were surprised, indeed, that our poor Master of Paupers was not acquainted with their reputation, — intimated mildly that it "argued himself unknown." Every one in Boston knew them, and in their own neighborhood. In fact, they pretended to come from a town not thirty miles away. They were pleased with poor Bessy, and wanted to adopt her; were eager, for certain personal reasons, to take her then, — something about the birthday of the dear child they had lost. The Master showed them the statutes, and they were quite amused at the idea of their producing credentials from the selectmen; it was much more probable that the selectmen would need testimonials from Mr. and Mrs. Pendleton. But if that were the law, of course they wanted to observe every formality. So, on the spot, they executed all the papers; and the Master, on his part, did the same; and they undertook, by the next day's mail, to send up the missing testimonial, whatever it was. And so they drove away with those handsome bays, and that beautiful " kerridge."

"If you had only seen the kerridge, Mr. Stephens!"

But Mr. Stephens cared no more for the carriage than did Boothby; nor did I. It became pretty clear, however, that we should not advance our point by making a row in public. We should only put the kidnappers more on their guard. For there were no such people as the Pendletons at Millbury, or whatever the town was that they hailed from. The elegant "kerridge" proved to have been hired at a livery-stable there, and there the trail was lost. The poor Master had traced it as far as that, when his testimonials had failed. But then he knew his own blunder, and his only hope then was that nobody would ever overhaul his affairs in the matter of Boothby kidnapped. The less he said the better. So, by the time the new firm of Boothby, Slater, Stephens, and I were on the trail, it was very cold. Who was to remember whether a man, woman, and child did or did not take the train to and through Worcester, or to and through Providence, on a given day, or what became of them?

The unlicensed and illegal foolery, now known as the detective system, was not then much developed, nor would it have helped us much if it had been. But a man was engaged, and paid, who had some shrewdness in such things, who followed out a good many false scents, one or two of which, at one time or another, promised a good deal. But each and all of them came to nothing. I, who have since seen a much fresher scent lost in Paris, by the much-vaunted French police, never wondered that, in the freedom of Massachusetts life, poor Bessy Boothby was lost through and through.

At this point, Asaph Ferguson, who had, to give

him his due, stuck to his work pretty steadily, and had never once interrupted, broke in, " Then you never found her ? Then I guess we had better go home. Don't you feel cold ? "

" I did not say we never found her. You are always a great deal too quick. I said she was clean lost, and so she was. The man who was paid to follow up the scent gave it up. Slater and Stephens paid poor Boothby his wages while he went trailing up and down the country ; but at last even he had no further lines of inquiry to propose, and he had to stop from mere failure of ingenuity. My part in the business had been simply to advise, and to write bullying letters to the Master of the poor-house. But, as I said, he had nothing more to tell, and he told it. If it had been in a fairy-tale, Mr. and Mrs. Boothby would have started on foot, resolved to seek for little Bessy through the world till they found her. But it was not in a fairy-tale. It was in a world where they worked for their living, and where they would have deserted five children in searching for one, and probably, also, would have gone away from the one while they were searching."

" Well," said Asaph, " let us go ashore. You can tell me the rest while we are dressing."

But, in fact, while we were dressing, the unsentimental creature began talking to me about minority representation, and so he lost his chance then to hear the rest of the story.

That evening he was telegraphed to go to Memphis to take some depositions. A nice place in the end of August! but good enough for such an unsentimental listener.

III.

ALTHOUGH I did end that last chapter in such a vindictive way, I was glad that poor Asaph Ferguson did not get yellow fever in Memphis. We were all glad to see him again; very thin, and very brown, and very hungry. We were spending September in a lovely house there is in Summer Place, in Lynn, just where Nahant Beach joins on. You are so high that you can see the fingers of the Right Arm of Massachusetts. I mean you can see Cape Cod itself sometimes. You are so high that you throw Egg Rock right down upon the water, and your horizon line is high above it. Yet your garden terraces run down close to the surf-beaten beach, and as you sit every day you can see ten thousand happy men, women, and children, savages again, dash into the surf, and renew their life as, in that simplest way, they measure themselves with the infinite.

Of course it was not long before we took Asaph down to the shore. It was one of those hot days with which September is so apt to begin. The habit was to undress at the house, and wear a sort of domino down to the beach, which you then and there left, with a black man, Theodore, to watch them all, lest you shared the fate of the unlucky Emperor Jovinian. Not a bad plan.

Ah, was not the water delicious! Were it always so, I would never have maligned Nahant bathing, as I may or may not have done in these pages. Were it always so, the human race would assemble on the shores of the sea, and "going into water," as the boys call it, would be the only duty of a new civilization. We played with the children, and gave them swimming lessons; we let the waves wash us up on the shore; we stood and let the surf roll on us, and then Asaph pretended he wanted to swim to Egg Rock. All nonsense; it is three miles away. But I knew his humor, and we stretched out to sea.

"Well," said he, "how did you find her?" You see, though he had pretended he did not care for Bessy Boothby, he had carried her all through those depositions. And here he was, almost ready to offer himself in marriage to her. That was what I gained by waiting. Did not I know my man?

"I did not say we found her," said I. "But I will tell you what happened. For where she is now I know no more than you do." Did I fancy it, or did a blank chill come on Asaph? Had he, perhaps, meant to offer himself in marriage, and started now because his hopes were blighted? Or did he, may be, strike one of those shiny medusas with his little toe? I know not.

But I told the rest of the story just as I now tell it to you.

I heard no more of Bessy Boothby for years. I wrote down in my note-book the facts I tell you of. They are there now. Then I forgot them. My life in Worcester ended. I moved to Boston, and became minister of a church there. I had been there a year or two, and was going up from the vestry to service with my gown on, one Sunday afternoon, when Mr. Herrick, the sexton, called me back, and said a gentleman wanted to see me.

" I can't help it," said I. " Tell him he must wait till after service."

" I have told him so, sir, but he says it is very important. It is Mr. Melcher."

" I don't care who he is. It is three o'clock, and the organ is now playing. He may see me here at half past four, or he may see me to-morrow."

" I wish you would say so, Mr. Hale. He will not go away."

So I pushed by the baize door, and said in pretty short metre to the man that he must see that it was time for service, and that I could not see him.

" I know I am very late, sir," said he ; " but it is really important I should have the child to-day, and they will not give her to me without your order."

" I know nothing of any child," said I, with the austerity of an archbishop. " I only know that it is after three o'clock, and I ought to be in the pulpit, and I wish you a good afternoon." And I turned away.

"Pray stop, Mr. Hale, pray stop. All I want is your signature. If you would only sign an order to the Children's Home, so that they will give me this Bessy Boothby."

"Give you who?" said I, turning round from my archiepiscopal stride.

"Give me this Bessy Boothby," said the poor man. "You are the director for this month, and they will not give her to me without your order."

"I am the director for September," said I; "to-day is September 30th. No. I don't think they would give her to you without my order! I should be sorry to see them!" For I thought of Bessy Boothby's history. "How came Bessy Boothby there? and who are you? and how do you know anything about her?"

"Why, I," said the man, "am the Representative in the General Court from Sandersville. And Mr. and Mrs. Boothby live in Sandersville. And I want to carry Bessy to them by the first train to-morrow. That's the reason I want your signature to-day."

"Mr. and Mrs. Boothby don't live in Sandersville," said I austerely, resolved to find the guilty kidnapper. "They live in Worcester."

"They used to live in Worcester," said the imperturbable M. G. C., "but now they work in Sanders's Mill in Sandersville."

"Please, sir," interrupted Mr. Herrick, the sexton, "the organ has been playing ten minutes."

"Yes, yes, I'll be up in a minute. We must make haste. How came Bessy Boothby at our Children's Home?"

"Why, the people at Charlestown, New Hampshire, thought she was not well treated. She had been adopted by a man and woman there who were no better than they should be. And the neighbors watched the child, and they did not like these people. And at last, I believe, the man died. And the woman did not seem to have much to live on, and the neighbors went in and told her that they did not mean to let her have the child."

Enter Mr. Herrick again. In a loud aside, "Please, Mr. Hale, Mr. Brown has played fifteen minutes; he has sent down to know if you are here."

"Tell him to play the Hundred and Nineteenth Psalm with Dr. Madan's variations." And Mr. Herrick departed.

The member of the G. C. began again: "The neighbors told this woman she should not keep her, I mean, should not keep Bessy Boothby. She said she did not want to, and they might have her. They wrote down to your asylum."

Enter Mr. Herrick. Loud aside again, "Will you write down the Psalm for Mr. Brown, Mr. Hale?"

"O no, no! Mr. Herrick, I will really be up in a moment. They wrote down — ?"

"They wrote down to your asylum, and your asylum took her, and she has been here a fortnight. But Mr. Boothby was always watching all the asylums, so he has found her, and all that we want is your order for letting her go back to him."

Sure enough, here was a note in Mrs. Gwynne's well-known hand, telling me that the whole case was looked up, and the parties perfectly authenticated; that she was satisfied, and the other director for the month was satisfied. If I had no other views for Bessy Boothby, she wished I would sign. So I signed, the member of the General Court went on his way rejoicing, I went up stairs and relieved Mr. Brown, and I believe that is the first and last time that I have ever been late at a service in the South Congregational Church, and, till now, I have never told anybody why.

But I think if they and Mr. Brown should have known that his long voluntary was the means of bringing Bessy Boothby to her father and mother one day earlier, they would all agree that the voluntary was an acceptable offering.

The next day but one I got a note telling me that Bessy and the other Boothbys were reunited.

If you want to know how happy was the reunion, you must draw on your imagination, for that is all I ever had to draw upon in that matter.

This was the story I told Asaph, and he said he thought we had better turn and pull home. So we did. And if he went and proffered marriage to Bessy

Boothby, it is since I saw him. But, as I count, she must now be about twenty years old.

Please observe, that if I had driven the man away without hearing his story, neither you nor I would ever have known what became of Bessy Boothby. For I went out of office that very day. The 30th of September was my last day of office for a year.

MOUSE AND LION.

CHAPTER I.

"THERE are two pretty girls," said I.

"Yes," said Mrs. Merriam. "They are pretty, and they are nice. They leave me next month, and I do not know what I shall do without them. They have been with me ever since the school began." For we were talking in her pretty parlor in Clinton Avenue, Brooklyn, where she had "kept school" now — and a boarding-school at that — for six years.

"Who are they?"

"Their names are Henrietta and Margaret. But the girls call them 'Ettie' and 'Grettie,' and they call themselves the Mouse and the Lion."

"Mouse and Lion?" inquired I. "Which is Mouse and which is Lion?"

"You think it a very mild Lion and a very tall Mouse, whichever name belongs to either. The truth is, and their great boast is, that they are absolutely of a size; and, if they could escape good old Katie's watch and ward, they could wear each other's frocks, shoes, gloves, and the rest, indefinitely. But she is flint, as you say, about that. Mouse and Lion?

Neither of them will often own to being Mouse, and each of them claims to be Lion. There are forty pretty stories the girls tell about it. Here is one : —

"Henrietta there, with the blue neck-tie, draws nicely. I make them all draw in ink a good deal, and one winter she got up with great care a set of copies from Retzsch's outlines of 'The Crusaders,' which were to be a birthday present to her mother. Then she patiently translated the whole German poem, which, if you know it, is pretty long, and copied it very neatly, so that the drawings and the text might arrive together on the very day of the birthday. There was a nice box, and every detail was carried out perfectly. Poor child, she and Gretchen there, got it out to show some one the night before, and Henrietta had it on her desk in her own room to improve something in the illumination of a letter, which she did. Before she put it up, she was called off, or turned round, or something ; her sleeve caught the corner of the open writing-desk ; the illuminating-ink bottle, of course, upset, and one blotch of crimson ink ran down, over, under, through every precious page of the thirty pages of copying, to which she had given the last month. It was one of those villanous successes of the " total depravity of things." There was not one sheet of her manuscript but had just a tinge somewhere !

"And, of course, her brother was to call for the box early the next morning, and was to carry it himself to St. Charetin.

"O, how the poor girls cried! Of course, they rushed across the passage to my room. I was just going to bed. But there was nothing to be done. I told them in the morning I would try to see all right, but that they must go to bed. Her mother would enjoy the drawings alone, and they were not hurt. And go to bed they did. Meggie undressed poor Etta,—they always sleep together; said her prayers for her, poor sobbing child; took her in her arms like a baby, cooed to her, cried with her, kissed her, soothed her, and really sung her to sleep with 'Sleep, baby, sleep.'

"And then, when she was sure she was asleep, and that I was asleep, she dressed herself in the dark, went up stairs, and got one of the girls to call down old Arvedson, our porter, gave him her orders,—after eleven o'clock at night,—made him go rout up some shop they knew about, and match the precious paper that was spoiled. About one o'clock he came home with it. And that child, before seven in the morning, had copied 'The Crusaders' again; and had it waiting, all but the first page, for Etta to see when she waked from her dead-beat. She had had wit to leave the first page for Etta's own handwriting, though neither you nor I could tell one from the other, were we bank cashiers.

"O dear! what a time it was again when they came, and Meggie confessed to me. You see it was the most outrageous thing ever done in the school. But Etta was so proud of her; and smoothed her hair, and kept turning round to look at her so grandly, and said such pretty things that poor Meggie did say, for once, 'Why, I am only the little mouse who gnawed your net for you.' And then Etta danced a saraband, and said, 'Am not I a fine lion?' And so I had to forgive Gretchen and send her to bed, not as punishment, but as reward; and the present was all ready when Horace came. And that was the first time the girls were ever called 'The Mouse and the Lion.' Sometimes one is Mouse, and sometimes the other. The other girls say they get into scrapes all the time, each for the fun of being helped out by the other. Margie says that when she is stupid at the blackboard she can always pull through if she knows Etta knows what she ought to do, and is looking into the back of her head. And, as Etta always does know, that is very good for Margie."

This was the first I ever happened to hear of these two girls, though I knew Mrs. Merriam so well. Mrs. Merriam was what we call "one of the original Ten." That means that she was one of ten of Henry Wadsworth's friends who had happened to meet in the North Colchester Station-house after his funeral. She told me this story of the "Mouse and the Lion." I often told it to one and another young friend of mine; and one day I asked her what had become of them both in five years more. So is it that she tells me their story; which, if you please, we will print without any more quotation-marks than shall be quite necessary.

CHAPTER II.

MRS. MERRIAM BEGINS.

I HAD determined to keep this school.

> "Thus from her lofty couch the tale began."

I had hired the house. I had sent my circulars north, east, west, and south. I had hired old Gustav Arvedson, and had engaged the teachers. I had answered many and many a letter of inquiry; and through many and many a hot summer day I had waited here, reading "Shirley," while no one came to inquire. At last it was October. School was to begin on the 5th, Monday. In no case, said the circular, will the number of pupils exceed twelve. No, indeed. It would not exceed twelve, that was very clear. For now, on the 1st of October, even if the girl came from Cuba, who spoke no English, and whose friends had been so undecided about her coming, there would be but eight.

Twelve iron bedsteads up stairs; twelve silver spoons and forks for the girls, — for we were above requiring them in the advertisement; twelve chairs for them in the dining-room; twelve other chairs in the school-room, — not desks, we were above school-desks also; and only eight, at the outside, to fill chairs, bedsteads, napkin-rings, forks, and spoons!

Well, people say I am good-natured! Perhaps I am. Of this I am sure, I am proud.

What I did was this. I took the newspaper. I sent out and bought two others — Brooklyn " Union," New York " Herald "; yes, I bought the " Herald." The " Tribune " I had. I looked and looked. And I made a list of the worst accidents, and the worst murders, and the worst "locals" that I could find for that day. I had on my little book at least twenty stories of misery. The next day I took a carriage, and the next, and the next. I went to house after house, to see the widows of men who had tumbled off scaffolds. I called on city missionaries, and coroners, and local reporters, and policemen, and police captains, and justices of the peace. I went to Castle Garden, and spent a day there among the children who had been left orphans by a horrid ship-fever passage of the " Montcalm." And at the end of my three days I had in the dining-room yonder, sitting in four of the chairs, four of the dirtiest girls you ever saw, all eating large ginger-cakes, looking in wonder at each other. Two of them were " spacheless," one of them was *muette*, and one of them was *stumme*, for immediate purposes ; that is, though they all had tongues in their heads, they were all frightened to death, and could not say one word to each other. And so the account was complete. " In no case will the number of pupils exceed twelve." And in no case will it be less than twelve, unless the Cuban girl or her friends break down. So

far I had succeeded. I had had these girls given to
me by their relatives, and bound to me by sundry and
various guardians *pro hac vice*, as such people are called
by processes, circumlocutory, but sure, of certain pro-
bate or surrogates' courts, and they were mine till they
were eighteen. So the school was full.

No! I do not mean to say that I had run in debt
about it. I might be a fool; but I was not a liar. I
had gone first of all to May Tileston. Found her;
that was a good omen. She was just as lovely as she
was sensible. I told her my scrapes and my plan. I
told her I wanted to pick four girls out of the gutter
and fill up with them. I told her that there was a
hint in "Whewell" that Charity would do a much
more practical thing if, instead of taking crowded Z
from his layer, and squeezing him into Y's layer,
which was almost as crowded, Charity, while she was
about it, would lift him bodily to A's level, where
there was no crowd at all, and where the world wanted
him. "Always plenty of room higher up," as Mr.
Webster said to the young lawyer. I told May that I
was going to give these four girls the best training
that I knew how to give; that, for bread and butter
and jam, they were to have as much and as good as
any of my scholars. "But," said I, "I cannot do
things by halves. They are not to be demeaned in
the school; and they are to have as nice clothes as the
others ought to have, and as much pocket-money as
the others ought to have, and to go to the opera as

often as the others ought to go." I told her that I
had not money enough for this; and I had come to
her to ask if she would not like to provide two hundred dollars a year for the dress and spending-money
of one of them. If she would, I would bully my
Uncle Salem to make him undertake one. I would
write to Mr. Ingham to see if he did not know some
one who would take one; and then I thought I would
go to Mrs. Van Astrachan.

"Child," said Mary, — and she looked like a sibyl,
she was inspired, — "do no such thing. Let me take
them all. I know just how much you want for each
of them. You want $ 237 a year. I know just how
much my Mary cost for those things the year she was
thirteen; these girls will cost the same. I will give
you now my check for $ 237; and I will send you my
check for that sum once a quarter, till you say "stop."
That shall be my part. You do yours, and it will be
lovely. Is it not charming? Tell me all about it.
Where shall you find the girls?"

So that part got settled. And so is it that Margaret came into my school. She was one of the two
"spacheless" ones who ate the gingerbread — of
Emerald parentage.

CHAPTER III.

THE BISHOP OF THYATIRA.

No, I do not know what the mothers of the others would have said. I never asked them. I do know that these four waifs and strays brought to the school just as many and just as few bad habits as the eight others did; for the Cuban girl came. She was an orphan too. In six months you could not have told which was waif and which was not. And the school got the benefit of good French talk, good German talk; and, as you saw in Margie, an element of native common sense and efficiency which perhaps it would not have had, had all the girls been born, as you say, in the purple.

Katy and I had two busy days in dressing our four new dolls, who had open-eyes-shut-eyes, and who in two days were no longer " spacheless." But even in those days there was ready-made clothing in New York for women-kind; and before the other scholars came, these little witches were as well dressed, their trunks and bureaux were as well furnished, and they were as pretty to look at as the best of the cabin-window scholars. I must not tell their story. Suffice it to say they were all of them a comfort to me. One of them, the youngest, was rather stupid; but they were all affectionate, and I was never sorry for a

minute that I took them. They were then eight, nine,
eleven, and twelve years old. Margaret was the oldest
of them all. Little Delia, who was Margaret's second
cousin, only left me last year.

Well, at first I kept the four "waifs" a little more
under my own eye out of school hours. Delia slept
with me; Margaret slept in that dressing-room which
opens from mine. But, as the school warmed up, and
the girls came to know each other, I saw that between
Henrietta and Meggie there was forming one of those
undissolvable harmonies foreordained in Heaven.
Fred. Ingham says they are the choicest illustration
of the Communion of the Saints. Mrs. Primrose used
to say they were like hook and eye, that the people
held together in all strain, because they were wholly
unlike each other. Certainly Etta and Gretchen are
wholly unlike, except in size. Etta is quick as a
flash, Gretchen is slow and very sure. Etta appre-
hends, and Gretchen comprehends. Etta will sit down
on the floor and tell Gretchen a whole string of her
observations, questionings, difficulties, and amaze-
ments; and Gretchen will listen, and listen, and
listen, and wonder how such things ever came into
Etta's head, and then she will wait a minute and pro-
nounce some really grand, all-embracing "Law of the
Instrument," in which every one of these difficulties
and problems finds its place, so that for the hour poor
inquiring Etta is wholly comforted.

Well, I say, I saw they were drifting together. I

think Tasso "was the book." Etta was to study
Italian, because her mother wished it; and I had
given her Margie as a companion in study. That was
one of the advantages of being absolute over the four
waifs, as you call them. The girls came together over
"Graglia," and by the third or fourth canto, without
compact, promise, or word exchanged, they were in-
dissolubly one. Their fate was sealed for time and
eternity.

From that time they looked out words in the same
dictionary, once for both; they learned the same
poetry; they read from the same Bible; they sang
from the same hymn-book. When the Staples sisters
left, there came, of course, a petition that they might
have for their own the double-bedded corner-room.
Then they could say all their prayers together; and
they promised, so prettily, that they would not talk
more than they could possibly help at night, — not
one bit more than I should think reasonable.

It was quite early in this "Communion of the
Saints" that an immense event occurred. The Bishop
of Thyatira, I will call him, came to call on me.
There was another single-breasted-coated gentleman
with him, to show him the way; and they came in a
carriage, and the quiet of the house was quite up-
turned. And it proved that the Bishop of Thyatira
was Irish by birth, though he had not been in Munster
since he was ten years old, but for a visit. He had
been in Rome, and I know not where else, and had at

last become a bishop *in partibus ;* and, at some unexplained lull in his duties of bishopping, he had set out to look up his father and mother and brothers and sisters. Now it turned out, by certain and infallible signs, that one of the sisters had gone to America; and some years after, the Bishop, passing through New York, on his way to Puget Sound, bethought him of her, and hunted up the same Margaret Tyler, or tried to do so; only to find that her husband was dead, and she. But some clew or other made it clear that our Gretchen was her daughter; and the Bishop, getting my address from some surrogate, persevered to Clinton Avenue, as I have said. Fortunately, Etta and Margie were both out. My hen's feathers were a good deal ruffled; but I did not show that to him, or his faithful Achates, no, nor to the girls after he had gone. But when I explained at tea-time, there was terrible commotion. Margaret was perfectly sure he was going to take her away to be a nun; in fact, she was not certain but she was to be built into a niche by masons, like Constance, on the title-page of her "Marmion." I never had such a time, — scolding and laughing and soothing, and trying to make her promise that she would behave properly when he came the next day. All she would say was that she would tear his eyes out, if he were her uncle fifty times over. And she did not believe he was her uncle. "There were twenty-nine Margaret Tylers in the Directory; why did he not go after some of their girls, to make nuns of them ? Would not I be in the room with her ? "

Not at all. I was never in the room with them when their relations called.

He was her relation, and she must receive him like a lady.

" But he will have thumbscrews under the sleeves of his surplice, and hot pincers in his boots, and I shall be haled before the Inquisition before you know it," sobbed and laughed poor Margaret. " Besides, if he was not a bishop, if he was only a young man with patterns from the thread store, I should be frightened to death. The other girls are used to uncles. But I ain't. I hate uncles. I do not see what they are good for."

There was no pacifying her but by telling her that Etta might be present at this fatal interview. And Etta in private promised her to take a paper-cutter of bronze, which was the only weapon they could find, and thrust it into the heart of the familiar, if he tried to " hale them away."

So the Bishop of Thyatira came again, with his friend. Two nice, gentlemanly men as you ever saw, though not without that " certain air of condescension " which Mr. Lowell observes in all foreigners. I ordered cake and fruit, and sent for the girls, and retired. Slight surprise, I think, on the Bishop's face at Etta's appearance. Had he, then, two nieces to care for ?

Indeed, I have wondered whether the visit were not

as much a bore to him as to me. He had doubtless
many other things on hand and in heart. Doubtless
he had discovered many other nieces and nephews;
doubtless he had many purchases to make for Puget
Sound; doubtless his time in New York was horribly
limited. Still, as matter of conscience, he was willing
to look up his niece. But were there two nieces?
"Why two bootjacks?" as Joe Miller has it.

Margaret was very shy, and dropped her eyes, and
only said, "Yes, sir," to his first question. But that
voluble little Etta, with her French blood all at the
fore, boldly fell on her knees and asked him for his
blessing on both of them.

Dear, nice, simple man, he was delighted! Margaret would not kneel down, but he put his arm round
her in a fatherly way, and gave them both a blessing
which I am sure did them no harm. And, before he
well knew it, Etta, the little minx, with a pertness
that turned my hair gray when she told of it, spoke
to him in French, and that pleased him, — for his
French was by this time much better than his Irish;
asked meek little questions about his mission, and the
Indians, and the routes thither; and got him talking,
dear simple soul, on the things that really interested
him, and put in her *Incroyables* and her *Est-il-
possibles* in the most engaging way, and lured him
from minute to minute, till the shy familiar, who did
not fully understand the position, had to inform his
lordship that they should miss their appointment with

my Lord Cross John (as the "Journal of Commerce" used to call Bishop Hughes, irreverently). The dear Bishop of Thyatira was quite amazed.

"O, he must not go! indeed, he must not go!" said the impetuous Etta, — Margaret dumb and amazed all the while, — his lordship must eat a banana. And would the friend of his lordship not eat an orange? Henrietta was very sorry, but the *pension* was strict; she could only offer them water. Would they drink a glass of water? If they observed, there was ice, American ice, in the water. And their lordships must not go before they had granted one great favor. They had brought down Margaret's "Thomas à Kempis" and Etta's "Fénélon." Would his lordship write his autograph in each of them? It would remind them of the day they had his blessing. She had pen and ink here. Would he not write a little text on the first page of each book? He was so kind. He would not forget them in his prayers? Or would he perhaps come again?

Well! I do not know. To this hour Etta is sure that in no point did she say more than she would have said to Bishop Simpson himself, or any lonely Methodist *padre* who came in. She says, if the Bishop chose to think she meant any more, it was because he was himself planning evil, and that his evil plans closed his eyes so that he did not see. Any way, the dear soul — for I now count him as one of the saints, for the simple reason that from that moment to this I have never seen his face — abandoned all thought of abduction, if he ever had any. He saw that his niece was well off. He saw there were Madonnas and Holy Families on the walls. He saw she had "à Kempis" and "Fénélon"; and, not knowing much of the Church Universal, he thought, perhaps, she was on the high road into that Catholic Church which is not universal. Any way, he left his autograph in the two books, with two lines from the "Glories of Mary." He went away extending an apostolic benediction on the ends of his two fingers to Etta and Gretchen. The familiar went with him. Etta shouted "Victoria" as the hall door closed, and Gretchen cried.

"How could you be so bold?" said I to Etta.

"Why, dear auntie," said she, "I had seen them at St. Charetin ever since I was as big as a fly. I was very glad of a chance to have a religious conversation with a bishop alone. They think it is their business to take care of young girls. So it is; unless it becomes the business of young girls to take care of them!"

So the Bishop of Thyatira went to Puget Sound.

CHAPTER IV.

MISS CHAMPERNOON'S DEFEAT.

OF course, I would never have permitted this for a moment. I was not afraid of the Bishop. The child was mine by all law and justice, and all the bishops and all the uncles in the world could not take her away. Etta steadily justified herself. "No; there was not any intent to deceive. There was only a determination that a bishop should know what a free religion was, and that we could get the good of anything without going into his tabernacle." But I would not approve of her French, and her taking all the talk away from Gretchen. "Why had she said 'Victoria'?" And she knew she was in disgrace. But I need not say that Gretchen loved her all the more for that. And to this hour Gretchen would tell you that but for Etta she would have been forced into the carriage that day and have been compelled to enter a convent on Nootka Sound. "You gnawed my net for me! you gnawed my net for me!" she said, sobbing and laughing, as she fell asleep that night in Henrietta's arms.

And so it always went on. The girls all led a very simple life, so that it took all a school-girl's wit to construct adventures out of their daily walks and history. As I came to be sure of them, of course I trusted them; and those whom I trusted went and came as your children go and come. Their adventures would hardly be more terrible than coming to the Wall Street Ferry without a penny — "without *one* penny, Mrs. Merriam" — for fare. And, if this happened when Etta waited there, why, by some miracle, Meggie invariably descended from the clouds with the needed coins; or, if Meggie were the penniless one, Etta was the angel. If Etta were bored to death at one of Mrs. Talmadge's sociables by that persevering Rollo Holiday, Margaret had arts known to herself of compelling him to speak to her. If William Williams wanted to make Margaret waltz with him, she was always at liberty to say she was engaged; and when the time came, lo! it was a standing engagement of many years, by which she waltzed with nobody but Etta. I do not think they ever prompted each other at recitations. But Etta said she did not know anything but what Meggie had told her; and Meggie really knew that she knew nothing but what Etta had taught her.

They led a very happy life, — happiest of all, I suppose, because it had this double aspect, in which each of them was saved from carrying along any of the selfish worries and burdens. Strange to say, if you would take their own version of life, the "great grief of all," as Etta called it, was a certain invitation for their last Christmas holidays. They had looked forward to great pleasure in spending these holidays

together here.   Holidays at school are not generally
thought so pleasant; but they said they had all New
York to see, and they had a novel to write, and wanted
to see a New York New-Year's day, and I know not
what all.   St. Charetin was far away; and word had
come that Etta might stay this time, if Mrs. Merriam
were willing.   Joy, joy, joy!   Joy sadly interrupted,
alas! by a very proper invitation from Etta's aunt, at
Llewellyn Park, that Etta and her young friend would
join their Christmas party.   Worst of all, a letter from
mamma to say that Etta, at least, must go!

O dear! how they hated it.   And at last I was
coaxed into sending word with them that they were
only to stay five or six days ; and then, with unutter-
able groans of terror and disappointment, they went
their way on what Mr. Ingham calls St. Victoria's day.
They returned in time for New-Year's calls, with a
hundred tales of perils from which Etta had extricated
Margie, and pitfalls from which Margie had saved
Etta.

Most terrible of all had been a state dinner.   This
awful event had parted them for hours !   Actually one
gentleman had handed out Henrietta, and another gentleman had handed out Margaret!   And the girls
could not sit by each other, nor even see each other,
and had to do their most proper and very best all alone.
The gentlemen were nice, however ; so they would
have got along very well, but that, of a sudden, in a
lull in the talk, a Miss Champernoon — a dreadful

Boston girl, who was thirty-five years old, looked forty-five, and pretended to be twenty-five — must needs speak to Henrietta, "right across that great table, Mrs. Merriam. Only think how brazen she was!" and say, "I see you do not play classical music, Miss Henrietta. Are you not fond of classical music?"

Poor Henrietta! Why had not the Champernoon fired the first barrel of her revolver at her? It would have been far less dreadful.

"But I hated her, Mrs. Merriam; and that just gave me strength to say, like a fool, that I was very fond of the *Stabat Mater*, from which I had played a scrap before dinner."

Miss Champernoon smiled in irony, and said patronizingly, "Of course, Rossini is very well. I think it very pretty myself. But does not Mrs. Merriam let you play any classical music?"

"Think of her sneering at you, Aunty dear," said Etta, telling of the tournament. "I was so mad I know I was red with rage, and I could not speak; and all was still, when, just think, Aunty dear, Gretchen struck in with, "Don't you call Mozart classical, Miss Champernoon? *Mitridate* is by Mozart. I believe you heard Henrietta play in that duet from *Mitridate*.

"Was n't it splendid, Auntie? And then that fierce beast turned upon her to devour her, and I went free. You should have seen old Boston's amazement when somebody spoke who had not been spoken to.

She raised her eyebrows with sheer astonishment, as she would if the poker had spoken to her, and looked half amused and all surprised, as if she would say, ' Really, this thing can make itself understood.' But she had to do something about *Mitridate*, for Gretchen had hit her well there ; so, with John Hancock's own grandeur, she said, ' O well, yes, I am fond of Mozart ; but, if Mrs. Merriam would let her young people sometimes hear Bach ; if, indeed, they could hear him well rendered.'

" And Gretchen said, Auntie, — just as if she had been a queen, and old Boston had been kissing her hand, — that Mrs. Merriam always took us to the Philharmonic concerts, and that she believed Mrs. Merriam thought that the classical music was best appreciated when people thoroughly enjoyed the romantic. And then she said to that impudent Champernoon, ' Do you remember what Marx says about the effect of the chapel music on Bach himself ? ' And old Champ had to confess she had never read Marx at all. So Gretchen conquered her, and trampled her into the ground. She did not speak for half an hour, and poor unworthy I was saved from instant death ! "

" My dear Peg," said I, " how did you dare quote Marx to anybody ? "

" O," said Peg, laughing, " it was a piece of cheap cyclopædia learning, as good as Ogre Champ's any day. We taught her how to come down on our dear Auntie ! "

This was the greatest victory of the visit; but all
the victories were, as theirs were always, Patroclus's
in the cause of Achilles, and Achilles's in the cause of
Patroclus. I do not know, looking back on it, but
I left them too much to each other. But how could I
have done differently? Each for herself was really
too shy, but each for the other was incapable of fear.
Rose Ferguson made a picture of Etta holding back four
omnibus horses, while Gretchen picked herself from
the mud; not that it ever happened, but Rose said it
would happen some day. Any way, whether I am
right or wrong, they had six happy, lovely years of it.
Part they must, part they did. But because they
knew how to bear each other's burdens they bore their
own none the less, when the time came. And so their
life was a double life, with a fourfold power; a life
many sided, indeed of infinite sides, because they had
seen the vision, and could now never live for themselves alone, or die for themselves alone.

Ah, well! and it was all too good to last. Etta had
to leave the school, and Margie would not stay longer.
She said she must go to the wars. Etta's mother was
eager that she should come and spend a year there.
But no, there were two reasons why not. Gretchen
said she must begin life, — that was what she called
the selfish reason; and she knew she must serve the
country, — that, after all, was the true reason. Then
Etta pleaded very hard with her mother that she might
go to the Sea Islands also, and teach the little black

folks, as Gretchen was going to do.   But, no.   She got
a kind, sensible letter from her mother, explaining
quietly that it was not her country ; that there were
plenty of people to be taught in regions where Etta's
home was, providentially ; and that she and Etta's
father had lived without their own child quite as long
as they wanted to.   I tried to explain to the two girls
that they could not dress and undress each other
always, and could not always fight each other's battles ;
but I knew perfectly well that I made a disgraceful
botch of it.   Of course, I did remind them that to true
love there is no parting ; that they could take care of
each other still, though the big world were between.
It was a sad enough parting ; but, for all that, it was.
Etta went to St. Charetin, and Gretchen went to Hilton Head ; and both of them were to correspond forever with each other, and almost as constantly with
me.   And, indeed, they did.   And so the story, which
is not a story, is almost at an end.

CHAPTER V.

TWO WEDDINGS.

AFTER two years, dear Meggie came back to me, — came home, as the dear child said. But twenty years old is twenty years old; and she had not been at the Sea Islands two years without finding her other destiny. She had met there with Tayler Wildair. He was a Pennsylvania captain at first, and afterward he had come back there on some sort of land commission; and they had found out, woe's me! that they were not to be two, but one. A loyal Christian gentleman was Tayler Wildair, is, and will be. All which, of course, had been written to St. Charetin.

And of course, at the same time, it appeared by gradual dawn of letters, first, that Mr. Munroe had spent an evening with the family at St. Charetin; then that Mr. Munroe and his friend, Lacretelle, had come on a short visit; then that Mr. Lacretelle and his friend had come on a longer visit; then that various sleigh-rides and hops and other entertainments were made for "Horace's friends" or for "the gentlemen," — for by this time Mr. Munroe was never mentioned; till at last it appeared that "Herbert" had asked Etta to marry him, and she said she would. And then, without difficulty, I guessed that Herbert's last name was not Lacretelle, but Munroe. Ah, well! She

would not be further from me in Kent than she was
in Canada.

And so Gretchen went to that wedding at St. Charetin, and was a bridesmaid. And I had the funniest
letter in the world from Etta, telling how, to the
last, Gretchen brought her out from scrapes which
she forever got into. And Mr. and Mrs. Munroe
took the steamboat for Montreal at their own river
landing, on their way to England; and poor, crying
Gretchen threw the last slipper after them, never
to see them again, most likely, and came back to
me.

And poor I had to be as cheerful as I could, and get
her ready for her own wedding. For dear Tayler had
an excellent appointment as acting president of a horse-
railway company in Melbourne; and they were to be
married at once, and he was to take her out in the
next Panama steamer. Really, the big earth was to
be between the two girls in its very biggest. And we
made the old Clinton Avenue house look as pretty as we
could; and little Delia and Tayler's sisters were brides-
maids, and dear Dr. Farley came and married them.
We were as cheerful as we knew how to be, and pretended to be a great deal more cheerful than we were.
Wildair had just got nice letters describing the new
home. It was to be a little out of the city, a semi-
detached house, not far from Admiral Kutusoff's, and
in sight of the cricket-ground, and quite a nice garden
and all that (how many such letters the girls show

me); and they would keep house very pleasantly. And I kissed my darling, and kissed her; and blessed her, and blessed her; and sent her half round the world, and thanked God for the millionth time for the day I read of her poor father's death in the New York "Herald."

CHAPTER LAST.

MY FIRST LETTER FROM MARGARET.

"AT SEA, GULF OF MEXICO, October 11.

"DEAR AUNTIE: . . . . I am better now, and able to enjoy the breeze on deck. A pleasant Mr. Dutton is here, who is on his way back to the Kermadeck Islands. Tayler knew him in the army; and he has a great deal to tell us about the pleasant native habits and all his island life. Of course, I know that Melbourne is very different; but still I begin to feel that I belong to the other side of the world. There are several English gentlemen going to the colony, but no ladies. Still, dear Auntie, I promise you I will be very brave, and at least, I will not be homesick before I get there. Tayler is so kind, and thinks of everything beforehand! They have just called me to see the Vanderbilt exchange signals with us; and now I must get ready for dinner.

. . . . " We all got safely across by eleven o'clock,
and we are to stay in this quaint old place till to-morrow morning ; because the steamer does not sail till
then, and Tayler says I shall see quite enough of my
state-room before I have done with it.   So I am talking Spanish with the chamber-girl. I have had my first
real disappointment.   I was quite sure of a letter from
Etta here ; and, indeed, thought there might be more
than one.   But none can be found.   Tayler has been
to the English consul.   Of course, a thousand things
may have prevented.   What I hope is, that she is in
Switzerland.   If Herbert only could get a fortnight's
holiday for that, it would be so nice for both of them.
What is provoking is, that one English mail has been
taken down by mistake to Lima, and will not be back
here till Monday, when we shall be far away.   Ah, well !
as you say, dear Auntie, what difference in a little paper,
more or less, when I know my darling prays God for
me twenty times a day, as I for her, and sees nothing
but to say what her own Gretchen would think of it :
Herbert says, you know, she buys her gloves to match
my dresses ! "

Then the letter became, in its next chapter, a sea
letter, with the sea changes not unfamiliar to the reader of a Pacific voyage, happily ended at Melbourne on
the —— day of November ; and then the wonders and
perplexities and fun of new housekeeping in a strange
land filled its last page, leaving room only for these
postscripts : —

"DEAR AUNTIE : Who do you think is in the other part of the house ? The things kept coming, and looked very queer and English. And when the carriage came with the people to our portico, you know, I could not help looking to see what my neighbor looked like, and when the coachman handed the lady down, who should she be but Etta !

"Always, your darling

"GRETCHEN."

"DEAR AUNTIE : Is it not splendid ?

"Your own, own darling

"ETTA."

THE MODERN SINDBAD.

THIRTY-ONE STATES IN THIRTY DAYS.

[MR. GREENFELL's journal was originally published in the Atlantic Almanac. A Western editor, while approving the promptness of the travellers, expressed his regret that persons of such intelligence should have taken so few notes, or published so few. Doubtless this is to be regretted ; but as Mr. Adams has well said, the moment people do anything which is worth telling, the doing consumes so much time that they have none left to write it down. It is for this reason that the task of writing devolves so often on people who have nothing to tell. The ease of travel in our times enables men of family to see strange lands without leaving their families at home. And it enables men who are in the midst of large business arrangements, by selecting what in business we call the dull season, to absent themselves from home for a few weeks, and in those few weeks to view, or as it is better called, *to do*, a continent. The mind looks back with sympathy, indeed, on the ignorance of the people a century ago, when John Carver took two years and a half to go from Boston to Detroit, from Detroit to Marquette, from Marquette to St. Paul, and from St. Paul back to Boston. If he had only invested in a single copy of Appleton's or the Official Railway Guide, he would have learned how to do it in a fortnight, and could have taken his family with him, most of the time in a palace car.

Another obliquity of ancient travel has been relieved by the invention of the time-table and the perfection of the Waltham watch, used, as may be learned from our advertising sheet, on all railroads in all habitable worlds. Sindbad the Sailor, besides great sufferings on the seas and on the lands, endured the greater misery of having to spend much of his time at stations. Whenever, by some unusual fortune, he did turn up at a point known to commerce, it inevitably proved that *the* ship for Balsora had sailed the day before, and that but one ship sailed in a year. So Sindbad had to adjust himself for the remaining three hundred and fifty-three days (the Mussulman calendar being lunar) to his journal and to his whittling. Supposing this happened to him seven times in each voyage, he must have spent forty-nine Mussulman years minus forty-nine days (say, on a rough calculation, forty-seven Christian years, four months, and twenty days) at these places, where they had no Atlantic Almanacs at the newsrooms, not even a Beadle's Dime Series, or New York "Observer"; and where, therefore, fortunately for us, he was obliged to make up his own serials, or die of *ennui*. Let it be mentioned, in passing, that if all people knew what good fun it is to make up your own novels, there would be but little market for the wares of those who write for the journals. It may be perhaps surmised that this will be the cause for the demise of the novel and the tale of the present generation, which may die out from the literature of another as completely as Amadis and Esplandian and Metis and Galien have died from this. Such loss of time at waystations may be considered now as substantially unknown ; and the traveller who leaves Soho Square on the 10th of June for his holiday, informing his junior partner that he shall be back on the 5th of August, is as sure that he shall keep that promise as he is that any other promise of Greenfell & Co. will not go to protest.

This preface is unnecessarily long for the introduction of the work which we have the honor to lay before the world. In point of fact, Mr. Greenfell had made his plans with such precision for the holiday which he had arranged for his wife and family, that he missed no single connection, and was able to visit thirty-one States of this continent in the course of thirty days, of which he spent three in Washington.   He has favored us with the sketch of his observations and those of his family, much more condensed than Sindbad's, if not so marvellous.   That one can leave home and return to it in safety, and make observations so philosophical upon a country so dissimilar in its institutions to his own, may certainly be regarded as one of the peculiar triumphs of our modern civilization.

We have not materially abridged the journal.   We trusted that work to the regular law of journals of travel, which, like streams of other sweet sirups, generally run fine by degrees and beautifully less.   As for removing from the journal the air of condescension which an American shows in England, and an Englishman in America, of his very nature, we have found that impossible.   It seems worth while to print it as it stands, as an illustration of the breadth and depth of the information which is gained under our modern systems of travel, so much more reliable than Sindbad's, although the published narratives may not be to the full as entertaining.

Mr. Greenfell landed at Halifax, and by the Carlotta steamer came to Portland on the 24th of June.   We omit the sea journal, and the accounts of Nova Scotia and New Brunswick, that we may begin with Maine.]

MR. GREENFELL'S JOURNAL.

I. THE NORTHERN STATES.

THE STATE OF MAINE

Is generally named first among the States of New England, which are generally named first among the United States.   This State, or a part of it, was the matter of discussion settled by the Ashburton treaty.

It is evident that another arrangement than that then made would have been much more convenient and natural. Here are Mrs. Greenfell and myself, with our children, on our way from Halifax to Montreal. We wish to go by the Portland and Montreal Railway. How foolish that our luggage should be inspected at the custom-house at Portland, and again when we enter Canada! How much simpler if Maine and the northern part of Canada had been assigned to England in that treaty!

We arrived in Portland in the Carlotta steamer from Halifax, looked round us as we rode to Mrs. Jones's inn, here called a boarding-house. We were glad, after the rough night, to sleep in good beds on shore. Took a walk in the morning; and in the afternoon, by the Grand Trunk Railway, started for Montreal at ten minutes past one, American time. Unfortunately, just as we left the inn, George found that he had not his hat. He had come from the Carlotta in his travelling-cap, and, till this moment, no one had observed that he had left the hat on the steamer. He hurried to the dock to find it, expecting to meet us at the station, but failed to overtake us. Undoubtedly he will overtake us by the next train. The station really looked somewhat like home. We were pleased to learn that the railway, which is a section of the Grand Trunk Road, is leased by an English company, and run by Englishmen. The servants were civil and attentive. The road is broad gauge. The carriages are all open, like those in Switzerland. We sat together, however, and found a good deal of amusement from watching our fellow-travellers.

The railway runs through Maine for nearly ninety miles, giving us good opportunity to study the industry and manners and customs of this State. The principal towns in Maine are Falmouth, Cumberland, Yarmouth Junction, North Yarmouth, Pownal, New Gloucester, Danville Junction, Mechanicsville, Oxford, Paris, Bryant's Pond, Locke's Mills, Gilead, and Bethel. Of these, Mechanicsville is much the most considerable. The others are small places, of which the chief trade seems to be in deal and timber, of which we saw much from the windows, and a sort of nut called peanuts, and lozenges, of which specimens were brought for sale into the cars. The population is very sparse. In the latter part of the ride, a young man next to me pointed out to me the White Mountains of New Hampshire.

NEW HAMPSHIRE.

A little before six we entered the State of New Hampshire, which is even less populous apparently than Maine. It was an unexpected pleasure to us to find that we had so arranged our route, purely by accident, that it gives us a complete view of the finest mountain region in the United States. We saw the highest peaks, which are named Washington, Adams, Jefferson, Carter, Madison, Monroe, King, Crawford, and Cherry, from successive Presidents of the United States, who have borne these names. We asked for Mt. Lincoln, Mt. Davis, and Mt. Grant, but were told they were not in sight. The lavish wastefulness of the people leaves fine water-privileges, close by the railway, unused, except for some deal saw-mills, which are worked by the fall. I called the attention of some of our fellow-travellers to very fine positions which might be used to advantage. We were not able to make any long explorations; but at Gorham the girls collected

> Trifolium repens (vulg., *White Clover*).
> Trifolium pratense (vulg., *Red Clover*).

They tell me that the timber is largely coniferous. At ten o'clock we arrived at Island Pond in Vermont; but as I shall have a fuller opportunity of examining that State when we revisit it, I will not here enter our observations. Servants came in, and arranged beds for us to sleep upon, while the train was in motion. It was quite dark in this latitude at ten; and as we were all tired, we slept, without much intermission, until half past six in the morning, when a loud voice informed us that we had arrived in Montreal.

MONTREAL.

This city, although not the capital of the Dominion, is a place of large trade and population. In a very curious cab, or *fiacre*, we rode at once to the St. Lawrence Hall, where, under the Union Jack, we felt once more quite at home. We had been more than twelve hours under the jurisdiction of another power. I sent a line to our old correspondent, Mr. William Brydges, who came round to the hotel soon after breakfast, and showed us every attention.

Here we spent Sunday, attending St. John's Church, with Mr. and Mrs. Brydges. The large number of Catholic churches gives a very foreign appearance to the Sunday.

Mr. Brydges and Mrs. Tyrwhitt have pressed us most cordially to make a longer stay, proposing excursions in every direction ; but our plans are definitely made, involving sailing from New York on the 24th proximo, and we were obliged to decline. I regretted leaving the more, because a telegram from George informed me that he could not join us until Tuesday morning. I replied by bidding him cross the country, and meet us at Concord, in New Hampshire, where our party will be complete again.

We bade these new friends good-by with great regret, and at half past three on Monday left Montreal for a military post called Rouse's Point, on the frontier of Canada and the United States. The railway carriages are still open from end to end, like that of the Grand Trunk ; the railway gauge, however, is narrower. The country is flat and fertile. The vegetation is abundant, and the prospect for a good crop of grain seems good. At a place called Lacadie, which Ellen thinks is the scene of one of Mr. Longfellow's poems, a peasant of the French population entered the carriage with a little girl : a black rag around her straw hat told the sad tale that her mother had died. The man seemed unused to children, but in his rough way comforted her with lozenges and pop-corn, a sort of white blossom with a yellow centre, eaten dry, though tasteless if it have no salt or sugar added.* At a larger town, called St. John's, he left the carriage and the child, asking me, of all persons, to see to her. The child screamed horribly, and I had neither nuts nor flowers. I looked through the window to see the wretched father drinking in the station-house. I called to him ; but he did not seem to understand my language, though he had spoken intelligible broken English only the moment before. The bell struck, the guard cried, " All on board !" the child screamed louder than ever, and for sixty horrible seconds I had the certainty that, in a land of whose customs I knew nothing, and whose laws are not well adjusted, I had assumed the charge of a female child. I turned to consult Mrs. Greenfell, when the face of the Canadian met and reassured me. He travelled with us as far as St. Armand.

Before leaving Montreal our trunks had been examined by a United States officer of customs ; and before we arrived at St. Alban's another officer looked through the carriages to see that we had no smuggled articles with us.

* We learned afterwards, from Bancroft's History, that this is a custom of the natives, who sent bags of this corn as token of hospitality.

VERMONT.

We had passed through the northeast corner of Vermont yesterday. To-day we entered it a little after six in the afternoon, on the extreme northwest, and by the Central Railway, followed up the valley of the Winooski River, and passed through the middle of the State, as the name of the railway implies. I understand that Winooski is the Indian for onion, and that in English this pretty little stream is called the Onion River. St. Alban's is a thriving town, with a fine station-house and a large inn. We made some stay there, and, from the number of people around the station, inferred the existence of a large population. It was the scene of a considerable action in the late war, in which the Confederates were victorious. We left about sunset, and soon found ourselves, in the gathering darkness, in the gorges of the Green Mountains, from which the State takes its name, having been named by French-Canadians, in whose language *vert* signifies green, and *mont* a mountain. Sleeping-berths were again arranged, — on quite a different plan from those of yesterday. I was able to take two compartments, as they are called. In one of them Mrs. G. slept in a lower berth, and I in the berth above, as we had done in our state-room in the Europa. In the other, Ellen and Maud divided the berths in the same way.

If all the towns in Vermont are as thriving as St. Alban's, it must be much more populous than Maine or New Hampshire. The darkness, however, in both our journeys through it, prevented our examining other places as carefully as we did that town. We left the State a little after midnight, at a place called White River Junction; but I did not wake, as I had intended, to witness the crossing of the Connecticut River. Tired out by the hospitalities of our Canadian friends, I slept till morning, and then found that we were approaching Lowell, in Massachusetts, having passed through New Hampshire without waking. I regretted this the less on my own account, because we had seen that State so thoroughly on Friday; but, to my perplexity and surprise, I found, on going wholly through the train, no sign of George, who was to have met us at Concord. I inquired carefully of the guard, who is here called the conductor, and he recollected no such person there. Whether he was there, and could not find us, or whether he failed to arrive there in time, I do not yet know.

From Lowell to Boston is twenty-six miles. We arrived between eight and nine, and drove at once to the Revere House. We were all sadly in need of baths, and glad to take them. They are supplied by what is called Cochituate. water, drawn by the city from a lake of that name. I asked if it was near Wenham Lake, but found no one who knew. At nine we met, with good appetite for breakfast.

THE COMMONWEALTH OF MASSACHUSETTS.

Thus far we had unfortunately missed the capitals of all the American States we had seen. The capital of Maine is Augusta, that of the Dominion is Ottawa, that of Vermont, Montpelier; and we had not been able to visit either of these towns. Concord is the capital of New Hampshire, and at that place we spent two hours this morning. I have already explained the misfortune by which it happened that I lost so favorable an opportunity in sleep. We are now more fortunate. Boston is the capital of the Commonwealth of Massachusetts. We saw from the train this morning a monument erected at Bunker Hill, the scene of one of the battles of the rebellion; and, so soon as I have finished writing, we are to go to see the State House, the Town House, the Coliseum, and the other public buildings. I get no tidings of George, but may do so after we have met Mr. Nevers. . . . .

I finish this entry at ten at night, in the waters of the State of Connecticut. A busy day has given me no earlier opportunity. We unfortunately missed Mr. Lousada, the Queen's consul, as we had missed Mr. Murray in Portland; but I sent my card to our correspondents, Nevers and Littlewood, and before we had done our breakfast Mr. Nevers called. He seemed disturbed, as they all do, to find our time so short, but ordered a carriage at once; and under his guidance we saw the city and neighborhood to much advantage.

We spent an hour or more in the State House. The Legislature has just adjourned; but we saw several of the officers of State, and for the first time I feel as if I understood the politics of this country. We visited the Coliseum, which is a place for musical entertainments, the Funnel Hall, which is a market and town house, where are some curious pictures and a carved wooden eagle. We drove out of town to the Park, made a visit to the Historical Library and another Public Library, to a Primary School and a Grammar School, drove to Cambridge and back, and afterwards met a pleasant company at Mr. Nevers's house at dinner. We called at Fields and Osgood's, my publishers. Unfortunately Mr. Fields is in Europe, and I missed the other partners; but by leaving the first three States of my book, I am able to secure copyright for them by printing them while I reside in this country. At half past five we took the train to Stonington, which enabled us to see most of the State of Rhode Island. We took a steam-packet at Stonington, in Connecticut, and have now had supper, and I am writing in the cabin while the ladies have retired. I am sorry to say George has not yet overtaken us. Just as we left the Revere House I got a telegram from him at Montreal. I have bidden him meet us at New York, and we look to see him to-morrow.

The population of Massachusetts is dense, given mostly to manufactures. One gentleman told me at dinner their only exports were ice and granite, another that their principal business was in ready-made clothing, yet another that they were mostly engaged in shipping houses ready-made to Rio Janeiro, and another that they looked on the manufacture of pianos as their strong point. I had no opportunity to examine statistics on these subjects. The conversation turned principally at dinner on the exercises at the Commencement at the University. We had had an opportunity of spending nearly quarter of an hour in the church there. We heard part of an oration on Philistinism, by Mr. McLeod, a Confederate officer, who on this occasion received the highest honors of this college. I am scarcely willing here to enter into an argument on the subject, as I did not hear the whole of his address. The Governor of the State, and one of the historians of the country, received the honorary degree of Doctor of Laws. Mr. Nevers had told me, in joke, that perhaps it would be given to me ; but this was only a pleasantry ; for my presence on the occasion was purely accidental, and could not have been known to the government of the University. We regretted that we could not remain to be present at the dinner of the Alumni.

RHODE ISLAND.

is the smallest State in the United States, and the richest in the world ; so I was told by a gentleman who sat next me. It has four capitals, of which we passed through two, Providence and Kingston. Near

Kingston, King Philip was taken prisoner in the late war. The spot was pointed out to me by a fellow-traveller. This interesting fact shows, what is not generally understood in England, that republican institutions have not been universal in America till a period quite recent. I asked what became of King Philip's family, and was told his sons were sold into slavery. They must, however, have been soon emancipated, as slavery now exists no longer.

CONNECTICUT

is known as the land of steady habits. We arrived in it at about five minutes before nine, coming from Westerly, in Rhode Island. Stonington should have been named " Easterly," as the most eastern town in Connecticut. It is a well-lighted State, lighted with gas. The people seemed prompt and orderly. We had no difficulty with the luggage, the vans which carried it being pushed upon the packet while we walked on board. We were interested in all we saw of Connecticut, and were sorry we could not remain longer.

II. THE MIDDLE STATES.

NEW YORK.

We woke early, and passed along the East River by many of the public buildings of New York to the dock on the other river called the North River, though it should be called the West River, because it is to the

west of the city.   We saw no cabs at the landing-
place, but I found in a large coach conveyance to the
Westminster Hotel.   Here I had telegraphed to George
to meet me ; and in the hope of seeing him we so far
changed our plans as to give up a day to this place,
but without avail, for what reason we do not know ;
but by some unfortunate detention he has been held
back, and we are obliged to leave without him.

Under the lead of our good friend, Mr. Ashcraft
Ashcroft, we were able to see the more important
points of the city.   I called with him on Mr. Buchanan, the consul of her Majesty, but unfortunately
missed him.   The next day Mr. Ashcroft was so kind
as to send me quite a full series of the New York
journals.   By studying them, and by full conversations with intelligent gentlemen afterwards, I obtained
some views more correct than I had had before, and I
insert them here, as I prepare my journal for the
press.

New York is nominally governed by several Boards,
and by a Mayor, all of whom, according to the most
of these journals, are chosen from the ranks of the
most profligate of men ; and they are all absolutely
governed by what is here known as " the ring."   This
" ring " also governs the Governor of the State, Mr.
Hoffman, who would seem to be another of the most
profligate of men.   Strange to say, " the ring " also
intimidates and controls General Grant and his Cabi-
net, who appear to be, as I am distressed to learn from

these writers, all men of the lowest personal character, and to the last degree vacillating in their purposes, living, indeed, in constant fear of this "ring" and of the press of New York City. It seems fortunate for the country and the world, therefore, that the charge of this press has fallen into the hands of the most pure and high-minded and courageous men living. They evidently do not fear "the ring," although "the ring" controls every other interest and institution in the country; the Exchange, the Church, and the schools, all being subservient to it. I cannot but wish that the press of all countries might be managed by wise men as beneficent as these writers represent themselves.

NEW JERSEY,

as will be seen by the accompanying map,* lies between the southeastern part of New York and Pennsylvania. Its principal production is said to be peaches; but I observed no peach-trees in the part which we crossed through. We were not, the children said, out of sight of a house all the way. We stopped first at Elizabeth, which I suppose to have been named in honor of good Queen Bess; but nobody I spoke to knew anything about the origin of the name. Here we crossed diagonally the road to Philadelphia. Plainfield is a place, of whose inhabitants I do not know the number, in a flat and warm region of country.

* We omit the map, which is a transcript of that in Appleton's Railroad Guide.

Somerville seems to be a manufacturing town ; I noticed a sign of a maker of oval photograph frames. After crossing a wooded ridge, we came out on Philipsburg, where we found large iron-works ; and here we crossed the river into

PENNSYLVANIA.

I regretted, when it was too late, that none of us had set foot in New Jersey after landing : we had in our eyes some of the soil.

In Pennsylvania we crossed to Harrisburg, the seat of government, where we saw the dome, or circular tower, of the State House. I was much interested, at the station, in seeing five or six stout workmen change the water-tanks which are provided for passengers in the "cars," taking out the empty ones, and filling them with Wenham ice and water, brought in by the hydrants by a long hose. Ellen calculated that the consumption of each "car" must be about fifty gallons. Of this I confess I drank a good deal myself. At Altoona, at eight and a half in the evening (twenty-two minutes after three, by London time), we again took sleeping-"cars," where, instead of blankets above the sheets, we had what are called comforters, — rugs quilted of cotton-wool. We are now so used to this system of travel that I did not wake till half past six in the morning (twenty-two minutes after one, London time), near Newcastle, in Ohio. In Pennsylvania we crossed the anthracite coal country, where we were quite cool ;

met a thunder-storm in the valley of the Susquehanna, not far below the Vale of Wyoming, which we were sorry not to see. The productions of Pennsylvania are coal, iron, wheat, and rye.

Of the flora of the day the report is, that the daisies are gigantic ; they have long, high stems. My daughters also observed in seed

Taraxacum Dens-leonis (vulg., *Dandelion*),

which they had before seen in blossom, and, in blossom now,

Ranunculus acris (vulg., *Buttercup*),
Linum usitatissimum (vulg., *Common Flax*),

and a white flower, and a purple marsh-flower, of which they did not know the names ; and unfortunately none grew near the dining-station, or in the neighborhood of Harrisburg.

WEST VIRGINIA.

Between one and two in the morning we passed that portion of West Virginia known as the Pan Handle. West Virginia sided with the Federals in the late war, and was rewarded by being set off from Virginia as a separate State of the Union. It was too dark for me to make much observation of the soil or the inhabitants, even had I been awake ; and we collected no specimens for the hortus-siccus. The climate seemed to us all very warm, and the air close ; there is an odor of coal-oil or naphtha in it, which may result from our proximity to the oil-wells. We left it by a bridge at Steubenville, over the Ohio River.* This river takes its name from an Indian word signifying the beautiful, and gives that name to the State of Ohio, which we next entered.

III. THE WESTERN STATES.

OHIO.

On leaving the atmosphere of the sleeping-" car," which, as I have said, was somewhat close, and going forward to stand upon the platform of the train, I was struck with the appropriateness of the name. The country seemed newer, to take the American word, than any we had yet passed ; yet we were seldom out of sight of houses or cabins. The log-cabin, as its name implies, is built of logs. At Denison the train stopped for half an hour for our breakfast. The coffee was very bad ; the steak was thin and tough ; the eggs were very good ; and we were very hungry. The table-cloth was spotless, to Mrs. G.'s great delight and mine. She expressed her pleasure to me, because we had learned from a fellow-traveller that intelligent travellers in this country always travelled on Monday or Tuesday, that they might have clean table-cloths and towels. I had regretted that we should not be able to

* We omit in the American edition a drawing of this bridge, which has been reduced by Miss Ellen from the company's "posters."

lie over till next Monday, after I learned this ; but our
arrangements would not permit.

The capital of the State, which we passed through,
is Columbus. Here is also the State Prison, which we
saw, but could not visit. It is the custom in America
to have the State Prisons in the towns where the legislative bodies meet, perhaps to keep them in terror. A
gentleman next me asked if there was not " something
extra " about the State House. I told him I did not
know ; but from the question I infer that the size of
the Legislature, or the extent of the government, may
require what we call " an annex " to the building.
We left Columbus with regret, for Indianapolis and
Chicago.

INDIANA.

A desire to see as many seats of government as
possible led me to take a longer route than necessary,
and to pass through Indianapolis. The name denotes
that it is the city of Indiana. It stands on a flat, and
is very hot. The streets are regularly laid out, as I
believe are those of most towns in America. As we
waited for the train to Chicago, Mrs. G. and I and the
girls took a little walk in the city. I am not sure
whether we saw the State House or not. I accosted a
native whom we met, and asked, " Would you show
me, please, the way to the State House ? " His reply
was, " Which ? " From this I inferred that, as at
Columbus, there are two State Houses, in different
parts of the town. Possibly the senate, which corre-

sponds to the House of Lords, sits in one, and the Commons in the other ; but I am sure it was not so in Boston.   Unfortunately we had no time to continue the inquiry.   We left this interesting capital without regret, at about dark.

The people of Indiana, as I had before learned, are called " Hoosiers ; " but when I addressed a lad in the railway carriage, and asked him if he were " a Hoosier," I found he was displeased.   I suppose he came from some other State, but he would not explain himself. In crossing from Indianapolis to Chicago, we passed over a long prairie country ; but unfortunately it was too dark for us to make out much of the scenery.

The wheat and oats are abundant in the States of Ohio and Indiana.   The Indian corn, which was the grain of the Indians, is so little advanced that we cannot as yet understand its growth.

ILLINOIS.

It seems to be our fortune to arrive in the large cities to breakfast ; and the girls say they shall remember America as the country of shower-baths and bathtubs.   We had, however, no such opportunity in Ohio ; and after forty-six hours of scarcely broken travel from New York, we were glad of the welcome of the Tremont House in Chicago.   We met at a late breakfast, at nine o'clock, and found a telegram from George. The fine fellow arrived at the Westminster at New York the day we left, too late for us.   He has taken the New York and Erie route to this city, and we shall meet him to-night. Till then we shall scarcely feel that our journey is begun.

I called on the consul as soon as breakfast was over, but missed him. With the ladies, however, I visited the new tunnel under the river which makes the harbor, which seemed to us short indeed in comparison with Sir Isambert Brunel's masterpiece, but is a creditable work for a new country. It is not yet quite completed. We went to the top of the City Hall, and, in company with a gentleman I met at the hotel by the name of Jones, we visited one of the curious elevators which pump up corn from the vessels and canal-boats, and deliver it again. We also visited the water-works which supply the city with water from the depths of the lake. Mr. Jones offered to show us the neighborhood of the city; and we rode along Wabash Avenue, their finest street, quite into the country. He showed me some fine sites for building, if I wished to settle here; but we told him that Mrs. G. would never be satisfied far from Bloomsbury Square.

Mr. Leadbetter called while we were out, and we dined at the hotel. We then agreed, as we had seen the city so thoroughly, and as I wished to visit Michigan, that we would ride out on the eastward train to Michigan City, which is on the frontier of that State, meet George, and return with him.

MICHIGAN.

I can hardly regret this determination, though we were not so fortunate as to meet my son. There are two trains through Michigan it appears, which, at the moment we started, I had not noticed in the Official Guide, which is the American Bradshaw. George had taken the Michigan Southern, and we were on the Michigan Central.

Michigan is a level State, so that, although Michigan City is scarcely within its lines, I was able to see a good deal of it by mounting on a wood-" car " while we remained at the station. The business seems to be conducted mostly by railway. The motto of the State is, *Si peninsulam amœnam quœris, circumspice*, " If you are seeking a pleasant peninsula, look round."

This I did for a few minutes, and confess I was somewhat disappointed. The bustle and confusion of a large railway junction is anything but pleasant. We had but a few minutes to remain in Michigan City. The eastward train there meets the express train from Cincinnati to Chicago ; and by this train we returned to that city, arriving a little before ten o'clock, but not having seen my son.

It subsequently proved that he had arrived in the city, and at the Tremont House, a little after eight o'clock. Some one at the office of the inn told him that we had taken the train for Davenport, in Iowa ; and, without sufficient inquiry, scarcely snatching his

supper, he rode to the station of that road to catch the
express. On our arrival at the hotel we were told that
a gentleman had inquired for us, but I supposed it was
Mr. Leadbetter again. Just as I was retiring for the
night, however, while looking casually on the register
which is kept open at all American inns, for the information of the police, public and private, I saw
George's familiar name. They assured me that he had
gone to Iowa. My first thought was to start in pur-
suit the next morning. But on consultation with Mrs.
G., we agreed it would be better to telegraph him to
meet us at La Crosse in Wisconsin.

I defer my conclusions on Illinois till we visit it
again.

WISCONSIN.

After a day in Wisconsin we feel that we see indeed
a new country. The girls no longer report that we are
" almost never " out of sight of a house. Long prairie
reaches where we are out of sight of a tree, stretches
of woodland, sometimes, which it seems hopeless to
break into, teach us what the settlers encounter.
Janesville, Madison, and Portage City are the largest
towns we have seen. La Crosse, where we are, is the
chief city of the Democratic party in America ; but I
have unfortunately no letters here, and, being an inland
town, there is no English consul. It is late as I write,
our arrival at the hotel being at midnight, so that I
can scarcely speak of the city. Sunday, the 4th of
July, is the anniversary of the separation of these

States from the crown of England, and is generally celebrated as a holiday. The celebration this year is postponed until to-morrow, except by the Germans, who prefer to celebrate to-day. We have attended service at the Episcopal church.

MINNESOTA.

We had here, on the whole, a favorable opportunity to examine the trade and productions of this new State, which received its State government as lately as 1857. After breakfast, as we walked from the hotel to see the flow of the great Mississippi River, we noticed a ferry-boat starting for La Crescent, a town opposite La Crosse on the western side. It must not be supposed that the inhabitants of Minnesota are Mahometans. But the name La Crosse having been given to the Wisconsin town by some early missionary, I suppose the name of La Crescent was seized upon here, in allusion to a popular prejudice here that towns on the west side of great rivers *increase*, while those on the east side are less rapid in their growth.

As we loitered by the river-side, the blowing of steam and ringing of the bell announced that a river steamer, the General Logan, was about to begin her voyage to St. Louis. The ladies are so tired of travel by land that I went on board to inquire as to her departure, and secured passage on her for my family. She will touch at the river landings, and we can take up George at Prairie du Chien (the Dog's Prairie), or at

Dunleith, or at Rock River. I have telegraphed him to wait us at one of these points.

Minnesota seems to be a State of dealers in timber and rough wood, of ferry-men and other boatmen. A railroad runs from La Crescent to Rushford.

IOWA.

We sent our luggage to the General Logan, but she did not leave her moorings till near two o'clock, although we were on board four hours, and were constantly assured that she would go "right away," which, in the language of this country, means "directly." The girls would have been glad to improve this time in botanizing. We have pleasant state-rooms opening on a balcony called the guard, which looks upon the river.

The recent rains have made the river very high; and, as the captain had no landing to make before we arrived at Prairie du Chien, we reached that town before evening. Meanwhile we had had an opportunity to see much of Minnesota and Iowa from the deck of the boat as we passed by. Harvest is just beginning through all this country; and in one or two cases, where farms approach the river, we could see the reapers, no longer with their sickles, but trotting round in their little go-carts, gathering in the wheat and other grain. It is still so wet, however, that there is some delay about the harvest. Before arriving at Prairie du Chien we were able to land at Iowa, at places known as Hogg's Landing and Wilmot's Creek. It does not differ, as far as we could see, from the country on the other side. The day has been very hot.

We had to wait but little at Prairie du Chien, and, soon after dark, were on our way again. The ladies enjoyed the comparative stillness of the steamboat berths, and we slept late. Going on deck, I found that our run had been very rapid in the night, and we were approaching the celebrated bridge at Rock Island. Here we expected to meet George; and we left our friendly Captain Parsons, and landed here.

We were again disappointed. I could learn nothing of George at any of the hotels. There is no railway below Rock Island on the river shore; and it seemed certain that he had attempted to strike us at Fulton, higher up the stream. I telegraphed him at that point to await us there. We were fortunate enough to be able to strike a pleasant evening train up the river, and, before dark, again had retraced our course and arrived in Fulton.

At Fulton, on the hotel book, was his name! The keeper of the hotel said he had inquired after the General Logan on arriving, and, learning that she had passed down the stream, had taken another boat which was passing, and had followed us to Rock Island! Ellen declares that at this very spot on the river the same adventure happened to Evangeline in one of Mr. Longfellow's poems. But Maud thinks this was lower down, at a spot which we shall visit in a few days. I telegraphed him at once not to attempt to overtake us here, but to await our arrival at St. Louis.

I was obliged to do this that we might secure passage by daylight in the train for Omaha in Nebraska, which leaves Clinton, opposite this place, at seven o'clock every morning. This we succeeded in doing; and after a little more than twenty-four hours, having tried the sleeping-" car " again, on yet a different arrangement, we find ourselves in Omaha.

NEBRASKA.

We have been travelling with four young men who are on their way to Porthos, where they have established their families. I was sorry not to visit that place with them, as it is to be the commercial capital of the whole country within a few years. I was very fortunate in meeting these gentlemen, who kindly gave me a full account of it. It is on the Missouri River, just half-way between the two oceans; and when railroads, now contemplated in each direction, are finished, it will be the great *entrepôt* of Eastern and Western trade. It is also half-way between the Gulf of Mexico and the parallel of 54° north latitude, and must be always a great centre of the trade North and South. Whether the Seat of Government is soon removed there or not, Porthos must become a great mercantile city, and nothing would have interested me more than a visit to it.

Of course, also, the temptation is very great to leave

Omaha westward, and cross the continent to San Francisco by the Union Pacific Railway just now opened. Four days would carry us to the Pacific Ocean, and in five more we could return to St. Louis, adding thus five to our list of States visited. But the plans we made in London do not permit this extension of time. To see the Southern States thoroughly will require all the time I have between this and July 24th, on which day our berths are taken in the New York steamer. With reluctance, therefore, we turn eastward at nine o'clock, Omaha time, which is twenty-four minutes after two by London time. We have travelled more than one quarter round the world.

Finding, after breakfast, a boat with steam up, about to start for the lower landings, we enjoyed a day's sail between Kansas and Missouri, arriving at St. Joseph early enough the next morning to take an express train for Kansas City. We entered this city by a new bridge over the Missouri River, finished and opened on Saturday last. We went on shore at Elwood, in Kansas, and by starlight had a fine view of that State.

We have thus made a survey of all the States generally known as the Loyal or Northern States in the late contest. Missouri, Tennessee, Kentucky, Delaware, and Maryland were generally in the hands of the Federals, but were known as Border States. These we are yet to visit, as well as the Gulf States and Arkansas and the Carolinas. I see that I have nowhere summed up our view of ILLINOIS. It is a State rapidly growing in population, with large supplies of provisions for all parts of the world.

IV. THE SOUTHERN STATES.

If I abridge my sketches of this interesting region, it is not that our notes were less thorough than in the region we have passed. Our route will be best understood if I speak of it once for all. Crossing Missouri in an afternoon and night, we took the fine steampacket Gray Eagle at St. Louis, and, in a sail down the Mississippi of a day and a half, reached Cairo, at the southern point of Illinois. At Cairo we spent Sunday, and, leaving early Monday morning by steampacket, landed at Columbus in Kentucky, whence to Memphis by rail is about nine hours; and thus we examined Kentucky and Tennessee. By a ferry-boat at Memphis we crossed into Arkansas; and thus at the landing we were able to study that interesting State. By rail again to Vicksburg, in Mississippi, is two hundred and ninety-one miles : here by ferry we crossed into Louisiana, returning to Vicksburg. Twenty hours more thence took us to Mobile, in Alabama, and a steamboat excursion to the opposite side of the bay permitted us to land in Florida. From Mobile to Montgomery, to Atlanta, in Georgia, through Augusta to Branchville and Wilmington in the Carolinas, is a fatiguing railway ride, by day and night, of sixty-eight hours, — three nights and two days. At Wilmington what is called the Great Northern Line took us to Weldon, thence to Richmond, in Virginia, and to Washington, the capital of the Federal States in the war, and now of the re-united country. Of all this region I will now speak in detail.

KANSAS.

Our impressions of Kansas are of a warm, low country with little timber. The settlements are new. The people seem to deal mostly in wood for steamboats.

MISSOURI.

We saw this State thoroughly, passing from Kansas City in the west to St. Louis in the east, and coasting the eastern line on the river. We passed through the capital, Jefferson. There is but one State House. The trade of the State seems to be mostly periodicals, cheap novels, novels bound in cloth, candies in papers of different kinds, figs in wooden boxes, chewing tobacco, and maple-sugar. These were offered to us freely in the " cars." The climate is warm.

KENTUCKY

was one of the doubtful States in the war, and is not thoroughly reconstructed. The climate is very hot.

TENNESSEE.

The same remarks apply to Tennessee. We saw cotton growing here for the first time. The girls were much interested in the growth of this useful plant. The weather was too hot for long excursions.

MISSISSIPPI.

This is one of the Gulf States. We found the climate hot, as we had expected. At the station at Vicksburg I offered, in pay for my tickets, some of the bonds of the State, which had been placed in my hands for negotiation by the father of my wife. The ticket-seller was very angry, and asked if I saw anything green. This was an allusion to the Federal currency, the bills of which are printed with a green back. I was obliged to give this instead of the bonds.

LOUISIANA.

The soil appeared to be fertile, but the climate, like that of the other Gulf States, is very warm. There are many venomous insects. We killed many mosquitoes. We saw here the remains of some of General Grant's works.

I must interrupt the order of my narrative, to say that at Vicksburg we were doomed to another disappointment in regard to George. At St. Louis we had felt sure of meeting him. But, on our arrival at the Planters' House, we found a note from him saying that his friend, Mr. Morley, had invited him to visit the stupendous iron-mines a few hours from the city. It so happened that the Gray Eagle had been recommended to me as a specially fine boat ; I telegraphed to George, therefore, to bid him cross from the Iron Mountain and meet us at Cairo, which he could do more easily than he could return to St. Louis. Unfortunately he missed my despatch, returned to St. Louis, failed to overtake us at Cairo, and, by I know not what misfortune, again at Vicksburg. We shall certainly find him at Washington.

ALABAMA.

This State is distinguished for its cotton, and for being the seat of the chief government of the Confederacy early in the war. I called on the English consul at Mobile, but he was absent. We found it too hot for much visiting, but in a pleasure steamer made an agreeable excursion to

FLORIDA.

This State was bought of Spain by the Americans. The land is low, and the climate hot in July, at which time we visited it.

GEORGIA.

In Georgia we came into higher country. Atlanta, which takes its name from the Atlantic Ocean, which is supposed to be named from the fabled Atlas, is a thriving manufacturing town, which has doubled since the war, when it was captured by Sherman. We saw many of the field-works of the General's. It was too warm, however, for much study of the scenes of interest.

SOUTH CAROLINA

is known as the Palmetto State. It is the State which fired the South. We thought it might well have done so, for the climate is oppressively warm. The chief production is cotton.

NORTH CAROLINA

is known as the Rip Van Winkle State, and was thought cool by the Confederates, as I was told by an officer of high rank. We thought it, on the other hand, very warm. The chief productions are pitch and pea-nuts. We had longer opportunity to see this State than most of the Southern States. We arrived at Wilmington at five o'clock, or thereabouts, Sunday morning. I would willingly have avoided travelling at all on that day; but at Branchville, where we had intended to spend it, there is absolutely no sleeping accommodation for travellers.

We attended St. John's church in the evening, but had not the pleasure of making any acquaintance. I did not like to call on the consul; and we spent the day quietly at our hotel.

VIRGINIA.

This was the largest of the Confederate States till the western half, West Virginia, was cut off. We found it even warmer than that State. Richmond is a beautiful city, with fine water-power, not much im-proved, on account of the heat of the climate. We passed through it about dark, but could see the prison and State House. I think there is but one State House, though there are two prisons.

From Richmond we went to Acquia Creek and the Potomac River; and there, after a continuous railway ride of five days and more, only broken by our excursion at Mobile, we gladly took berths on the steamboat again, for Washington. This closes our review of the Confederate States, all of which, except Texas, we have been able to visit.

DISTRICT OF COLUMBIA. WASHINGTON.

At Washington we found the weather extremely hot, and not well fitted for excursions. The ladies, however, did not regret this so much, as they were a good deal exhausted by the rapidity of our recent movements. I called on our minister, Mr. Thornton; but he had, unfortunately, removed to Newburyport, in Massachusetts, with his family, for the hot weather. President Grant was also absent at Long Branch, a watering-place not far from New York; so that we lost the opportunity to see him.

The Congress is not in session. It sits every alternate summer; but, unfortunately for us, this is the summer when it does not sit. I regretted this the less, having had the opportunity I have described to study the legislative customs of the country in Massachusetts.

We visited the Patent Office, where are a great number of models of inventions; the Capitol, which is a large building of marble; the Smithsonian Institute, which stands in a large garden; and what is known as

the East Room at the White House. The West Room,
I know not why, is not shown to visitors.

If I were to come to America again, I think I should
spend all my time in this or some other city. I have
now so far acquainted myself with the outline of the
country that I feel better prepared for a more quiet
post of observation. We waited here for George till
the last moment; but were obliged, on the morning of
the 23d, to leave without him.

MARYLAND.

Leaving home, as we came to call Washington,
at seven o'clock on the morning of Friday, we arrived in New York at five o'clock the same afternoon. This enabled us to cross the State of Maryland from southwest to northeast, and to pass
through the historic city of Baltimore. Baltimore is
known as the Monumental City, as I learned from the
newspapers; but, though we saw one or two shot-
towers, we saw neither monument, nor do I know
for what they were built. Judging from the population at the station, the white and black races are about
evenly represented.

DELAWARE.

We have been very much interested in this State.
The stay of the train at Wilmington is nearly ten
minutes; and we were able to walk into one of the
streets of that curious old town. An ancient church

is in sight from the train. Delaware is mostly inhabited by negroes, who seem to spend most of their lives at the station, with nothing to do there.

PENNSYLVANIA AND NEW JERSEY.

I have little to add to the account of these States which I have already given. Philadelphia is a large city, built mostly of brick. We passed through Trenton, the capital of New Jersey. It has but one State House.

Arrived once more at the Westminster Hotel, after our parting absence of a month, to our great joy we met George! He had arrived at Washington before us, direct from Memphis. At the Legation they had assured him that we had been and gone. It must have been that Greenfell of Liverpool, of Greenfell, Atwood, & Greenfell, who is somewhere in this country, had called, and left his card. George, therefore, had hurried to this city, and resolved, as he said, not to leave the Westminster for an instant, day or night, till we should arrive.

It was the easier for George to do this, because in the same hotel was residing a charming young lady from New Madrid, in Missouri, with whose family he had travelled from Memphis. Anticipating the pleasure it would give his mother and me to gain a daughter in America, George had offered to this dear girl all he had to offer, while they rested a day in Washington. With the approval of her estimable parents, she had accepted the proposal; and, as I write these lines, at twelve o'clock at night, I have just left the young people together, having wished them every blessing.

George will remain some months in America. His mother, his sisters, and I sail to-morrow morning.

His hat looks well, but not so well as when he started.

———————

To resume my observations. I do not wonder that the inhabitants of this country are thin and short-lived. I have not slept well five nights since I landed here. I do wonder that they are so tall, for their beds are but six feet long. I do not wonder that they are dyspeptic; for a constant diet of sandwiches, figs, candies, and praslins must be very injurious in the course of years. I do wonder that they make money; for the necessity of telegraphing is constant, and the charges are exorbitant.

I have visited thirty-one States of the Union, and have conversed with citizens of all the others. I have visited also the District of Columbia, and Washington, the capital of the country. I have also visited Montgomery and Richmond, the two capitals of the Confederacy. I have visited fourteen of the capitals of States, if I am right in the impression that Kingston is one of the capitals of Rhode Island. In Boston I was able, just after the adjournment of the Legislature,

N

to see the arrangements of the different branches of the government.

But there is no place like home. And of this we are more satisfied than ever. We have acquainted ourselves with the customs of a republic, and are more than ever willing to adapt ourselves to those of the good city of London.

Saturday, July 24*th.*— Thirty days from our landing from the Carlotta, in Portland, we set sail for England, in the stanch ship City of London. Happy be the omen of a name so like home !

A TALE OF A SALAMANDER.

It was a clear, cold night in February, when a young man, well muffled, returned to his comfortable, book-lined study from making a social, neighborly evening call. He evidently professed to be a student; for the room was filled with heaps of books and papers, and the table strewed with the happiest abundance of unarranged volumes. Indeed, it was not merely a profession : it was clear that he had studied, and studied hard. The comfortable look which he assumed as he sank into his easy-chair, and dragged his light table up to him to write, showed that he felt himself at home, and that he knew what the piles of books around him were, and was glad to return to their society. He warmed his hands at his bright fire, opened his note-book, looked at the last entry he had made, tore it out and burnt it, and wrote rapidly a few lines ; then dropping his pen, began to stare at his fire eagerly, and sunk into a deep revery. The entry in the diary was this : —

"Mr. Austin told a queer tradition to-night about the glass-houses in the valley. This is what the workmen there call the salamander night. It seems that all glass-blowers believe that a salamander will emerge from any fire which burns more than forty days and nights; and that accordingly, from fear of seeing one, they always extinguish the fires in their furnaces on the fortieth night after they have kindled them. To-night there is no glare from the valley; and Austin says that this is the cause. It is an odd idea."

Hardly had he written the last words, when, by a sudden transition of feeling, he began to think in a much more respectful manner of the tradition of the glass-blowers. "What strange ideas we have," said he to himself, "about popular opinion. I argue, men who call themselves wiser than I argue, that there is a distinction between right and wrong, because every one in the world has, in some way, made it. I argue, and they argue, that there is a God, on similar grounds. I believe, and they really believe, that there is an external world; that effect depends on cause, not because we can prove it, but because we always have believed it, and because all the rest of the world believes it. And yet, when the affair in question is of rather less consequence, all the weight of popular opinion goes for nothing. Nine hundred and ninety-nine thousand and odd men out of a million in this world believe in the visible reappearance of departed spirits; and yet because Sir David Brewster never saw a ghost, I must believe that thousands of men who have, have been dreaming. And yet, out of the thousand people nearest me at this moment, I could not, I suppose, find ten who would dare to sleep to-night in the burying-ground yonder. I might take voyage after voyage, and never find a sailor who would tell me he knew there was no such thing as a mermaid; and yet because some German doctor, who never saw or tasted salt water, asserts that the thing is an anatomical impossibility, I am expected to fold my hands quietly, and say, 'What superstitious beings sailors are!' I might travel among our North American Indians, and hear all their traditions and opinions related without variation through all the different tribes; yet no civilized person would blame me for pronouncing on my own authority, without attempting a whisper of argument, without a shadow of premise, or an attempt at reasoning, that they were all contemptible because merely the superstitious prejudices of ignorant savages." He went on to call up crowds of instances where general prejudice had proved right, and the wise men not far from wrong: such as Dr. Lardner's views on steam navigation; the reappearance of the dragons of the romancers, so long banished from reputable society, in the Sauria of the geological cabinets; the tale of Charles II., his fish, and the Royal Academy; the great sea-snake of the Norse traditions; the sailor's tales of the Flying Dutchman and the commentary of modern science; the Italian tradition about the existence of Herculanæum and Pompeii, long before it was discovered that they were not wholly destroyed.

He remembered how many of the antiquated prescriptions of the old empirical physicians had been condemned by modern science only to rise again to light as that science advanced further. All the old charlatans of past centuries gave doses of burnt sponge to their consumptive patients : modern science thought it as ridiculous as if they had given hemlock, till Sir Humphrey discovered iodine in sponge, and Dr. Somebody found iodine one of his most powerful remedies. He remembered how ably naturalists had demonstrated the non-existence of the Unicorn, who fights so gallantly for the crown, beyond the fancy of the heralds or the sign-painters, unless in the unwieldy form of the clumsy rhinoceros ; and that the demonstration was hardly over when they were called to examine the animal itself, in the Gnus, or horned horses, of modern menageries.

"So," said he to himself, " in this matter of the furnaces there, Mr. Austin talks of the workmen's superstition ; and his little bride laughs, and calls it a pretty idea ; and staid Mr. Dubbado frowns, and says the ignorance of the laboring classes is distressing ; and good Parson Drury says their superstition is more so ; and I, cold-blooded wretch, talk of the superiority of this legend, in matter-of-factness and dignity, to the milk-and-water traditions that fill out the annuals. Why have not these workmen a better right to know what they are about than we have ? What right have we to say that they are making fools of themselves ? They have always dealt with fire : we never have. Their fathers did the same : ours never did. Their tradition must have some shadow of foundation. Some shadow ? — a strong foundation. Must have ? — does have one. I will prove it myself. Why be afraid of a poor salamander ? I will begin my experiment to-night. Forty days from this will be — the 27th of March." He worked himself into such an excitement by the train of thought of which we have only given an outline, that he spoke these last words aloud, pacing backwards and forwards across his room. He immediately began to investigate his library to see if he could find there any aid in his undertaking.

The table was soon piled with volumes ; and although in many of them he had found nothing to satisfy his curiosity, yet his eye rested on two or three with peculiar satisfaction. Lord Bacon says, " The salamander lives in fire, and has power to extinguish it." Said the student, " Lord Bacon was a wise man, though he puts that in his book which he cannot prove."

Pliny says, " The salamander is an animal shaped like a lizard, never coming forth but after heavy showers and in overcast weather. It is so deficient in feeling that its touch extinguishes the fire around it, as ice would." And Pliny was a wise man, but at the same time a timid one ; for he adds a farrago of nonsense about the poisonous properties of the animal. The student turned all this over in his mind, and praised Bacon and ridiculed Pliny ; for he was but a man ; and

Bacon had countenanced, while Pliny had rather frowned at, his undertaking. He read but little more; he paused a moment on Pliny's matter-of-fact account of the phœnix, and found in it corroboration for his newly formed theory; he read a little in some Oriental fables, and found frequent mention of his new pet; and then, turning aside from his books, throwing himself back in his well-stuffed easy-chair, and gazing on his brilliant fire, he began to think.

He began to think, not in tangible words, or rhetorical sentences, like the hero of a second-rate novel, not aloud, like the hero of a tragedy, but, like a sensible, imaginative man, in air-castles, in brilliant fancy bubbles, his mind in an instant running where the swiftest shorthand of the tersest language could not overtake it in years. He wondered why men should suppose that earth and water were the only life-supporting elements; and then incidentally he asked himself whether any spirits of air were hovering round him at the instant, and watching his actions and reflections. Were there any around him, and who were they? Should he never be watching over friends, seeing their conduct and thoughts, and guiding their destiny, himself invisible? He liked to believe it: he did believe it; and he went on to think of his dear mother and sisters. What were they doing now? Were they not thinking of him, and of the time when he should return home again? The bright fire recalled him to his salamander friend; and, as he gazed, he despised the fearful superstition which had induced men to give up the knowledge of a known animal once known; to relinquish a secret they had discovered; to sink into ignorance where they had had sure knowledge; and then his fancy ran through a long labyrinth of ideas leading from the hint of lost knowledge, of which the books of Livy, the Alexandrian Library, the six books of the Sibyl, the lost sacred volumes of our religion, the manufacture of Greek fire, stained glass, Venice glass, the voyages of the old Northmen, the wanderings of the Ten Tribes, and a hundred other such mysteries, were the turning corners of the clew. No pen could sketch the different mazes into which he ran from every one of these corners in the minute before his bright light once more bade him recollect himself. Then he wondered whether he ought to pity the salamander. Had he always lived there? was he solitary or social? were his forty days an imprisonment or a pleasure; and were his happiest moments those when he escaped from, or returned to, his fire? Perhaps the few minutes of escape were the only moments allowed him to recollect himself and his own nature: he might be different, entirely different, when without from when within the flame; and if so, how long might his exile last? And here the student paused to think of the Saturday night's hour in the legend of the Onyx Ring, and to wish once more that his might have been the finger to wear that jewel. Recurring again to the salamander, he asked himself what could be its nature.

Would it be mild or ferocious ? would it perceive his
presence ? would it attempt to avoid him ? might it not
seek his protection ? and then flashed across his mind
the question, Might it not be intelligent, intellectual ?
might it not have a mind, a language ?   Why should
it not ? did it not ?

And here the student was carried away by the intensity of his feelings : he rose from his chair, and began
pacing his room, backward and forward, and attempted
to form a slight imagination of the glorious results of
such a discovery as he hoped.   But he was too much
excited by the suddenness and grandeur of the idea to
think composedly or connectedly.   Wild visions connected with it were constantly rising before him.   That
he should converse with a being from another element
of our world — an element hitherto neglected, despised,
in natural history, yet the most singular and wonderful of all — was not improbable ! Thus much was clear.
Further than this it would be hard to follow him.   He
revelled long in wild dreams of the imagination, till
at length, exhausted by the excitement aroused by the
new idea, he felt quite willing to retire to sleep.

Days passed on, and the student gained more control of his ideas than he had had on the night when the
wonder of his embryo discovery had first burst on him.
Day and night his fire burned with an unusual glow,
never extinguished on any emergency. Yet he did not
neglect his usual routine of study ; but often, when his
head ached and his eyes tired from poring over the

dreary tomes that made his mental daily bread, he would not strive to rouse himself when the letters grew dim before him, but would let his mind run astray to his fiery friend. Often and often did· he think of his singular destiny; often and often did he endeavor to imagine his habits of life, duty, and action; and then he would laugh at himself for trying to conjecture that respecting which a few weeks at latest would give him full information. And often from the animal he would turn to think of the pleasure of the discovery, — the pleasure, the honor of it: his ambition could point to nothing higher than the just elevation of the man who should discover to mankind an animal from a new world, perhaps an intellectual, moral, social being. What floods of new light might this one discovery not pour on disputed questions in ethics, physics, and metaphysics! Man has attained to a certain point of knowledge, derived from some few intuitions and certainties, by one fixed course. Who could tell at what point some other being might arrive, from some other intuitions, by another course? How much would their mutual discoveries elucidate the doubts and fears of each! How honorable his station, in the opinion of both races, who should be the means of opening so desirable a communion, who, disregarding popular prejudice or fear, should throw open the little door between two such vast worlds of thought! The student gloried in the dreams of such ambition; and after his first delight at his happy discovery, such dreams often followed.

It was in such a frame of mind that he one day
wrote home to his mother. His letter, which had been
cheerful in an unusual degree, closed with these
words : —

" And if, my dear mother, that should turn up of a
sudden which should give us all once more the com-
petence that for your sake I have so often regretted,
which should give me at once that station in society,
that reputation, which has so often been declared my
due by the kindness you and my sisters feel for me,
without my passing through much more of that
heavy drudgery of study which has so often made me
repine, — God knows how unreasonably, — it would
be not more singular than many things which have
happened in this world of ours. Who knows that it
may not be so ? "

With this letter he walked to the post-office.
There he received one from home, full of that kind
affection that none but a real family circle can inspire.
The day was one of those lovely, spring-like days
which February will have, when Miss Mitford and
such fortunate people find violets, when everybody
thinks of May, and the dullest person's spirits rise
much higher than par. The student read his letter at
the post-office, then continued his walk. He was
cheered by his good tidings from home and the pleas-
antness of everything around him, and he enjoyed the
beauty of the day to the utmost. He had left his
room close and hot, for the fire still burned as brightly

as ever; and he was glad to breathe the clear, fresh air, and fancy it springtime. He walked to the glass-houses, recently his favorite stroll. He liked to look in at the windows and see the workmen moulding the melted glass, and to wonder at the intensity of the heat of their furnaces, — they strengthened what were now his favorite theories; and on this day he watched them with more than usual eagerness. As he walked home he built his castle higher than ever in the air, and was in the most cheerful frame of mind when he entered the house in which were his lodgings.

In the passage-way, as he entered, he met Mrs. Mumler, his landlady, brush and water-pail in hand. He was about to pass her with his usual civil salutation merely, when she stopped to say, "I have been arranging your room, sir; and as the day was fine and you were out, I gave it a good airing, threw open the windows, cleared out all the fire, and have polished up the grate nicely. I knew you would want no fire before night; but it can be made at any time."

The student had just self-possession enough to thank her for her well-meant exertions, and then hurried into his room, looked at the cheerless polished grate, and, throwing himself into a chair, he cried like a child.

He was not, however, a man to be easily discouraged : his fire soon burned brightly again; and, although he often checked the wildness of his imaginations by recollections of his disappointments, he still revelled in the new field of the fancy world that his strange idea had thrown open upon him. His general reading assumed the train of his new ideas. He would pore eagerly over the passages in the chronicles of the old voyagers which told him how Columbus paced the deck of his vessel on the night of his magnificent discovery, when he had seen the light on the shore of St. Salvador, and knew that the next sun would disclose to him a new world. He ransacked volumes to read the private history of Nicholas Flamel, the reputed discoverer of the philosopher's stone, and felt that he could recall his feelings when he first saw the copper sous which he was working upon take the form and reality of gold. In his more doubtful moments he called up Robert Fulton's feelings, when he had started on the Hudson in his new steam-barge amid the derision of the spectators, and had had the mortification to see it stop after the first few evolutions of the engine. But as he read further, he would flatter himself that he was rather in Fulton's condition when, after he had put in the defective rivet, the boat moved slowly and with dignity up the stream ; and he asked himself what might be the importance of his discovery, which should introduce a new living creature to man's knowledge, and that, perhaps, as he loved to persuade himself, an intelligent creature, when Fulton's mere application of the glorious handiwork of Watt had produced such an influence on the externals of society.

One bright evening, as he returned from a call on Mr. Austin, he had been star-gazing, admiring the full moon, and the brilliant, pure, good-natured look of Jupiter, till he began to think of Newton and his glorious discoveries. He remembered his disappointment when all his hopes for those discoveries were crushed by the error of one of the details on which his theory rested, and wondered if his fate would be to wait like Newton twenty years between the idea which suggested, and the success which should consummate, his daring discovery. And then he remembered that, when Newton came to the conclusion of the whole, he had not nerve to go through the mechanical details of calculation necessary to substantiate his theory, but was obliged to trust a friend with these minutiæ. He remembered how, when the centring was to be struck from the great arch at Notre Dame, the architect was too heartsick from anxiety to conduct the operation himself, but awaited, half dead, the report of his nephew, who took his place. He felt as if he should feel the same weakness, and was thinking over all the short list of his acquaintances to decide whom he should call in, in such an emergency, when he reached his home. The passages and staircase were crowded; the house was filled with smoke; and when he reached his room he learned that, from a defect in the flue, the lathing above the grate had taken fire and endangered the safety of the house. He was obliged to rejoice, however, with the rest, that they had so soon succeeded in extinguishing the flames, although his own grate looked as cheerless as ever.

"There's nothing of the least value hurt," chattered Mrs. Mumler, as she left the room with the last of the extinguishers. "We will soon have your room looking as nicely as ever."

"Nothing of value!" muttered the student. "What is value, then?" and he threw his head on his arms, and was lost in bitter thought.

The room was repaired, and the fire burned once more. The student watched it as carefully as ever; but he was not the sanguine enthusiast that he was on the first week of his experiment. He was resolved to continue his experiment as a duty which he owed himself and his race; but many days passed before he could raise his imagination of its cheering results so high as he had done before. Weeks passed on, however, and his spirits rose. Another *salamander day* was observed at the glass-house, and the fire was again extinguished there. Spring drew nearer; but his grate was still filled with coals, and he constantly gave out peremptory orders, in the sternest tones that his mild voice could assume, that his fire should never be extinguished. Three, four weeks he counted; five, — and then he began to reckon in days with a painful anxiety for the coming of the fortieth. He felt as if he were the hero of the old Arabian tale, the fate of whose life was to be determined in forty days, and who lived to the last hour to be killed by the fall of a fruit-knife.

The student knew that the result of all his hopes and expectations was at hand. He could not wonder at the creations of the old romancers ; for he could imagine now that every kind of difficulty, in these few days, might come between him and the accomplishment of his desires. He felt that he should hardly recover from another disappointment. Again he turned to the history of Columbus, and imagined his feelings when his rebellious sailors would give him but three days' longer westward sailing. What might not three days bring forth ?

Years before, he had been in a burning house ; and, while he heard the blows of an axe falling on the locked door to open him an escape, he had felt his head grow more and more giddy from the clouds of smoke around him, and had known that, unless he could preserve his senses a few minutes longer, his hours were counted. He felt once more the agonizing doubt which he had felt then ; but now it was for days, while it was then only for minutes. When the idea of his experiment had first crossed his mind, it was merely as a casual theory, which, inquiring and philosophical as he was, he did not choose to let escape him. As day by day had passed, he had roused himself to a more distinct conception of its importance, and vacillated between more sanguine hopes, and more disheartening doubts, as to its success. The disappointments he had undergone had made his doubts preponderate ; but they had not at all diminished the eagerness with which he awaited the result. It was now no longer to him merely a curious inquiry in science nor even an investigation whose results upon society and philosophy might be important : it was the one subject in which all his thoughts and hopes and imaginations centred. He thought of little else, he dreamed of nothing else ; now his hopes beat high and exultingly, and now he felt deeply despondent. He felt the strongest desire for the approach of the fatal hour, and yet the greatest dread of its passage ; for it might pass in vain.

The fortieth day came. Without, it was mild and lovely as the brightest day of April could be. Within his room the air was thick and close and hot ; and he sat there with the fearfully anxious air of a gambler who is determined to play out a desperate game. He had resolved that he would not leave his fire that day. Who could tell with precise accuracy of the appearance of the animal ? It could know nothing of day and night ; and by a moment's carelessness he might render fruitless the care of weeks. There he sat, hour after hour, haggard, anxious, and impatient, entirely unable to fix his attention on anything but that raging flame.

They say that the Duke of Wellington, at Waterloo, looked oftener at his watch than anywhere else ; for he knew that if his squares would hold firm till night he need care for nothing more. The student looked constantly at his. He knew that by midnight the agony must be over; and he knew that he could not bear such suspense much longer. As he sat, he attempted to imagine what would be the most hospitable reception he could give to the stranger; and as he had always supposed that his only object in leaving the fire at all was to refresh himself from its intolerable heat, he placed a large vessel of water on the hearth as the most agreeable attention with which he could receive him. He lighted no lamp when evening came on; for he would not torture it by light in the moment of its need. He tried to read: he might as well have tried to fly. Read! He could think of nothing but his suffering friend, could feel nothing but sympathy for him in that hour of his agony. He took his pen to write a few words of memoranda in his note-book; but before he knew it, he had dropped it from his hand, and was gazing earnestly, without flinching, on the raging flame.

It was about eight o'clock in the evening when he heard a rap at his door, which opened immediately without his call. Mrs. Mumler had come, terrified and flurried, to say that her youngest child had just fallen into the kitchen fire, and to beg that he would be good enough to go for the physician, for he was the only person besides herself in the house, and she was really afraid that the poor child was dying.

Reader, should you have hesitated? The student did not; his kindness of heart and true charity were strong even then against all temptation. He showed, too, a surprising zeal; for he went and returned sooner than any one could have believed possible. He brought the physician, saw that his prescriptions were attended to, begged Mrs. Mumler to send him anywhere else that she might wish, and returned to his vigils by the fire.

The first person who ever imagined the possibility of a transit of Venus was a young man named Horrox, who calculated that of 1639. His authorities were so vague that he could only compute that it would occur on Sunday, the 24th of November. Sunday morning, accordingly, he began to watch to see Venus cross the face of the sun; but he saw the surface still clear and untouched when he heard the bell for church; and he had enough of what he thought principle to leave his darling observation, and go to the worship of his God. After service he returned to the watch with the consciousness that the whole which he had anticipated for years might have passed while he was at church. The student had a similar overwhelming feeling as he returned from the bedside of that suffering child. He knew that it was possible, probable, that all his brightest hopes had looked forward to might have occurred and gone by in the hour while he was gone. The salamander might have left the fire and returned, in his absence: the chances were that he had done so; and yet, though the probability of success was much less than before, he must still gaze on. He would have sacrificed anything to relieve that doubt. He remembered how Copernicus roused himself from his death-bed to see the last sheet of his great work, and lay down to die. He felt that, with his certainty that his great object was accomplished, he could die. He remembered Horrox, and tried to console himself with his success. He knew that he had watched again till the afternoon church service, and then, doubtful whether the transit had or had not taken place, went once more to his devotions. When he returned, he was amply rewarded: he saw distinctly that the planet had just entered on the sun's disk; and the sight was enough to make him forget all his self-devoted sacrifice. The half-heartbroken student tried to believe that his fortune would be the same. At all events, he knew he had done his duty.

As he sat pondering thus, he fancied he heard another call from his landlady. He ran to the door, and opened it. No one had spoken: it was only fancy. Just as he closed the door, a bright glare lighted up the room and then was gone, while he heard a sharp hissing from the water on the hearth. He felt that the moment had come; and as soon as the thick clouds of steam had passed off which were rising from the water, he bent down to examine his welcome friend.

*   *   *   *   *

On the evening of the 16th of May, the student was taking, with his friend Mr. Austin, his first walk after his recovery from the violent fever which had

preyed on him for some weeks, and had nearly over-
come his constitution, weakened as it had been by his
previous watchings. Through his whole illness the
Austins had shown him every kindness. They were
his nearest friends, and they had shown themselves
truly such; and this evening Mr. Austin had induced
the invalid to take a little stroll, to breathe the fresh,
dry, spring air, and see the beauty of the sunset.

The student was not, however, in good spirits.
Even the freshness of springtime failed to exhilarate
him. Austin, who was desirous to turn his reflections
from off some of the disagreeable features of his present situation, on which he seemed inclined to dwell,
had spoken cheerily of an anticipated visit from his
relations, of the beauty of the sunset, of the freshness
and brightness of everything as spring opened, — but
without removing the heaviness on his young friend's
mind, till, as they made a sharp turn in the road
which led over a hillside, he pointed out the glass-
works in the valley below them, and said, "It is
another *salamander night*. Do you see, the furnaces
are extinguished."

The poor student shuddered ; but he evidently made
an exertion to take some more decided part in the conversation, and, in a manner at least, to guide it. "So
it is," he said. "By the way, do you own any stock
in those works ? Fettyplace told me he thought it
was surer property than most such."

"I own a few shares, which pay pretty well. Why

do you ask ? Do you think a factory with a legend attached, more reputable than a more commonplace one ? "

The invalid exerted himself to say, " O, I hardly thought of the legend ! Pray, how is Mrs. Austin to-night ? "

" Well, perfectly well. Do you remember how amused she was, that evening last winter, when I told her and you the glass-blowers' tale ? She was quite delighted with it, and went so far as to go over to the workmen's cottages, and talk with some of their wives about it. She said she had never met with a real-life superstition before."

" I suppose not, from her early education. Has she heard from her friends lately ? "

" Her cousin is staying with her now. They have both of them been counting days till to-night should come. My wife has told her *live superstition* so often that she feels a strong interest in it now, and has inspired her friend with the same. Indeed, although I have known the tale so long, it never made half the effect upon me that it has lately, since she has talked so much about it. I wonder that you, who are so imaginative, have never thought of it since that night last winter."

" O, it has passed my mind, sometimes. What is your new cousin's name ? "

Austin did not heed this forced interrogatory, suggested by a desperate but vain desire to change his

train of thought and conversation. " I wonder," said
he, " if there may not be some ground for this workmen's superstition. Strange that it should exist without any, stranger that no one should test it! Why
should no one ? I will, myself. A month's watching,
or a trifle more, may make an important discovery. I
claim your congratulations for my idea. You pretend
to be a philosopher and a theorizer ; and yet I shall be
before you, after all, in a useful discovery ! Useful ! a
glorious discovery ! Faith ! what a grand thing it
would be — don't you see it ? — to draw a real salamander from his prison ! Why, to me it seems grand
beyond conception. If you had thought of it, with
your energy, you would have made yourself a great
man before now, by this simple idea. What will Mrs.
Austin say ? You shall watch with me the fortieth
night, and see him."

He turned to his young friend as he spoke, and saw
that he was ghastly pale and almost fainting. In reply
to the fears he expressed, that he had made him walk
too far for a person in his weak state of health, the
student said, with an almost fearful energy, " No ! no !
I am better now. But, Frank, don't try it ! don't try
it !"

" You are tired," said Austin, quite alarmed. " We
have walked too far. Let us cross home by this short
cut. After a night's rest you will feel stronger."

" Frank Austin, you think my mind is wandering.
I am as sane at this moment as you are ; and I beg

you, as you love yourself, and your own peace of mind through life, as you love me, as you love your wife, not to try this rash experiment. Experiment? Say, rather, this fearful certainty."

"What do you mean? Why do you take it so seriously? The idea has but just struck me as a mater of curious inquiry. I supposed you would like to start such a fine, bold theory, you are so good at scheming," said Austin, hoping to bring back his young friend's ideas to a firmer tone.

"The idea struck *me* nearly three months since. With me, as I say, it is no longer an experiment, but a certainty; and the only gratification my trial has left me is the ability it has given me to warn my friends against following my example. More than this I can not, ought not, say. But let me implore you, Austin, to give up the idea. Not that you could not carry through the experiment as well as any man; not that you, or any man, could not bear the suspense of it; but there is more than this, and you ought not, you must not, attempt it. Austin," he added more calmly, laying his hand on his friend's shoulder, "you will not? promise me you will not."

"Certainly," said Austin, glad to see him more calm: "it was only a passing fancy. Since you make a point of it, I do not care for it."

And they returned home.

THE QUEEN OF CALIFORNIA.

[IN the winter of 1862, I read for the first time the Spanish romance of the " Sergas of Esplandian." It is sometimes cited as the fifth book of Amadis of Gaul, but is by Garcia Ordoñez de Montalvo, the translator of Amadis, — a workman very inferior to Lobeira, who must be rated, I think, very highly among the writers of narrative. Coming to the allusion, in this forgotten romance, to " the island of California, very near to the Terrestrial Paradise," I saw at once that here was the origin of the name of the State of California, long sought for by the antiquarians of that State, but long forgotten. For the romance seems to have been published in 1510, — the edition of 1521 is now in existence, — while our California, even the peninsula of that name, was not discovered by the Spaniards till 1526, and was not named California till 1535.

At the next meeting of the American Antiquarian Society, I called their attention to this derivation of the name ; and it has since been universally recognized as the origin of the name now so familiar to us. The romance of " Esplandian " is now so rare that I translated for the Atlantic Monthly all the parts which relate to the Queen of California, and I now republish them. The reader may be interested in examining first the history of the discussion of the subject, and then of the romance.]

THE name of California was given by Cortez, who discovered the peninsula in the year 1535. For the statement that he named it, we have the authority of Herrera.* It is proved, I think, that the expedition of Mendoza, in 1532, did not see California: it is certain that they gave it no name. Humboldt saw, in the archives of Mexico, a statement in manuscript that it was discovered in 1526; † but for this there is no other authority. It is certain that the name does not appear till 1535.

No etymology of this name has been presented satisfactory to the historians. Venegas,‡ the Jesuit historian of California, writing in 1758, sums up the matter in these words: "The most ancient name is California, used by Bernal Diaz, limited to a single bay. I could wish to gratify the reader by the etymology and true origin of this name; but in none of the various dialects of the natives could the missionaries find the least traces of such a name being given by them to the country, or even to any harbor, bay, or small part of it. Nor can I subscribe to the etymology of some writers, who suppose the name to be given to it by the Spaniards, on their feeling an unusual heat at their first landing here; that they thence called the country *California,* compounding the two Latin words *calida* and *fornax,* 'a hot furnace.' I

* Decade VIII. Book VI.

† It would be very desirable to have a new examination of the manuscript alluded to.

‡ The work of Venegas is chiefly due to the labors of Father Andres Marcos Buniel, according to Greenhow.

believe few will think the adventurers could boast of so much literature."

I believe the Californian authors of our own time agree with Venegas in rejecting this forced etymology. The word to be made from it should be " Calidafornacia." Dr. Bushnell, who says the heat of the interior valleys is that of a baker's furnace, speaks of a region which Cortez never saw. It must be recollected, that, though Bernal Diaz only uses the name for the bay, we have Herrera's better authority for saying that Cortez gave it to the peninsula. But neither peninsula nor bay is the oven described by Dr. Bushnell.

Clavigero, in his " History of California," after giving this etymology, offers as an alternative the following, as the opinion " of the learned Jesuit, D. Giuseppe Compoi " : " He believes that the name is composed of the Spanish word *cala*, which means ' a little cove of the sea ' ; and the Latin *fornix*, which means ' the vault of a building.' " He thinks these words are thus applied, " because, within Cape St. Lucas there is a little cove of the sea, towards the western part of which rises a rock, so worn out that on the upper part of the hollow is seen a vault, as perfect as if made by art. Cortez, therefore, observing this *cala*, or cove, and this vault, probably called this port *California*, or *cala* and *fornix*, — speaking half in Spanish, half in Latin."

Clavigero suggests, as an improvement on this somewhat wild etymology, that Cortez may have said *Cala fornax,* " Cove furnace," — speaking, as in the Jesuit's suggestion, in two languages.

I am told that the Rev. Dean Trench, in one of his etymological works, suggests the Greek καλὴ πορνεία, — implying that the province seemed to the early settlers to have the attractions of a " beautiful adultery." I have not myself found this passage ; but I remember that Mr. Powers, the sculptor, represents California as a naked woman, seductive in front, but concealing a thorn-bush in her hands behind ; and he describes his statue as intended to represent her false seductions. Of this etymology, it is enough to say that Cortez and his men knew nothing of the seductions, — never finding gold or anything else tempting there ; and that the theory requires more, yet worse, scholarship at their hands than that of *calida fornax.*

Of all such speculations, Mr. Greenhow says very fitly, " None of them are satisfactory, or even ingenious."

It is in the worthless romance of the " Sergas of Esplandian," the son of Amadis of Gaul, — a book long since deservedly forgotten, — that there is to be found the source from which the adventurers transferred the name " California " to the new region of their discovery.

Towards the close of this romance, the various Christian knights assemble to defend the Emperor of the Greeks and the city of Constantinople against the attacks of the Turks and Infidels. On this occasion, in a romance published first in 1510, — twenty-five years before Cortez discovered the American California, — the name appears with precisely our spelling, in the following passage : —

Sergas, ch. 157. — " Know that, on the right hand of the Indies, there is an island called California, very near to the Terrestrial Paradise, which was peopled with black women, without any men among them, because they were accustomed to live after the fashion of Amazons. They were of strong and hardened bodies, of ardent courage, and of great force. The island was the strongest in the world, from its steep rocks and great cliffs. Their arms were all of gold ; and so were the caparisons of the wild beasts which they rode, after having tamed them ; for in all the island there is no other metal. They lived in caves very well worked out ; they had many ships, in which they sailed to other parts to carry on their forays." . . . .

In the paper to which these paragraphs are an introduction, I have translated every passage in the " Esplandian " which relates to the Queen of California, — the name appearing, as will be seen, in several distinct passages in the history.

This romance, as I have said, is believed to have been printed first in 1510. No copies of this edition, however, are extant. But of the edition of 1519 a copy is preserved ; and there are copies of successive

editions of 1521, 1525, and 1526 ; in which last year
two editions were published, — one at Seville, and the
other at Burgos.   All of these are Spanish.

It follows, almost certainly, that Cortez and his fol-
lowers, in 1535, must have been acquainted with the
romance ; and, as they sailed up the west side of Mexico, they supposed they were precisely at the place
indicated, — " in the right hand of the Indies."   It
will be remembered also, that, by sailing in the same
direction, Columbus, in his letter to the sovereigns,
says, " he shall be sailing towards the Terrestrial Paradise." *   We need not suppose that Cortez believed
the romance, more than we do ; though we assert that
he borrowed a name from it to indicate the peninsula
he found " on the right side of the Indies, near to the
Terrestrial Paradise."   If it is necessary to analyze
very carefully his motive for borrowing a name from a
romance then so generally known, it will be enough
to say that this romance credited the " Island of California " with great treasures of gold, and that it placed
it very near the East Indies, in quest of which all the
adventurers of that time were sailing.   There is, however, no more reason for giving a serious motive for
such a nomenclature than there is for the motive
with which La Salle or his companions gave the name
of La Chine to the point in Canada from which they
hoped to reach China.

It is not strange that ecclesiastical historians, like

* See Appendix to this paper.

Venegas, should, in the eighteenth century, have lost sight of this origin of the name. It was not until 1683 that the Jesuit fraternity succeeded in planting an establishment there. Even then, their establishment was not permanent. For a century and a half, therefore, after Cortez's discovery, the province was of no value to any one, and its name was of as little interest. Long before the Jesuits planted it, the romance which gave it name was forgotten.

After 1542 no edition of the "Sergas of Esplandian" was printed in Spain, so far as we know, till 1575; and, after that of 1587, none for two hundred and seventy years more. The reaction had come. When the curate burned the books of Don Quixote, he burned this among the rest : he saved "Amadis of Gaul," but he burned "Esplandian." "We will not spare the son," said he, "for the virtues of his father." These words show Cervantes's estimate of it as early as 1605. It is not surprising, then, that an ecclesiastic like Venegas should not know, in 1758, the wild geography of the romance two centuries and more after it was written. D'Herbelay, the early French paraphraser of this romance, retains the whole story of the queen, but transfers the situation of California to the source of the River Borysthenes, near the descent of the Riphean Mountains.

The only effort to introduce it to modern readers, in any European country, until the recent Spanish reprint of 1857, is in the wretched paraphrase by Tressan, published in France in the last century. This author, as if to add to the probability of the tale, omits the name " California" in each of the passages relating to it ; so that, even in his forgotten work, we do not get hold of the lost clew.

The original work is now so rare that the copies in the valuable collection of Mr. Ticknor (now in the Boston Public Library) were till lately the only ones in Massachusetts. To that kind courtesy which opened his invaluable stores to every student, and illustrated it from the treasures of his own studies, am I indebted for all the authorities of value which I am able to cite here. In the large public libraries of the city of New York, I found in 1862 no copy of any of these romances, which made the lay literature of the first century after printing was invented ; but in the small yet well-selected library of the Free Academy of New York, and in that of Congress, are the " Amadis " and " Esplandian," in the recent Spanish edition edited by D. Pascal de Gayangos ; and the same edition is now, in 1872, in the Boston Library.

In ascribing to the " Esplandian " the origin of the name " California," I know that I furnish no etymology for that word. I have not found the word in any earlier romances. I will only suggest that the root *Calif*, the Spanish spelling for the sovereign of the Mussulman power of the time, was in the mind of the author as he invented these Amazon allies of the Infidel power.

The following is the account above referred to, with everything from the " Esplandian " which relates to the " Queen of
California."

I can see the excitement which this title arouses as it
is flashed across the sierras, down the valleys, and into
the various reading-rooms and parlors of the Golden
City of the Golden State. As the San Francisco
" Bulletin " announces some day, that in the " Atlantic
Monthly," issued in Boston the day before, one of the
articles is on " The Queen of California," what contest,
in every favored circle of the most favored of lands,
who the Queen may be! Is it the blond maiden who
took a string of hearts with her in a leash, when she
left us one sad morning? is it the hardy, brown adven-
turess, who, in her bark-roofed lodge, serves us out our
boiled dog daily, as we come home from our water-
gullies, and sews on for us weekly the few buttons
which we still find indispensable in that toil? is it
some Jessie of the lion-heart, heroine of a hundred days
or of a thousand? is it that witch with gray eyes, cun-
ningly hidden, — were they puzzled last night, or were
they all wisdom crowded? — as she welcomed me, and
as she bade me good by? Good Heavens! how many
Queens of California are regnant this day! and of any
one of them this article might be written.

No, *Señores!* No, *Caballeros!* Throng down to the
wharves to see the Golden Era or the Cornelius's Cof-
fin, or whatever other mail-steamer may bring these
words to your longing eyes. Open to the right and

left as Adams's express messenger carries the earliest copy of the "Atlantic Monthly," sealed with the reddest wax, tied with the reddest tape, from the Corner Store direct to him who was once the light and life of the Corner Store, who now studies eschscholtzias through a telescope thirty-eight miles away on Monte Diablo! * Rush upon the newsboy who then brings forth the bale of this Journal for the Multitude, to find that the Queen of California of whom we write is no modern queen, but that she reigned some five hundred and fifty-five years ago. Her precise contemporaries were Amadis of Gaul, the Emperor Esplandian, and the Sultan Radiaro. And she *flourished*, as the books say, at the time when this sultan made his unsuccessful attack on the city of Constantinople, — all of which she saw, part of which she was.

She was not *petite*, nor blond, nor golden-haired. She was large, and black as the ace of clubs. But the prejudice of color did not then exist even among the most brazen-faced or the most copper-headed. For, as you shall learn, she was reputed the most beautiful of women; and it was she, O Californians! who wedded the gallant Prince Talanque, — your first-known king. The supporters of the arms of the beautiful shield of the State of California should be, on the right, a knight armed *cap-à-pie*, and, on the left, an Amazon sable, clothed in skins, as you shall now see.

* In a letter from Starr King, written not long before I wrote these words, he spoke of seeing the color of Monte Diablo change when the eschscholtzias were in bloom.

Mr. E. E. Hale, of Boston, sent to the Antiquarian Society last year a paper which shows that the name of California was known to literature before it was given to our peninsula by Cortez. Cortez discovered the peninsula in 1535, and seems to have called it California then. But Mr. Hale shows that, twenty-five years before that time, in a romance called the "Deeds of Esplandian," the name of California was given to an island "on the right hand of the Indies." This romance was a sequel, or fifth book, to the celebrated romance of "Amadis of Gaul." Such books made the principal reading of the young blades of that day who could read at all. It seems clear enough that Cortez and his friends, coming to the point farthest to the west then known, — which all of them, from Columbus down, supposed to be the East Indies, — gave to their discovery the name, familiar to romantic adventurers, of *California*, to indicate their belief that it was on the "right hand of the Indies." Just so Columbus called his discoveries "the Indies"; just so was the name "El Dorado" given to regions which it was hoped would prove to be golden. The romance had said, that, in the whole of the romance-island of California, there was no metal but gold. Cortez, who did not find a pennyweight of dust in the real California, still had no objection to giving so golden a name to his discovery.

Mr. Hale, with that brevity which becomes antiquarians, does not go into any of the details of the life and adventures of the Queen of California as the romance describes them. We propose, in this paper, to supply from it this reticency of his essay.

The reader must understand, then, that, in this romance, printed in 1510, sixty years or less after Constantinople really fell into the hands of the Turks, the author describes a pretended assault made upon it by the Infidel powers, and the rallying for its rescue of Amadis and Perion and Lisuarte, and all the princes of chivalry with whom the novel of " Amadis of Gaul" has dealt.   They succeed in driving away the Pagans, " as you shall hear." In the midst of this great crusade, every word of which, of course, is the most fictitious of fiction, appear the episodes which describe California and its Queen.

First, of California itself here is the description : —

" Now you are to hear the most extraordinary thing that ever was heard of in any chronicles, or in the memory of man, by which the city would have been lost on the next day, but that where the danger came, there the safety came also.   Know, then, that, on the right hand of the Indies, there is an island called California, very close to the side of the Terrestrial Paradise,* and it was peopled by black women, without

* This was according to the cosmogony of the days when Columbus sailed on his fourth voyage, in which he hoped to pass through what we now know as the Isthmus of Panama, and sail northwestward. He wrote to his king and queen that thus he should come as near as men could come to " the Terrestrial Paradise."   On this curious subject I venture to add to this article a paper which I submitted to the American Antiquarian Society, at its meeting in April, 1872.

any man among them, for they lived in the fashion of Amazons. They were of strong and hardy bodies, of ardent courage and great force. Their island was the strongest in all the world, with its steep cliffs and rocky shores. Their arms were all of gold, and so was the harness of the wild beasts which they tamed and rode. For, in the whole island, there was no metal but gold. They lived in caves wrought out of the rock with much labor. They had many ships with which they sailed out to other countries to obtain booty.

"In this island, called California, there were many griffins, on account of the great ruggedness of the country, and its infinite host of wild beasts, such as never were seen in any other part of the world. And when these griffins were yet small, the women went out with traps to take them. They covered themselves over with very thick hides, and when they had caught the little griffins, they took them to their caves, and brought them up there. And being themselves quite a match for the griffins, they fed them with the men whom they took prisoners, and with the boys to whom they gave birth, and brought them up with such arts that they got much good from them, and no harm. Every man who landed on the island was immediately devoured by these griffins; and although they had had enough, none the less would they seize them, and carry them high up in the air in their flight; and when they were tired of carrying them, would let them fall any-where as soon as they died."

These griffins are the Monitors of the story, or, if the reader pleases, the Merrimacs. After this description, the author goes on to introduce us to our Queen. Observe, O reader, that, although very black and very large, she is very beautiful. Why did not Powers carve his statue of California out of the blackest of Egyptian marbles? Try once more, Mr. Powers! We have found her now. *Εὑρήκαμεν.*

"Now, at the time when those great men of the Pagans sailed with their great fleets, as the history has told you, there reigned in this island of California a Queen, very large in person, the most beautiful of all of them, of blooming years, and in her thoughts desirous of achieving great things, strong of limb, and of great courage, more than any of those who had filled her throne before her. She heard tell that all the greater part of the world was moving in this onslaught against the Christians. She did not know what Christians were; for she had no knowledge of any parts of the world excepting those which were close to her. But she desired to see the world and its various people; and thinking, that, with the great strength of herself and of her women, she should have the greater part of their plunder, either from her rank or from her prowess, she began to talk with all of those who were most skilled in war, and told them that it would be well, if, sailing in their great fleets, they also entered on this expedition, in which all these great princes and lords were embarking. She animated and excited them, showing them the great profits and honors which they would gain in this enterprise, — above all, the great fame which would be theirs in all the world; while, if they stayed in their island, doing nothing but what their grandmothers did, they were really buried alive, — they were dead while they lived, passing their days without fame and without glory, as did the very brutes."

Now, the people of California were as willing then to embark in distant expeditions of honor as they are now. And the first battalion that ever sailed from the ports of that country was thus provided.

"So much did this mighty Queen, Calafia, say to her people, that she not only moved them to consent to this enterprise, but they were so eager to extend their fame through other lands that they begged her to hasten to sea, so that they might earn all these honors, in alliance with such great men. The Queen, seeing the readiness of her subjects, without any delay gave order that her great fleet should be provided with food, and with arms all of gold, — more of everything than was needed. Then she commanded that her largest vessel should be prepared with gratings of the stoutest timber; and she bade place in it as many as five hundred of these griffins, of which I tell you that, from the time they were born, they were trained to feed on men. And she ordered that the beasts on which she and her people rode should be embarked, and all the best-armed women and those most skilled in war whom she had in her island. And then, leaving such force in the island that it should be secure, with the others she went to sea. And they made such haste that they arrived at the fleets of the Pagans the night after the battle of which I have told you; so that they were received with great joy, and the fleet was visited at once by many great lords, and they were welcomed with great acceptance. She wished to know at once in what condition affairs were, asking many questions, which they answered fully. Then she said, —

" ' You have fought this city with your great forces, and you cannot take it; now, if you are willing, I wish to try what my forces are worth to-morrow, if you will give orders accordingly.'

" All these great lords said that they would give such commands as she should bid them.

" ' Then send word to all your other captains that they shall to-morrow on no account leave their camps, they nor their people, until I command them ; and you shall see a combat more remarkable than you have ever seen or heard of.'

" Word was sent at once to the great Sultan of Liquia, and the Sultan of Halapa, who had command of all the men who were there ; and they gave these orders to all their people, wondering much what was the thought of this Queen."

Up to this moment, it may be remarked, these Monitors, as we have called the griffins, had never been fairly tried in any attack on fortified towns. The Dupont of the fleet, whatever her name may have been, may well have looked with some curiosity on the issue. The experiment was not wholly successful, as will be seen.

" When the night had passed and the morning came, the Queen Calafia sallied on shore, she and her women, armed with that armor of gold, all adorned with the most precious stones, — which are to be found in the island of California like stones of the field for their abundance. And they mounted on their fierce beasts, caparisoned as I have told you; and then she ordered that a door should be opened in the vessel where the griffins were. They, when they saw the field, rushed forward with great haste, showing great pleasure in flying through the air, and at once caught sight of the host of men who were close at hand. As they were famished, and knew no fear, each griffin pounced upon his man, seized him in his claws, carried him high into the air, and began to devour him. They shot many arrows at them, and gave them many great blows with lances and with swords. But their feathers were so tight joined and so stout, that no one could strike through to their flesh." (This is Armstrong *versus* Monitor.) " For their own party, this was the most lovely chase and the most agreeable that they had ever seen till then; and as the Turks saw them flying on high with their enemies, they gave such loud and clear shouts of joy as pierced the heavens. And it was the most sad and bitter thing for those in the city, when the father saw the son lifted in the air, and the son his father, and the brother his brother; so that they all wept and raved, as was sad indeed to see.

"When the griffins had flown through the air for a while, and had dropped their prizes, some on the earth and some on the sea, they turned, as at first, and, without any fear, seized up as many more; at which their masters had so much the more joy, and the Christians so much the more misery. What shall I tell you? The terror was so great among them all that, while some hid themselves away under the vaults of the towers for safety, all the others disappeared from the ramparts, so that there were none left for the defence. Queen Calafia saw this, and, with a loud voice, she bade the two Sultans, who commanded the troops, send for the ladders, for the city was taken. At once they all rushed forward, placed the ladders, and mounted upon the wall. But the griffins, who had already dropped those whom they had seized before, as soon as they saw the Turks, having no knowledge of them, seized upon them just as they had seized upon the Christians, and, flying through the air, carried them up also, when, letting them fall, no one of them escaped death. Thus were exchanged the pleasure and the pain. For those on the outside now were those who mourned in great sorrow for those who were so handled; and those who were within, who, seeing their enemies advance on every side, had thought they were beaten, now took great comfort. So, at this moment,

as those on the ramparts stopped, panic-struck, fearing
that they should die as their comrades did, the Christians leaped forth from the vaults where they were
hiding, and quickly slew many of the Turks who were
gathered on the walls, and compelled the rest to leap
down, and then sprang back to their hiding-places, as
they saw the griffins return.

"When Queen Calafia saw this she was very sad ; and
she said, ' O ye idols in whom I believe and whom I
worship, what is this which has happened as favorably
to my enemies as to my friends ? I believed that with
your aid and with my strong forces and great munition
I should be able to destroy them.   But it has not so
proved.' And she gave orders to her women that
they should mount the ladders and struggle to gain
the towers and put to the sword all those who took
refuge in them to be secure from the griffins.   They
obeyed their Queen's commands, dismounted at once,
placing before their breasts such breastplates as no
weapon could pierce, and, as I told you, with the
armor all of gold which covered their legs and their
arms.   Quickly they crossed the plain, and mounted
the ladders lightly, and possessed themselves of the
whole circuit of the walls, and began to fight fiercely
with those who had taken refuge in the vaults of the
towers.   But they defended themselves bravely, being
indeed in quarters well protected, with but narrow
doors.   And those of the city, who were in the streets
below, shot at the women with arrows and darts, which

pierced them through the sides, so that they received many wounds, because their golden armor was so weak." (This is Keokuk *versus* Armstrong.) * " And the griffins returned, flying above them, and would not leave them.

" When Queen Calafia saw this, she cried to the Sultans, ' Make your troops mount, that they may defend mine against these fowls of mine who have dared attack them.' At once the Sultans commanded their people to ascend the ladders and gain the circle and the towers, in order that by night the whole host might join them, and they might gain the city. The soldiers rushed from their camps, and mounted on the wall where the women were fighting ; but when the griffins saw them, at once they seized on them as ravenously as if all that day they had not caught anybody. And when the women threatened them with their knives, they were only the more enraged, so that, although they took shelter for themselves, the griffins dragged them out by main strength, lifted them up into the air, and then let them fall, — so that they all died. The fear and panic of the Pagans were so great that, much more quickly than they had mounted, did they descend, and take refuge in their camp. The Queen, seeing this rout without remedy, sent at once to command those who held watch and guard on the griffins,

* It is perhaps already forgotten that the plated ship Keokuk did not withstand the Armstrong bolts as well as the turrets of the Monitors.

that they should recall them, and shut them up in the vessel. They, then, hearing the Queen's command, mounted on top of the mast, and called them with loud voices in their language ; and they, as if they had been human beings, all obeyed, and obediently returned into their cages."

The first day's attack of these flying Monitors on the beleaguered city was not, therefore, a distinguished success. The author derives a lesson from it, which we do not translate, but recommend to the students of present history. It fills a whole chapter, of which the title is, "Exhortation addressed by the author to the Christians, setting before their eyes the great obedience which these griffins, brute animals, rendered to those who had instructed them."

The Sultans may have well doubted whether their new ally was quite what she had claimed to be. She felt this herself, and said to them, —

" 'Since my coming has caused you so much injury, I wish that it may cause you equal pleasure. Command your people that they shall sally out, and we will go to the city against those knights who dare to appear before us, and we will let them press on the most severe combat that they can, and I, with my people, will take the front of the battle.'

" The Sultans gave command at once to all of their soldiers who had armor, that they should rush forth immediately, and should join in mounting upon the rampart, now that these birds were encaged again.

And they, with the horsemen, followed close upon
Queen Calafia, and immediately the army rushed forth,
and pressed upon the wall; but not so prosperously as
they had expected, because the people of the town were
already there in their harness; and, as the Pagans mounted upon their ladders, the Christians threw them back,
whence very many of them were killed and wounded.
Others pressed forward with their iron picks and other
tools, and dug fiercely in the circuit of the wall.
These were very much distressed and put in danger by
the oil and other things which were thrown upon
them, but not so much but that they succeeded in
making many breaches and openings. But when this
came to the ears of the Emperor, who always kept
command of ten thousand horsemen, he commanded
all of them to defend these places as well as they could.
So that, to the grief of the Pagans, the people repaired
the breaches with many timbers and stones and piles
of earth.

" When the Queen saw this repulse, she rushed with
her own attendants with great speed to the gate Aqui-
leña, which was guarded by Norandel.* She herself
went in advance of the others, wholly covered with
one of those shields which we have told you they wore,
and with her lance held strongly in her hand. Norandel, when he saw her coming, went forth to meet her,
and they met so vehemently that their lances were

* Norandel was the half-brother of Amadis, both of them being
sons of Lisuarte, King of England.

broken in pieces, and yet neither of them fell. Norandel at once put hand upon his sword, and the Queen upon her great knife, of which the blade was more than a palm broad, and they gave each other great blows. At once they all joined in a *mêlée*, one against another, all so confused and with such terrible blows that it was a great marvel to see it; and if some of the women fell upon the ground, so did some of the cavaliers. And if this history does not tell in extent which of them fell, and by what blow of each, showing the great force and courage of the combatants, it is because their number was so great, and they fell so thick, one upon another, that that great master, Helisabat, who saw and described the scene, could not determine what in particular passed in these exploits, except in a few very rare affairs, like this of the Queen and Norandel, who both joined fight as you have heard."

It is to the great master Helisabat that a grateful posterity owes all these narratives and the uncounted host of romances which grew from them. For, in the first place, he was the skilful leech who cured all the wounds of all the parties of distinction who were not intended to die; and, in the second place, his notes furnish the *mémoires pour servir*, of which all the writers say they availed themselves. The originals, alas! are lost.

" The tumult was so great that at once the battle between these two was ended, those on each side coming to the aid of their chief. Then, I tell you that the things that this Queen did in arms, like slaying knights, or throwing them wounded from their horses, as she pressed audaciously forward among her enemies, were such, that it cannot be told nor believed that any woman has ever shown such prowess.

"And as she dealt with so many noble knights, and no one of them left her without giving her many and heavy blows, yet she received them all upon her very strong and hard shield.

"When Talanque and Maneli * saw what this woman was doing, and the great loss which those of their own party were receiving from her, they rushed out upon her, and struck her with such blows as if they considered her possessed. And her sister, who was named Liota, who saw this, rushed in, like a mad lioness, to her succor, and pressed the knights so mortally that, to the loss of their honor, she drew Calafia from their power, and placed her among her own troops again. And at this time you would have said that the people of the fleets had the advantage, so that, if it had not been for the mercy of God and the great force of the Count Frandalo and his companions, the city would have been wholly lost. Many fell dead on both sides, but many more of the Pagans, because they had the weaker armor.

"Thus," continues the romance, " as you have heard, went on this attack and cruel battle till nearly night. At this time there was no one of the gates open, ex-

* Maneli was son of Cildadan, King of Ireland.

cepting that which Norandel guarded.   As to the
others, the knights, having been withdrawn from them,
ought, of course, to have bolted them; yet it was very
different, as I will tell you.   For, as the two Sultans
greatly desired to see these women fight, they had bidden their own people not to enter into the lists.   But
when they saw how the day was going, they pressed
upon the Christians so fiercely that gradually they
might all enter into the city; and, as it was, more than
a hundred men and women did enter.   And God, who
guided the Emperor, having directed him to keep the
other gates shut, knowing in what way the battle fared,
he pressed them so hardly with his knights that, kill-
ing some, he drove the others out.   Then the Pagans
lost many of their people, as they slew them from the
towers, — more than two hundred of the women being
slain.   And those within also were not without great
loss, since ten of the *cruzados* were killed, which gave
great grief to their companions.   These were Ledaderin
de Fajarque, Trion and Imosil de Borgona, and the two
sons of Isanjo.   All the people of the city having returned, as I tell you, the Pagans also retired to their
camps, and the Queen Calafia to her fleet, since she
had not yet taken quarters on shore.   And the other
people entered into their ships; so that there was no
more fighting that day."

I have translated this passage at length, because it
gives the reader an idea of the romantic literature of
that day, — literally its only literature, excepting books

of theology or of devotion. Over acres of such reading, served out in large folios, — the yellow-covered novels of their time, — did the Pizarros and Balboas and Cortezes and other young blades while away the weary hours of their camp life. Glad enough was Cortez out of such a tale to get the noble name of his great discovery.

The romance now proceeds to bring the different princes of chivalry from the West, as it has brought Calafia from the East. As soon as Amadis arrives at Constantinople, he sends for his son Esplandian, who was already in alliance with the Emperor of Greece. The Pagan Sultan of Liquia, and the Queen Calafia, hearing of their arrival, send them the following challenge : —

"Radiaro, Sultan of Liquia, shield and rampart of the Pagan Law, destroyer of Christians, cruel enemy of the enemies of the Gods, and the very Mighty Queen Calafia, Lady of the great island of California, famous for its great abundance of gold and precious stones : we have to announce to you, Amadis of Gaul, King of Great Britain, and you his son, Knight of the Great Serpent, that we are come into these parts with the intention of destroying this city of Constantinople, on account of the injury and loss which the much honored King Amato of Persia, our cousin and friend, has received from this bad Emperor, giving him favor and aid because a part of his territory has been taken away from him by fraud. And as our desire in this thing is also to gain glory and fame in it, so also has fortune treated us favorably in that regard, for we know the great news, which has gone through all the world, of your great chivalry. We have agreed, therefore, if it is agreeable to you, or if your might is sufficient for it, to attempt a battle of our persons against yours in presence of this great company of the nations, the conquered to submit to the will of the conquerors, or to go to any place where they may order. And if you refuse this, we shall be able, with much cause, to join all your past glories to our own, counting them as being gained by us, whence it will clearly be seen in the future how the victory will be on our side."

This challenge was taken to the Christian camp by a black and beautiful damsel, richly attired, and was discussed there in council. Amadis put an end to the discussion by saying, —

" ' My good lords, as the affairs of men, like those of nations, are in the hands and will of God, whence no one can escape but as He wills, if we should in any way withdraw from this demand, it would give great courage to our enemies, and, more than this, great injury to our honor; especially so in this country, where we are strangers, and no one has seen what our power is, which in our own land is notorious, so that, while there we may be esteemed for courage, here we should be judged the greatest of cowards. Thus, placing confidence in the mercy of the Lord, I determine that the battle shall take place without delay.'

" 'If this is your wish,' said King Lisuarte and King Perion, ' so may it be, and may God help you with His grace !'

" Then the King Amadis said to the damsel, —

" 'Friend, tell your lord and the Queen Calafia that we desire the battle with those arms that are most agreeable to them ; that the field shall be this field, divided in the middle, — I giving my word that for nothing which may happen will we be succored by our own. And let them give the same order to their own ; and if they wish the battle now, now it shall be.'

" The damsel departed with this reply, which she repeated to those two princes. And the Queen Calafia asked her how the Christians appeared.

" 'Very nobly,' replied she ; 'for they are all handsome and well armed. Yet I tell you, Queen, that, among them, this Knight of the Serpent [Esplandian, son of Amadis] is such as neither the past nor the present, nor, I believe, any who are to come, have ever seen one so handsome and so elegant, nor will see in the days which are to be. O Queen, what shall I say to you, but that, if he were of our faith, we might believe that our Gods had made him with their own hands, with all their power and wisdom, so that he lacks in nothing ?'

" The Queen, who heard her, said, —

" 'Damsel, my friend, your words are too great.'

" 'It is not so,' said she ; 'for, excepting the sight of him, there is nothing else which can give account of his great excellence.'

" ' Then I say to you,' said the Queen, ' that I will not fight with such a man until I have first seen and talked with him ; and I make this request to the Sultan, that he will gratify me in this thing, and arrange that I may see him.'

" The Sultan said, —

" ' I will do everything, O Queen, agreeably to your wish.'

" ' Then,' said the damsel, ' I will go and obtain that which you ask for, according to your desire.'

" And, turning her horse, she approached the camp again, so that all thought that she brought the agreement for the battle. But as she approached, she called the Kings to the door of the tent, and said, —

" ' King Amadis, the Queen Calafia demands of you that you give order for her safe conduct, that she may come to-morrow morning and see your son.'

" Amadis began to laugh, and said to the Kings, —

" ' How does this demand seem to you ? '

" ' I say, let her come,' said King Lisuarte : ' it is a very good thing to see the most distinguished woman in the world.'

" ' Take this for your reply,' said Amadis to the damsel ; ' and say that she shall be treated with all truth and honor.'

" The damsel, having received this message, returned with great pleasure to the Queen, and told her what it was. The Queen said to the Sultan, —

" ' Wait and prosper, then, till I have seen him ; and

charge your people that in the mean time there may
be no outbreak.'

" ' Of that,' he said, 'you may be secure.'

" At once she returned to her ships; and she spent
the whole night thinking whether she would go with
arms or without them. But at last she determined
that it would be more dignified to go in the dress of a
woman. And when the morning came she rose, and
directed them to bring one of her dresses, all of gold,
with many precious stones, and a turban wrought with
great art. It had a volume of many folds, in the manner of a *toca*, and she placed it upon her head as if it
had been a hood [*capellina*]; it was all of gold, em-
broidered with stones of great value. They brought
out an animal which she rode, the strangest that ever
was seen. It had ears as large as two shields; a broad
forehead which had but one eye, like a mirror; the
openings of its nostrils were very large, but its nose
was short and blunt. From its mouth turned up two
tusks, each of them two palms long. Its color was
yellow, and it had many violet spots upon its skin, like
an ounce. It was larger than a dromedary, had its
feet cleft like those of an ox, and ran as swiftly as the
wind, and skipped over the rocks as lightly, and held
itself erect on any part of them, as do the mountain-
goats. Its food was dates and figs and peas, and nothing else. Its flank and haunches and breast were very
beautiful. On this animal, of which you have thus
heard, mounted this beautiful Queen, and there rode

behind her two thousand women of her train, dressed in the very richest clothes. There brought up the rear twenty damsels clothed in uniform, the trains of whose dresses extended so far that, falling from each beast, they dragged four fathoms on the ground.

" With this equipment and ornament the Queen proceeded to the Emperor's camp, where she saw all the Kings, who had come out upon the plain. They had seated themselves on very rich chairs, upon cloth of gold, and they themselves were armed, because they had not much confidence in the promises of the Pagans. So they sallied out to receive her at the door of the tent, where she was dismounted into the arms of Don Quadragante ;* and the two Kings, Lisuarte and Perion, took her by the hands, and placed her between them in a chair. When she was seated, looking from one side to the other, she saw Esplandian next to King Lisuarte, who held him by the hand ; and from the superiority of his beauty to that of all the others, she knew at once who he was, and said to herself, ' O, my Gods ! what is this ? I declare to you, I have never seen any one who can be compared to him, nor shall I ever see any one.' And he turning his beautiful eyes upon her beautiful face, she perceived that the rays which leaped out from his resplendent beauty, entering in at her eyes, penetrated to her heart in such a way, that, if she were not conquered yet by the great

* Quadragante was a distinguished giant, who had been conquered by Amadis, and was now his sure friend.

force of arms, or by the great attacks of her enemies, she was softened and broken by that sight and by her amorous passion, as if she had passed between mallets of iron. And as she saw this, she reflected that, if she stayed longer, the great fame which she had acquired as a manly cavalier, by so many dangers and labors, would be greatly hazarded. She saw that by any delay she should expose herself to the risk of dishonor, by being turned to that native softness which women of nature consider to be an ornament; and therefore resisting, with great pain, the feelings which she had subjected to her will, she rose from her seat, and said, —

"'Knight of the Great Serpent, for two excellences which distinguish you above all mortals I have made inquiry. The first, that of your great beauty, which, if one has not seen, no relation is enough to tell the greatness of; the other, the valor and force of your brave heart. The one of these I have seen, which is such as I have never seen nor could hope to see, though many years of searching should be granted me. The other shall be made manifest on the field, against this valiant Radiaro, Sultan of Liquia. Mine shall be shown against this mighty king your father; and if fortune grant that we come alive from this battle, as we hope to come from other battles, then I will talk with you, before I return to my home, of some things of my own affairs.'

"Then, turning towards the Kings, she said to them,

" ' Kings, rest in good health. I go hence to that place where you shall see me with very different dress from this which I now wear, hoping that in that field the King Amadis, who trusts in fickle fortune that he may never be conquered by any knight, however valiant, nor by any beast, however terrible, may there be conquered by a woman.'

" Then taking the two older Kings by the hand, she permitted them to help her mount upon her strange steed."

At this point the novel assumes a tone of high virtue (*virtus*, mannishness, prejudice of the more brutal sex) on the subject of woman's rights, in especial of woman's right to fight in the field with gold armor, lance in rest, and casque closed. We will show the reader, as she follows us, how careful she must be, if, in any island of the sea which has been slipped by, unknown, by the last five centuries, she ever happen to meet a cavalier of the true school of chivalry.

Esplandian himself would not in any way salute the Queen Calafia, as she left him. Nor was this a copperhead prejudice of color; for that prejudice was not yet known.

" He made no reply to her, both because he looked at her as something strange, however beautiful she appeared to him, and because he saw her come thus in arms, so different from the style in which a woman should have come. For he considered it as very dishonorable that she should attempt anything so differ-

ent from what the word of God commanded her, that
the woman should be in subjection to the man, but
rather should prefer to be the ruler of all men, not by
her courtesy, but by force of arms, and, above all, because he hated to place himself in relations with her,
because she was one of the infidels whom he mortally
despised and had taken a vow to destroy."

The romance then goes into an account of the preparations for the contest on both sides.

After all the preliminaries were arranged, " they separated for a little, and rode together furiously in full
career. The Sultan struck Esplandian in the shield
with so hard a blow that a part of the lance passed
through it for as much as an ell, so that all who saw it
thought that it had passed through the body. But it
was not so, but the lance passed under the arm next
the body, and went out on the other side without
touching him. But Esplandian, who knew that his
much-loved lady was looking on [Leonorina, the
daughter of the Emperor of Constantinople], so struck
the Sultan's shield that the iron passed through it and
struck him on some of the strongest plates of his
armor, upon which the spear turned. But, with the
force of the encounter, it shook him so roughly from
the saddle that it rolled him upon the ground, and so
shook the helmet as to tear it off from his head ; and
thus Esplandian passed by him very handsomely, without receiving any stroke himself. The Queen rushed
upon Amadis, and he upon her, and, before they met,

each pointed lance at the other, and they received the blows upon their shields in such guise that her spear flew in pieces, while that of Amadis slipped off and was thrown on one side. Then they both met, shield to shield, with such force that the Queen was thrown upon the ground, and the horse of Amadis was so wounded that he fell with his head cut in two, and held Amadis with one leg under him. When Esplandian saw this, he leaped from his horse and saved him from that peril. Meanwhile, the Queen, being put to her defence, put hand to her sword, and joined herself to the Sultan, who had raised himself with great difficulty, because his fall was very heavy, and stood there with his sword and helmet in his hand. They came on to fight very bravely; but Esplandian, standing, as I told you, in presence of the Infanta whom he prized so much, gave the Sultan such hard pressure with such heavy blows, that, although he was one of the bravest knights of the Pagans, and by his own prowess had won many dangerous battles, and was very dexterous in that art, yet all this served him for nothing; he could neither give nor parry blows, and constantly lost ground. The Queen, who had joined fight with Amadis, began giving him many fierce blows, some of which he received upon his shield, while he let others be lost; yet he would not put his hand upon his sword, but, instead of that, took a fragment of the lance which she had driven through his shield, and struck her on the top of the helmet with it, so that in a little while he had knocked the crest away."

We warned those of our fair readers who may have occasion to defend their rights at the point of the lance, that the days of chivalry or the cavaliers of chivalry would be very unhandsome in applying to them the rules of the tourney. Amadis, it will be observed here, does not condescend to use his sword against a woman. And this is not from tenderness, but from contempt. For when the Queen saw that he only took the broken truncheon of his lance to her, she fairly asked him why.

"'How is this, Amadis?' she said. 'Do you consider my force so slight that you think to conquer me with sticks?'

"And he said to her, —

"'Queen, I have always been in the habit of serving women and aiding them; and as you are a woman, if I should use any weapon against you, I should deserve to lose all the honors I have ever gained.'

"'What, then!' said the Queen, 'do you rank me among them? You shall see!'

"And taking her sword in both her hands, she struck him with great rage. Amadis raised his shield and received the blow upon it, which was so brave and strong that the shield was cut in two. Then, seeing her joined to him so closely, he passed his stick into his left hand, seized her by the rim of the shield, and pulled her so forcibly that, breaking the great thongs by which she held upon it, he took it from her, lifting it up in one hand, and forced her to kneel with one knee on the ground; and when she lightly sprang up, Amadis threw away his own shield, and, seizing the other, took the stick, and sprang to her, saying, —

" 'Queen, yield yourself my prisoner, now that your Sultan is conquered.'

" She turned her head, and saw that Esplandian had the Sultan already surrendered as his prize. But she said, ' Let me try fortune yet one more turn'; and then, raising her sword with both her hands, she struck upon the crest of his helmet, thinking she could cut it and his head in two. But Amadis warded the blow very lightly and turned it off, and struck her so heavy a stroke with that fragment of the lance upon the crest of her helmet that he stunned her, and made her sword fall from her hands. Amadis seized the sword, and, when she was thus disarmed, caught at her helmet so strongly that he dragged it from her head, and said, —

" ' Now are you my prisoner ? '

" ' Yes,' replied she; ' for there is nothing left for me to do.'

" At this moment Esplandian came to them with the Sultan, who had surrendered himself; and, in sight of all the army, they repaired to the royal encampment, where they were received with great pleasure, not only on account of the great victory in battle, which, after the great deeds in arms which they had wrought before, as this history has shown, they did not regard as very remarkable, but because they took this

success as a good omen for the future. The King
Amadis asked the Count Gandalin to lead their prisoners to the Infanta Leonorina, in his behalf and that of
his son Esplandian, and to say to her that he begged
her to do honor to the Sultan, because he was so great
a prince and so strong a knight, and, withal, very
noble; and to do honor to the Queen, *because she was
a woman;* and to say that he trusted in God that thus
they should send to her all those whom they took captive alive in the battles which awaited them.

"The Count took them in charge, and, as the city
was very near, they soon arrived at the palace. Then,
coming into the presence of the Infanta, he delivered
to her the prisoners, and gave the message with which
he was intrusted. The Infanta replied to him, —

"'Tell King Amadis that I thank him greatly for
this present which he sends me; that I am sure that the
good fortune and great courage which appear in this
adventure will appear in those which await us; and
that we are very desirous to see him here, that, when
we discharge our obligation to his son, we may have
him as a judge between us.'

"The Count kissed her hand, and returned to the
royal camp. Then the Infanta sent to the Empress,
her mother, for a rich robe and head-dress, and, having
disarmed the Queen, made her array herself in them;
and she did the same for the Sultan, having sent for
other robes from the Emperor, her father, and having
dressed their wounds with certain preparations made

by Master Helisabat. Then the Queen, though of so great fortune, was much astonished to see the great beauty of Leonorina, and said, —

"'I tell you, Infanta, that in the same measure in which I was astonished to see the beauty of your cavalier, Esplandian, am I now overwhelmed, beholding yours. If your deeds correspond to your appearance, I hold it no dishonor to be your prisoner.'

"'Queen,' said the Infanta, 'I hope the God in whom I trust will so direct events that I shall be able to fulfil every obligation which conquerors acknowledge toward those who submit to them.'"

With this chivalrous little conversation the Queen of California disappears from the romance, and consequently from all written history, till the very *dénouement* of the whole story, where, when the rest is "wound up," she is wound up also, to be set a-going again in her own land of California. And if the chroniclers of California find no records of her in any of the griffin caves of the Black Cañon, it is not our fault, but theirs. Or, possibly, did she and her party suffer shipwreck on the return passage from Constantinople to the Golden Gate? Their probable route must have been through the Ægean, over Lebanon and Anti-Lebanon to the Euphrates ("I will sail a fleet over the Alps," said Cromwell), down Chesney's route to the Persian Gulf, and so home.

After the Sultan and the Queen are taken prisoners, there are reams of terrific fighting, in which King

Lisuarte and King Perion and a great many other people are killed ; but finally the " Pagans" are all routed, and the Emperor of Greece retires into a monastery, having united Esplandian with his daughter Leonorina, and abdicated the throne in their favor. Among the first acts of their new administration is the disposal of Calafia.

" As soon as the Queen Calafia saw these nuptials, having no more hope of him whom she so much loved [Esplandian], for a moment her courage left her ; and coming before the new Emperor and these great lords, she thus spoke to them : —

" ' I am a queen of a great kingdom, in which there is the greatest abundance of all that is most valued in the world, such as gold and precious stones. My lineage is very old, — for it comes from royal blood so far back that there is no memory of the beginnings of it, — and my honor is as perfect as it was at my birth. My fortune has brought me into these countries, whence I hoped to bring away many captives, but where I am myself a captive. I do not say of this captivity in which you see me, that, after all the great experiences of my life, favorable and adverse, I had believed that I was strong enough to parry the thrusts of fortune ; but I have found that my heart was tried and afflicted in my imprisonment, because the great beauty of this new Emperor overwhelmed me in the moment that my eyes looked upon him. I trusted in my greatness, and that immense wealth which excites and unites so many, that, if I would turn to your religion, I might gain him for a husband; but when I came into the presence of this lovely Empress, I regarded it as certain that they belonged to each other by their equal rank; and that argument, which showed the vanity of my thoughts, brought me to the determination in which I now stand. And since Eternal Fortune has taken the direction of my passion, I, throwing all my own strength into oblivion, as the wise do in those affairs which have no remedy, seek, if it please you, to take for my husband some other man, who may be the son of a king, to be of such power as a good knight ought to have; and I will become a Christian. For, as I have seen the ordered order of your religion, and the great disorder of all others, I have seen that it is clear that the law which you follow must be the truth while that which we follow is lying and falsehood.'

" When the Emperor had heard all this, embracing her, with a smile he said, ' Queen Calafia, my good friend, till now you have had from me neither word nor argument; for my condition is such that I cannot permit my eyes to look, without terrible hatred, upon any but those who are in the holy law of truth, nor wish well to such as are out of it. But now that the Omnipotent Lord has had such mercy on you as to give you such knowledge that you become his servant, you excite in me at once the same love as if the King, my father, had begotten us both. And as for this you ask, I will give you, by my troth, a knight who is even more complete in valor and in lineage than you have demanded.'

"Then, taking by the hand Talanque, his cousin, the son of the King of Sobradisa, — very large he was of person, and very handsome withal, — he said, —

"' Queen, here you see one of my cousins, son of the King whom you here see, — the brother of the King my father: take him to yourself, that I may secure to you the good fortune which you will bring to him.'

"The Queen looked at him, and, finding his appearance good, said, —

"' I am content with his presence, and well satisfied with his lineage and person, since you assure me of them. Be pleased to summon for me Liota, my sister, who is with my fleet in the harbor, that I may send orders to her that there shall be no movement among my people.'

"The Emperor sent the Admiral Tartarie for her immediately, and he, having found her, brought her with him, and placed her before the Emperor. The Queen Calafia told her all her wish, commanding her and entreating her to confirm it. Her sister, Liota, kneeling upon the ground, kissed her hands, and said that there was no reason why she should make any explanation of her will to those who were in her service. The Queen raised her and embraced her, with the tears in her eyes, and led her by the hand to Talanque, saying, —

"' Thou shalt be my lord, and the lord of my land,

which is a very great kingdom ; and, for thy sake, this island shall change the custom which for a very long time it has preserved, so that the natural generations of men and women shall succeed henceforth, in place of the order in which the men have been separated so long. And if you have here any friend whom you greatly love, who is of the same rank with you, let him be betrothed to my sister here ; and no long time shall pass, before, with thy help, she shall be queen of a great land.'

" Talanque greatly loved Maneli the Prudent, both because they were brothers by birth and because they held the same faith. He led him forth, and said to her, —

" ' My Queen, since the Emperor, my lord, loves this knight as much as he loves me, and as much as I love thee, take him, and do with him as you would do by me.'

" ' Then, I ask,' said she, ' that we, accepting your religion, may become your wives.'

" Then the Emperor Esplandian and the several Kings, seeing their wishes thus confirmed, took the Queen and her sister to the chapel, turned them into Christians, and espoused them to those two so famous knights ; and thus they converted all who were in the fleet. And immediately they gave order, so that Talanque, taking the fleet of Don Galaor, his father, and Maneli that of King Cildadan, with all their people, garnished and furnished with all things necessary, set sail with their wives, plighting their faith to the Emperor that, if he should need any help from them, they would give it as to their own brother.

"What happened to them afterwards, I must be excused from telling ; for they passed through many very strange achievements of the greatest valor ; they fought many battles, and gained many kingdoms, of which, if we should give the story, there would be danger that we should never have done."

With this tantalizing statement, California and the Queen of California pass from romance and from history. But, some twenty-five years after these words were written and published by Garcia Ordoñez de Montalvo, Cortez and his braves happened upon the peninsula, which they thought an island, which stretches down between the Gulf of California and the sea. This romance of Esplandian was the yellow-covered novel of their day ; Talanque and Maneli were their Aramis and Athos. " Come," said some one, " let us name the new island California : perhaps some one will find gold here yet, and precious stones." And so, from the romance, the peninsula, and the gulf, and afterwards the State, got their name. And they have rewarded the romance by giving to it in these later days the fame of being godmother of a great republic.

The antiquarians of California have universally, we believe, recognized this as the origin of her name, since Mr. Hale called attention to this rare romance.

As, even now, there are not perhaps half a dozen copies of it in America, we have transferred to our pages every word which belongs to that primeval history of California and her Queen.

NOTE.

[From the Proceedings of the American Antiquarian Society, October, 1872.]

THE COSMOGONY OF DANTE AND COLUMBUS.

When Columbus sailed on his fourth voyage, he wrote to Ferdinand and Isabella a letter which contains the following statement with regard to the South Sea, then undiscovered, known to us as the Pacific Ocean : —

" I believe that if I should pass under the equator, in arriving at this higher region of which I speak, I should find there a milder temperature and a diversity in the stars and in the waters. Not that I believe that the highest point is navigable whence these currents flow, nor that we can mount there, because I am convinced that there is the terrestrial paradise, whence no one can enter but by the will of God."

This curious passage, of which the language seems so mystical, represents none the less the impression which Columbus had of the physical cosmogony of the undiscovered half of the world. It is curious to observe that the most elaborate account of this cosmogony, and that by which alone it has been handed down to the memory of modern times, is that presented in Dante's " Divina Commedia," where he represents the mountain of Purgatory, at the antipodes of Jerusalem, crowned by the Terrestrial Paradise. It is this paradise of which Columbus says, " No one can enter it but by the will of God."

Of Dante's Cosmogony a very accurate account is given by

Miss Rossetti in her essay on Dante, recently published, to which she gives the name of " The Shadow of Dante." Her statement is in these words : —

" Dante divides our globe into two elemental hemispheres, — the Eastern, chiefly of land; the Western, almost wholly of water. In the midst of the inhabited land-hemisphere he places Jerusalem, within the same hemisphere, so that its central and Hell's lowest point is exactly under Jerusalem ; he places Hell in the midst of the uninhabited sea-hemisphere ; he places Purgatory, as the antipodes to Jerusalem, distant from it by the whole diameter of the globe. Thus, on and within the earth, are situated the temporal and the eternal prison-house of sin. Neither, in Dante's view, formed part of God's original creation, wherein sin was not ; but the fall of Lucifer at once produced the one and prepared the other, convulsing and inverting the world which God had made. The rebel Seraph fell headlong from Heaven directly above the Western hemisphere, till then a continent, in whose midst was Eden ; and Earth, in the twofold horror of his sight and presence, underwent a twofold change. First, to veil her face, she brought in upon herself the vast floods of the Eastern sea-hemisphere, transferring to their place all her dry land, save Eden, which thus was left insulated in mid-ocean. And secondly, to escape his contact as he sank and sank through her surface, through her bowels, till the middle of his colossal frame, having reached the centre of gravity, remained there fixed from the sheer physical impossibility of sinking any lower, she caused a vast mass of her internal substance to flee before his face, and, leaving eternally void the space it once had occupied to form the inverted pit-cone of Hell, she heaved it up directly under Eden, amid the new waste of waters, to form the towering mountain-cone on whose peak the Terrestrial Paradise should thenceforth, to the end of time, sit by, above all elemental strife, and whose sides should, after the Redemption of Man, furnish the Purgatorial stair whereby his foot might aspire once more to tread, his eye to contemplate, his regained inheritance."

The allusion thus made by Columbus to the mystical cosmogony on which Dante wrought, is, I suppose, the last serious allusion made to it, as to a matter of fact, by any geographer. On the other hand, I am not aware that any of the distinguished critics of Dante have called attention to the fact, that, so late as the year 1503, a navigator so illustrious as Columbus was still conducting his voyages on the supposition that Dante's cosmogony was true in fact. All readers of later voyages will remember how often, without any reference to this cosmogony, the islands of the Southern Pacific have been spoken of as a terrestrial paradise. It may be worthy, therefore, of remark, that the precise antipodes of Jerusalem, which, according to the cosmogony of Dante, would be the place of the summit of the terrestrial paradise, is just south of Tahiti and southwest of Pitcairn's Island, the two points where different enthusiasts among modern navigators have fancied that their terrestrial paradise was found. These islands are, in fact, the nearest land to the spot which Columbus, in the half mystical and half geographical letter which I have cited, indicates as the terrestrial paradise.

It is to be remembered, also, that it has been proved that the Pacific islands have grown up on the crests of extinct volcanoes.

Mr. Longfellow's note to the " Purgatorio " thus describes the mountain which Columbus expected to find there : —

" The mountain of Purgatory is a vast conical mountain, rising steep and high from the waters of the Southern Ocean, at a point antipodal to Mount Sion, in Jerusalem. Around it run seven terraces, on which are punished severally the Seven Deadly Sins. Rough stairways, cut in the rock, lead up from terrace to terrace, and on the summit is the garden of the Terrestrial Paradise." — *Longfellow's first Note to the Purgatorio, Vol. II, Div. Com., p.* 159.

E. E. H.

CONFIDENCE.

DEAR little Janet! And you want me to tell her
story? Why, she would say there was no story to
tell.

I say " Dear little Janet ! " For all that, she is a
woman grown now ; and the last time I saw her there
was a great bouncing Donald in her lap. For a' that,
and for a' that, she will always be " little Janet " to
me.

There never was a child who showed so fully what
the woman was to prove. The first time I ever saw
her was one day when her father had fallen in with
me on a cross-road in the Piscataquis valley : that is
far away, forty miles above Bangor in Maine. He was
on his hay-cart : I was sitting on a log. We nodded
to each other ; and he, seeing my knapsack and stick,
asked if I would not mount with him, which I did ;
and so, before long, we came up to his cheerful, ram-
bling, great shingle-palace of a house, where I had
already promised to pass the night with him. We
brought up in front of the barn, from which we had
already heard shouts of " Coop ! Coop ! " Who should

appear at a little three-cornered window in the gable but little Janet, flaxen curls flying wild about her head. "Hurrah!" said "Miss Janet." "Hurrah!" said her father: "jump, birdie!" and, before poor cockney I well understood the order, the child flew out of the window, down into his arms, and they both rolled over and over in the hay. I have seen many a jump into hay-carts, — nay, have made my share; but I never saw such a flight as that. And even then it was not the distance which seemed most surprising: it was the absolute promptness, so perfectly fearless : —

> " Hers not to make reply,
> Hers not to question why."

He said " Jump!" and she jumped, not because she calculated the height, or had done it before, but because he told her to, and she loved and trusted him. That was little Janet all over.

Now, steadiness like that and readiness like that breed steadiness and readiness. It seems queer to me that I had never seen Janet before, I have seen her so much and so often since. I had not seen her long, before I found that I trusted her as implicitly as she did me : indeed, there was not a man who worked on the farm who had not absolute confidence in the child, or was not sure of her promptness, punctuality, and affection. Nor was it men or women alone who felt so. The horses and the cows — nay, the pigs and the hens — all knew her cheerful voice and her ready attendance and her steady hand. Jotham said she could collar and harness that cross brute " Mad March "; that she would climb into the manger, and put the wretch's collar on, and put the bit in his mouth, because she was such a lady. I know she could do it; and of course Mad March let her do it; for he could have eaten her, had he been carnivorous, and hardly know he had tasted food. But it was not because she was a lady, but because her easy confidence, as I say, created the same confidence in all.

Do you remember Miss Yonge's pretty story of Miss Keble ? The little wrens trusted her so entirely that they came to pick the red berries which were printed on her muslin dress ; and when they found they could not get any of them off, they flew down, and crept up under the skirt, thinking they should get at the berries on the other side. I have seen the little birds do that with Janet, — not such wrens as those, because there are none in Maine, but some little witches not so much bigger than an English wren, whose name I do not know. Wren or no wren, they knew Janet, even if she did not know their name nor they hers.

The pretty picture Mr. Billings has made of her just represents both sides. I mean, she trusted the birds, and the birds trusted her. In the picture you see just how it was. This little whistler has fascinated her, and she has fascinated him. He knows she will not hurt him ; and it almost seems as if she were listening

to him, and learning from him, as, in the " Arabian
Nights," and in the German fairy-tales, the girls of the
real blue blood understand all the language of cater-
pillar, cricket, grasshopper, toad, frog, weasel, pussy-
cat, tomtit, ostrich, camelopard, and all other verte-
brates or invertebrates.   Dear little Janet ! she is as
good a fairy as the best of them.

After the haymow flight, when she was as big a girl
as Mr. Billings has made her, we had many a tramp
together up brook, through moose-wood, and over
mountain.   I have seen her pass from rock to rock on
one of the ridges of Ktaadn, with no thought of taking
a staff, with no kind of uneasiness, though she were
just on the sheer edge of that precipice which you
remember, perhaps, on the southern face of Ktaadn.   I
have seen it fifty miles away.   Yes : and I have seen the
child's father fell a pine-tree a hundred and fifty years
old, that we might walk dry-shod across a stream ; and,
the moment it fell, little Janet was the first to swing
herself upon the trunk, to run across as lightly as one
of her own little birds would ; and in ten seconds was
beckoning and waving her hand from the rocks on
the other shore.   We could not hear a word she said
for the rush of the rapids in the gorge below.   Her
father, who worships her, — as well he may, — used to
tell a story of an experience of theirs in a sort of out-
lying station he had, half shanty and half lumber-camp,
just on the edge of the woods.   Mrs. Trevor had gone
up with him and Janet and the children ; and they

were to have a sort of picnic frolic for three or four days. But one of the little boys was not well; so their mother had taken them all home, leaving Janet to cook for her father, who had something in hand. Poor fellow! In the middle of the second morning, as he pried up a heavy sill from its resting-place, the ground gave way under him, his bar slipped, and he and the log rolled down together in the hole he had made, — poor Trevor underneath, and his leg broken just above the ankle. Janet was with him in two seconds; but she could not free him, nor could five others like her. "She did not wait long," he said. Off she went like a bird, down to McMurtrie's pasture, a mile and a half down the intervale: — over the root-fence, into the pasture, and then, threading through the high ferns, she began to call, "Dan! Dan! Dan!" Now, Dan was a vicious old stallion whom McMurtrie chose to keep ranging in his pasture and in the woods. When McMurtrie or any of his men wanted Dan, which was perhaps four times in a summer, it took a peck of salt, and lurings and chasings, lariats and lassos indescribable, to woo him and to win him. And now this child — for Janet was still not woman grown — only called Dan two or three times, and down through the underbrush came the great hulking creature, glowering at her; and, as she slowly walked up to him with a handful of raspberries, he did not turn away; and then and there he stood and she stood, — she on a rough boulder, he nibbling at the fruit; she rubbing his head between the ears, he whinnying with satisfaction that he had company. And at last, when Janet thought the *entente cordiale* was attained, she coolly put her little green scarf through his mouth, behind his great teeth, and, before he knew it, she had flung herself on his back and was away. They were not long making the six miles to the village. As she came in by the saw-mill, she met Dr. Kittredge. She told him her story; and in three minutes he and four or five other men were in a lumber-wagon on their way to the rescue. Kittredge told me this himself. They asked the girl if she would not go with them; but Janet said, No: somebody must take Dan back to the pasture; and so she went ahead of the party. Poor Trevor was released in less than two hours from the time he fell.

But you want to know how Wildair first met her. It is John Wildair, remember, — not Taylor: Taylor is in Australia. John is Taylor's brother. That is just the way with you young people. All you care about is the love-making and the wedding. Now, I might entertain you for an hour with pleasant accounts of how the Trevors came into the Piscataquis valley, and how I came to be there, and of the origin of the Trevor family; and you would skip it all to see how the story turned out, and who married them. Only Helen, of all of you, would read about the early history of Cornwall; and she would do it, not because she wanted to know, but from love of me.

Well, John Wildair first saw Janet on board a Kennebec steamer, — literally on board, if you will rightly consider the derivation of that term. John Wildair was sitting on the deck, at Bath, watching as the passengers came on board. And two men brought an old lady, in a chair, down the wharf and upon the deck; and Janet came with her, and wrapped her up warm, and coddled her, and made her feel quite at home. Then the old lady wished she had some of the oranges which a German woman was selling on the wharf; and Janet ran ashore to buy them. While the German fiddled about the change, the boat cast off, the captain's bell struck, and they had fairly pulled the gangway in, when Janet came running back with her fruit.

Did she stop ? Not she !

" Please run it on again," she said ; and the wharf-hands obeyed her, — just as Dan obeyed her in the pasture. And the little bird, as I called her before, ran right over the board, — the boat moving the end along steadily as she did so, — and sprang upon the deck, as perfectly unconscious as if she had been walking the floor. Years after John Wildair tried to make her remember it : but she did not remember it at all ; said, indeed, there was nothing to remember. She said there was no danger, and consequently no courage ; that the plank would remain on the boat fully five seconds, and the slowest woman in Christendom could have crossed in two. Still, John Wildair wondered when he saw her do it; and, as I believe, admired her, then and there, that she did not spend ten seconds first in inquiries of the wharf-men whether or no it would be safe to cross the gangway.

But John was destined to see her again far, far away.

Tom Trevor went to the war in the Forty-seventh Maine Rifles. Tom was the wild-cat, black-haired brother that dared everything and went everywhere. And after that horrid carnage at Bell's Ford, when the lists of the Forty-seventh were printed, Tom's name was among the missing. Dead, perhaps? Janet said, "No, not dead." She was sure he was not dead. If he had been shot, some man would have seen him fall, and would have told of it; for they all liked Tom. No: Janet, with all her own clear-sightedness, which is what Mr. Billings and I call "Confidence," pronounced that he was in a Rebel prison. Then the next thing for her to do was to go and find him. Her father would not hear of it; for, as I said, he worshipped Janet. But, because people are fain to obey those whom they worship, he had to do as Janet bade him before he knew it; and in fewer days than it has taken me to tell this story, as we say when we write in the Dime Series, Janet was in Washington, besieging Knapp at the Sanitary, and Stanton in his den, and General Townsend in his, for some sort of pass that would carry her across the lines. Little good did she get of that. Of course, there was no pass for her of any kind or sort; and they all told her, with great tenderness, that she would have done much better to stay at home.

But Janet did not go home, for all that. By this time they knew, and she knew, that Tom Trevor was in Richmond, in Hospital No. 21, where were our wounded prisoners. Whether he was there because he was sick, or because he was wounded, she did not know, nor could anybody learn; but he was there. What Janet did was to go up to Harper's Ferry. Then she turned up at Stanton and Lexington, and, one fine day, appeared in Lynchburg, — quite comfortably within Rebel territory, — very seedy, and speaking very bad English and very good French. She called on all the ministers in Lynchburg; she waited at Lynchburg till she could be sure whether they would not want her as a teacher in the academy. Meanwhile she knit stockings like fury for the wounded; and in the hospital there was not a volunteer nurse as ready and careful as Janet, nor so universal a favorite as she. And so it happened, that when, in the spring of '64, Butler struck in so suddenly at Bermuda Hundred, and fought the battle of the fog; and when the wounded began to be sent to the rear from the Wilderness and Spottsylvania; when Dr. MacGregor and Mr. Harris went down to Richmond with fresh spring vegetables for the wounded, — Mlle. Lacretelle, whom you and I know better as Janet, went with them, with express charges to look after certain wounded of the Twenty-ninth Virginia. Nobody could go in without Dr. MacGregor's pass; but he would take Mlle. Lacretelle anywhere.

That was the way it happened that Janet, after she had carried to Adam Clement the stockings his mother had sent, and to Jesse Burton the head-rest Mary sent, and the boxes of home-baked cakes to Jo Stratton and Walt Victor, and the letters to twenty others, whom she found in one hospital and another, appointed herself to duty one day at Hospital No. 21, with a note from Dr. MacGregor to our good friend, Dr. Sample, who was in charge there. The note said that she was a perfect nurse, and could speak French and German well. Sample had little to do with French or with German; but he had no surplus of perfect nurses. And so it was, that, one morning when Tom Trevor was waiting for his breakfast of mush and molasses, it was brought to him, not by the nice, red-turbaned black woman who brought it Monday, but by a tiny little white woman, in the full dress of a sister of charity. Tom hopped a foot off his bed when the sister of charity turned round on him; but the sister of charity magnetized Tom also, so that his " Janet!" died unspoken. But from that moment, I can tell you, Tom began to get well.

So did John Wildair, who lay in the next bed; and so did all the Smiths and the Joneses and the rest, with whom this story has nothing to do. Never was there such a sunshiny place as was that ward of No. 21, till they were all packed up and packed off, and sent back into the country.

And then! Why, by that time Mlle. Lacretelle had her way as perfectly as any red-tapist of them all. Not Dr. Sample nor Dr. MacGregor could draw up requisitions with more formality, insist on precedent more precisely, or do as he chose more certainly, than could the French nurse. She never asked for anything that was not right; and, when she asked for anything, she asked as if she were certain it was to be granted. So the end was, that it always was granted. Tom Trevor was assigned to Lynchburg. Dear me! how John Wildair wished that he could be assigned to Lynchburg. He would have given his hand had he dared to ask her to assign him to Lynchburg. And the only reason he did not dare was his fear that she would find out, by his asking, how it was as a matter of life and death for him to go there. Queer human nature! He hoped she knew she was all in all to him; and yet that was the one thing he did not tell her, and was so afraid she would find out. Why was he afraid? Why? O, it is the old, old story. What if she did find out, and then moved Tom into Ward A, and let Rebecca come into Ward B in her place,— what would John Wildair do then, poor thing? So John Wildair did not say one word; and so he was assigned to Lewisburg when they were assigned to Lynchburg.

Die of a broken heart? Not a bit of it. He did

not die at all; he got well. He bribed a black brother to let him out of a window; and he stole a horse, and rode him thirty miles before daylight. Then he slept all day in a barn; and then he stole another horse, and then another: and so he turned up at Harper's Ferry; and so he was in Battery Seven in front of Petersburg; and so he marched under Ord to Appomattox Court House; and so, when Janet brought poor Tom, still limping, down to our lines, and hunted up the Forty-seventh Maine, John Wildair was in command, because he ranked every officer left in the field. And did not John Wildair tell her then how glad he was to see her!

Yes. And she was glad to see him! And John had her and Tom sent back to the field-hospital in an old carryall, and in the evening came down to see how Tom had borne the journey. And after that he took Janet out to see the sunset behind the river; and they walked and they walked, and John told her how desolate all life had been to him since she and Tom went to Lynchburg, and begged her, by the love he bore her, never to leave him again, without saying he might come after her.

I don't know what he said to her; but I know, that, after the Forty-seventh was paid off, I married them both, and that there, according to all rule, this story ought to end.

When Mr. Billings sent the painting to John to look at, and said it was named "Confidence," Janet asked if " Confidence " was not Latin for " Brass." But John said " No " : he said that it was a word which meant Faith and Love mixed together. And we hung the picture above the mantel in the dining-room ; and, as we sat looking at it, the brothers and sisters came in for prayers, and old Chloe brought in the little Donald. And old Grandfather Trevor opened the old Bible he brought from Cornwall, and he read, —

" I give unto you power to tread on serpents and scorpions, and over all the power of the enemy, and nothing shall by any means hurt you."

THE END.